SMOLDER

Crown of Fae Book Three

SHARON ASHWOOD

PRAISE FOR SHARON ASHWOOD

Sharon Ashwood is all that is good and right in the paranormal romance genre.

— BITTEN BY BOOKS

Fast paced and captivating... chemistry is immediate and undeniable, and the love scenes are scorching hot.

— PUBLISHERS WEEKLY

Multiply the Wow Factor, the Dark Forgotten saga must continue!

— SINGLE TITLES

This is a splendid way to spend your precious leisure time!

— ROMANTIC TIMES BOOK REVIEWS TOP PICK!

A prince. A prisoner. The last embers of hope.

Leena is a fae and a fire dancer, as wild as her mountain home. But war with the Shades has crushed her tribe, and she is forced to use her powers for her captors' entertainment. She obeys to protect her family, until the Shades enslave her young brother in a nightmarish spell.

Rich, arrogant, and devastatingly handsome, Morran is feared as an ally of the Shades. Known as the Phoenix Prince, he is a prisoner of a different kind, cursed to forget his bloodline's legacy of magic. His familiar is the firebird, but it has been stolen—along with his memories, his power, and his sanity.

If Leena can heal the prince, she has a chance to rescue her brother—but it's been centuries since Morran was cursed. Can she find the key to warming his heart again? And once the Phoenix Prince is free, who says she'll be able to tame him?

N
IMRAGEN
GRAY MOUNTAINS
WESTERING RIVER
MARGIT BAY
POMANDINE
BLACK LAKE
HAWKSGATE RIVER
HEARTRUIN RIVER
ELDABAN
GREAT DESERT
SERPENT RIVER
RAVAGED LANDS
THE FAERY REALM

HIGHCLAW CASTLE
THE WHEEL
THE TEETH
BLACKFLEET RIVER
WOLFRUN HALL
ILDARAN RIVER
ILDARAN FALLS
VERRINDER RANGE
CELADOR FOREST
FLEETFOOT
PENRIVA HOUSE
PENRIVA BAY
OUTWARD ISLES
KYLEEN
VALE CASTLE
GREAT DESERT
FEREDITH RIVER
PLAINS OF GOLD
PALACE OF THE PHOENIX
TYMEERA
EVANTRA

❦   I   ❦

"Servant Leena, you know the punishment."

The guard stood in Leena's path like a wall of steel and leather. Behind him was the door to the sandstone banquet hall, where she should have arrived twenty minutes ago. Evening approached, and the pillars of the porch cast long shadows on the dusty ground. The day's heat had been blistering, but now a soothing breeze stirred the white shawl that protected her face and arms from the sun.

Leena had been born in the mountain wilderness, far from Eldaban's sweltering streets. Now she was here, with little money and less status. Tardiness meant a beating.

Anxiety spiked, but she bowed her head in silent apology. All she wanted was to report for duty with no one the wiser that she was a little late.

"Lord Dorth expects better," the guard said.

A rude retort slid through Leena's mind, but she kept it to herself. Instead, she made another humble bow. "Delay could not be avoided."

"Were you at the temple?" he asked.

"I was." Leena straightened. She was tall and slim with an

athlete's lean muscles, and well able to meet his gaze without looking up.

She knew Guardsman Remmik and his wife. Like so many of Eldaban's citizens, they had come to the Temple of the Flame in Eldaban when fever ran amok last spring.

The Kelthian fae—Leena's people—survived through their healing skills. When she was young, her tribe had arrived in the city's crowded slums to escape the war. They were seen as little more than barbarians—red-haired, pale-skinned shepherds, illiterate and ill-suited to Eldaban's desert sun. And, in truth, they were hot-tempered and destitute, but they'd brought along their medical talents.

Remmik studied Leena for several moments, a battle between rules and mercy plain on his broad face. Leena had trained as a fire dancer and a maker of medicines. She'd been the one who'd given his wife a healing potion. Sadly, serving as a priestess of the temple didn't bring in coin—and she was late for work.

Leena struggled not to squirm. The guardsman's tired eyes were a match with the creases in his face. They all looked haunted these days. Everyone had lost the war, just in different ways.

Finally, Remmik stepped aside. "Go on and be quick about it."

"Blessings, Guardsman." She slipped past him, turning right to dart through the smaller entry only the servants used.

It was stifling inside the hall, the air thick with the scent of food and warm bodies. Leena pushed through the crowd of servers and kitchen boys. Some were human, while others were the solid, dark-eyed earth fae common in Eldaban. A few were slender Kelthians in their brightly colored tunics.

Leena's destination was a small antechamber beside the main dining area, where she would wait until called on to provide entertainment. Lord Dorth had little use for the temple healers, but he paid good wages for their dancers—and Leena was the best. Judging by the crush of people, the fat lord of Eldaban had spared no expense tonight. There had to be an important guest.

She hurried down the corridor, with its high ceilings and marble floors. Her sandals clip-clopped as she ran, but the sound was lost in the hubbub of voices. The guests were just arriving. She still had time to get to her place, but only if she moved fast. There would be hell to pay if the Master of Revels noticed her absence.

Two burly fae passed with enormous platters, the golden dishes barely visible beneath heaps of food. The scent of herbed lamb and fresh bread made Leena's stomach cramp. She hadn't eaten since dawn, and there would be no time now. Swallowing the saliva flooding her mouth, she hurried on.

Her luck held. She skidded to a halt outside the door she wanted, smoothed her hair, and drifted in as if nothing were amiss. The room was full of performers, all faces she knew. There were musicians and jugglers, fire-eaters and acrobats. She slid onto a bench beside her friend, Elodie. Like Leena, she was a red-haired fire fae of the southern mountains. Unlike Leena, she was compact and generously rounded, her tight copper curls spilling over her bare shoulders.

"Where were you?" Elodie demanded, giving her a quick, one-armed hug. "You're lucky the guests were delayed."

"There were wounded." Leena sucked in a deep breath, doing her best to stop panting from the run. "There was a skirmish outside the city walls."

"Were the wounded from Eldaban, or were they true defenders of Faery?" Elodie asked bitterly.

It was an old argument. The enemy of all the fae—the one true enemy—were the Shades. The turncoat Lord Dorth of Eldaban had sided with the invaders, betraying the Kelthian tribe as well as the rest of the fae resistance. To be fair, it was the only reason his city still stood.

"I can't blame the townsfolk," Leena said. "They didn't choose this fight."

"They could have refused."

"And we could have left Eldaban the moment Dorth swore to serve the Shades, but we've been glad to have shelter. Healing is how we pay our debt."

Elodie opened her mouth to protest, but a black cat leaped onto the bench between them.

"Kifi," Elodie squeaked, clearly startled.

"I know who the general is bringing to dinner," the cat said in a small, childlike voice.

"Who?" Leena asked. "And what are you doing wandering the streets?"

"Temple cats are allowed to roam," Kifi replied loftily, settling her sleek form between the two women.

"You are a temple cat in training." Elodie's tone was severe. "You don't have permission to wander the streets."

Ignoring the comment, Kifi curled her tail about her paws. "Do you want my news or not?"

"Who is Lord Dorth entertaining?" Leena asked, mostly to end the argument.

"General Juradoc, of course."

He was the leader of the Shade army that occupied the lands around Eldaban. The name made Leena shudder.

"He has someone with him by the name of Morran." The cat blinked golden eyes. "That one walks like a man with a storm cloud as his crown."

"What does that mean?" Leena asked. Temple cats could be frustratingly vague, as if that were their job. "And who is he?"

Kifi's answer was cut short by a loud, throbbing fanfare. The trumpeters had signaled the start of the banquet. Instinctively, Leena sat straighter, her pulse quickening at the sound. Pounding drums followed as the host and his guests paraded in. From where she sat, Leena could see the hall through the partially open door. She glimpsed Lord Dorth, his tunic stiff with gems and golden braid.

The Master of Revels circulated throughout the room, giving

the performers their instructions. Tovas was squat and warty, as much goblin as fae.

"Be ready," he said in a stage whisper, giving Leena and Elodie a wink. "The high and mighty are in a mood. We've got to be perfect tonight. Elodie, my sweet?"

Elodie hopped to her feet. She began checking the performers' costumes, ensuring laces were tied and buckles properly secure. There would be no mishaps on her watch.

The acrobats and jugglers were the first entertainment, meant to welcome the nobles filling the hall. They erupted from the room with a shout, balls flying as they somersaulted through the air. Leena's feet twitched, aching to follow, but her turn would come. When she and Elodie took the floor, they would be the climax, the jewels of the feast, giving onlookers a glimpse of the sacred Flame. Nothing could follow that act.

Kifi crawled into her lap, her slight form surprisingly heavy. "There were portents about this evening. Dire events. I heard it at the temple."

"Such as?"

"I'm not sure." Kifi yawned, showing sharp fangs. "I was chasing a spider at the time."

"You're a terrible temple cat."

"I am a perfect cat."

"And therein lies the problem."

Leena rose, Kifi draped in her arms, and stood closer to the door where she could see all the guests without being seen herself. The banquet tables formed a vast square along the edges of the cavernous room. The high table, where the dignitaries sat, occupied a raised dais at the front. Behind that were double doors to a marble balcony overlooking Eldaban's main square.

Leena had a good view of the elaborate table settings and damasked silk cloth. Scarlet hangings draped the walls, the jeweled embroidery glittering with rubies. Servants hurried from the kitchens, adding food to the already-groaning tables. It seemed enough to feed the entire city twice over. Leena's stomach growled again, earning her a sharp look from Tovas.

In the center of the room, the acrobats leaped and twirled for the guests. There were humans and fae, lords and merchants. Some of the fae were small and winged, while others sported horns or limbs covered in supple vines. One thing, however, was constant. Despite their fine clothes and practiced smiles, everybody looked nervous.

The figures at the high table had their heads together, conversing among themselves. These were the nobles Leena had to please. Kifi stretched to get a better view as well, her whiskers tickling Leena's cheek.

"There is Lord Dorth. He's scowling as if he's eaten bad fish," the cat said. "And there is Morran."

"Huh," Leena replied, at a loss for words.

He was taking his seat, somehow managing to occupy more than his allotted space at the table. Fae did not age, but, even so, she could tell Morran was just entering his prime. The language of his body was there for her dancer's eye to read—the dominating, impatient quality of his movements, every gesture quick and certain. He had the bearing of a commander, not a follower.

And such good looks were rare, even among the fae. His hair was pure black, thick and curling as it fell across his brow. While his skin was a warm golden brown, his eyes were the deepest chocolate. Yet, Leena's instant attraction was short-lived. There was no kindness in the set of his mouth or those heavy-lidded eyes. Despite the perfection of his features, Morran's expression was deadly cold.

Foreboding slithered down her back, as if the man were fated to do her harm. Leena glanced at the window at the back of the chamber, where it overlooked the street. An irrational part of her wished she could fit through the tiny opening. She'd hurried to arrive tonight, yet now she yearned to be far away.

Morran had arrived with a contingent of guards in black-and-gold tabards. They were traitors, fae from across the land who had sworn allegiance to General Juradoc. They scattered through the room, standing back as the guests settled at the tables.

A handful of Shades commanded those guards. They wore black robes over their black armor, the hoods pulled forward to hide their faces. A few carried long, crooked staffs tipped with elaborate carvings. Warriors and sorcerers—both deadly. Shade magic left everything it touched lifeless ash.

And General Juradoc was the deadliest of the Shades who had invaded the south of Faery. Robed and hooded in inky black, he stood to one side of the high table, across the room from where Leena watched. He made no move to join Morran or Lord Dorth, though a throne-like chair sat between them. As far as Leena knew, Shades didn't eat or drink.

At the sight of the enemy, Kifi gave a soft hiss.

"Hush," Leena whispered.

The cat's ears flattened. "The general smells like a butcher's pail left in the sun."

As if Juradoc had heard them, the Shade's hooded face turned Leena's way. There were plenty of rumors about what lurked beneath the Shades' robes—the enemy was an army of rotting corpses, skeletons, or nothing at all. Twin pricks of violet light glimmered in place of Juradoc's eyes. The gaze snagged on Leena, holding hers for one heartbeat, then two.

He shouldn't have been able to see her, not from where she stood beyond his line of sight. And yet, Juradoc's presence seemed mere inches away. Intimately close. Terrifying.

Leena's muscles drew tight. Kifi mewed a complaint and jumped to the ground, then leaped to the windowsill.

"Go," Leena whispered. "Go back to the temple."

"Flame guide you." With a flick of her ears, the cat was gone.

A wise creature, Leena thought, drawing breath as Juradoc's gaze released her at last. She stepped back, colliding with Elodie. Her friend braced Leena's shoulders, giving her support.

"Easy," Elodie said in a low voice. "We are just dancers, here to entertain. We are safely beneath the general's notice."

Leena wasn't so sure. The sensation of that stare lingered like a slug's sticky trail.

The acrobats had finished, and the hall fell quiet. Lord Dorth rose, his round face shining with the heat. He drew breath, clearly preparing for a speech.

Juradoc flicked a gloved hand. A flash of green light seared Leena's eyes, followed by a clap of thunder loud enough to rattle the dishes on the tables. Someone shouted in alarm. Another person shushed them.

Elodie gripped Leena's arm. "What's going on?"

Juradoc strode to the middle of the room, black robes swirling in his wake. The startled acrobats sank into a deep bow. Juradoc dismissed them with a gesture, and they all but sprinted from the room. Leena envied them the chance of escape.

"Enough with these paltry entertainments," Juradoc said, his voice harsh as he turned toward Lord Dorth. He spoke the fae language well, but with an odd accent. "You insult us with such frivolity."

The words fell like barbs, chasing any pleasure from the room. Juradoc circled the space, his steps unhurried. "We allowed Eldaban to live, unlike the Ravaged Lands to the south. Nothing survives there now."

Elodie's indrawn breath filled the silence. The smoking ruins of the south had once been their home.

Juradoc kept pacing. The banquet guests were motionless, their expressions appalled. Morran picked up his goblet, sipping the wine slowly. He sat back in his chair with an air of boredom, giving an approving nod to the vintage.

"My captains and I were generous," Juradoc continued, a snarl creeping into this tone. "We stayed our hand because Eldaban bought our mercy. You swore the ancient power you shelter within your walls would be ours for the taking. And yet, tonight, you try to amuse us with *clowns*."

"Blame the Master of Revels," Dorth stuttered, his small eyes wide. "He insists on leading up to the highlights, building anticipation."

Leena winced, suddenly worried for Tovas.

"Building anticipation?" Juradoc's tone dripped with incredulity. He stopped, robes eddying around him. "Are we peasants at a fair?"

Blood draining from his cheeks, Lord Dorth sat without uttering another word. Leena almost pitied him.

"Do not think for a moment that we can be handled or impressed by trifles." The Shade came to a stop before the high table, raising a hand to point at his host. "Do not presume upon my goodwill."

Juradoc jumped onto the dais with a surprising lightness, then reached across the overflowing table to snatch the goblet from Morran's hand. The Shade turned to the crowd, the heavy metal cup held aloft. Jewels winked along its golden rim.

Then, a pulse of green fire covered it—so quick, it was gone in a blink. But then the heavy gold powdered to black ash, sifting through Juradoc's gloved fingers like sand.

Shade magic consumed all while leaving nothing behind.

Leena's throat closed as memories of her home's devastation crowded in. Entire villages and fields had turned to dust. The Shades had stripped the life from the mountains, leaving nowhere to live. Nothing but barren rubble.

Eldaban didn't stand a chance. The banquet hall was still as a tomb.

"I grow bored with your cringing," Juradoc sneered. He jumped off the dais as lightly as a temple cat. "Summon the fire dancers."

Lord Dorth made a frantic gesture. In response, Tovas spun to face Leena and Elodie. "Get out there, now."

Leena froze, struck by a horrible certainty. Juradoc had spied her tonight, and he knew what she could do. He'd seen the Flame inside her.

What Shades saw, they took. Terror threatened to turn her knees to jelly.

"Hurry." Elodie pulled Leena's shawl away, tossing it aside.

Mouth dry, Leena kicked off her sandals. She needed nothing special to perform. Her straight, coppery hair fell to her hips, and her simple blue dress was all the costume she owned.

"There's no need for panic." Elodie's tone was firm. "This is what we do."

She was right. The Flame was the soul of the fire fae, and it was as pure and unrelenting as the sun. It wasn't so flimsy that one enemy, not even a Shade, could steal or sully it. They were priestesses, and the spirit burned hot and proud inside them. Leena would personally show the enemy she was unbowed.

By the time they were ready, Juradoc had retreated to a place by the wall, giving them the floor.

There was no music to accompany their entrance. Elodie went first—a spark of energy unleashed. Her white dress hung to her knees, leaving her tanned legs bare. She spun, curls flying, coming to rest only when she reached the far end of the room. Then Leena leaped forward, her motions long and liquid. She and Elodie were excellent foils, playing off each other like instruments in a duet.

Yet, when she turned to face the high table and bow in reverence, she faltered. Until now, she'd seen Morran only in profile. From this angle, she could see his face clearly. Her first impression was the same as before—an unbidden wave of attraction. His cheekbones were high, his dark brows slightly slanted. The overall impression was of strength and intelligence. A dark blue tunic stretched across his broad chest, embroidered in gold and silver thread with a firebird surmounted by a crown.

Shock momentarily numbed Leena into stillness. There was

only one man who could wear that sigil—the Phoenix Prince, Lord of Tymeera. He was the mightiest of the fire fae and a warrior without equal. He had beaten the Shades back for years, protecting the south with magic and sword until his sudden disappearance.

Without him, Kelthia had lost everything—and here he was at Juradoc's side. He'd betrayed them all. The knowledge was like a fist to her belly, robbing her of breath.

When Morran's gaze met hers, his eyes were as dead as stone.

Morran caught the dancer's gaze for a moment. Even at a distance, the bright amber of her eyes shone like ancient gold. Her soft lips parted in a gasp of surprise, as if he were an unexpected apparition—one that inspired both hope and despair.

Morran looked away. He offered no hope—he was an abyss.

With swift, precise moves, he filled his plate from the dishes heaped before him. A servant replaced the goblet Juradoc had destroyed. When Morran looked back, the dancers had already launched into their performances. The soft silks of their dresses flowed around their limbs, reminding him of exotic plumage.

What had the Kelthian woman seen in him? What had made her cheeks flush and then turn white as chalk?

Familiarity tugged at his thoughts, but he was certain he'd never met either dancer. Both were young, beautiful, and supple, promising energetic pleasures. Need stirred, but so did caution. No one set such a luscious temptation before Morran of Tymeera without a motive. Juradoc wanted something. Or Dorth did. No man climbed the dung heap of power without a facility for plots.

Morran kept his face utterly blank. If he remembered only one thing, it was never to show curiosity, much less weakness. As long as he kept the jackals guessing, he wasn't prey.

He picked at his food, choosing only the plainest fare. Dorth's taste for rich sauces and heavy spice was appropriate for a feast, but provided a convenient disguise for poison. A minion filled first Dorth's goblet, then his, from the same golden pitcher. That meant this round of wine was probably safe.

The dancers were moving faster now, circling each other with hands touching. They twined and parted, surrendering to a rhythm that began to pulse in his own veins. There was no music, no drumbeat to keep time. Bare feet stamped across the floor, the strong, sure steps speaking of strength as much as grace. Slender arms beckoned and waved. The movement spoke of desert winds scattering sand across the horizon.

Morran's pulse beat faster. He remembered now—these two fire fae—goddesses in their beauty—were dancers of the Flame. Their art meant something to him, but he couldn't recall what. There was a void where that knowledge had once belonged, as with so much else.

He was hollow, a night without stars inside the shell of his body, but the dance reminded him that sand, stars, and fire were part of who he was.

Had been.

Was. He was *still* the Lord of Tymeera, protector of the great city-state at the mouth of the Feredith River. He had come from a land of sudden floods and scorching heat.

Home. The idea clutched at his heart, rousing him for the time it took to lift his goblet and taste Lord Dorth's expensive wine. Then the notion was gone again, falling into the void where memory should have been.

He watched the taller of the two dancers, her legs long and her back lean. She was the type of woman he liked, willowy and athletic. And all that red hair—he could imagine the warm silk of it against his skin.

Magic gathered in the room, summoned by the dance. Even in his detached state, Morran could feel it like a vision of flames through smoked glass. Something was going to happen.

He'd been thinking about—what was it?

He turned his knife so the tip rested against the thumb of his opposite hand. Slowly, gently, he pushed the blade home until it hurt, without breaking the skin. The pain cleared his thoughts, but not enough to knot together whatever it was he'd been trying to recall.

He pushed enough to pierce the skin, and a pearl of blood fell onto his plate. *Home.* Yes, that was it. He'd seen it in the dancer's face as clearly as if she'd shouted out loud. She had known he was the Phoenix Prince. She wanted him to pick up his sword once more.

"How do you like the entertainment?" Dorth asked, abruptly smashing through Morran's thoughts.

Ideas scattered. With some confusion, he wondered why he was bleeding.

Morran took another mouthful of wine. It was a heavy red, with notes of ash and ripe cherry. He set the cup down before turning to address Dorth. The man was sweating, his round cheeks flushed with food and heat.

"I like the show well enough," Morran said, giving nothing of his frustration away. "Your dancers are very... flexible."

Dorth waved a hand. "I'm sure they are a poor substitute for those at your palace."

Morran shrugged, a slight lift of one shoulder. Inside, he groped like a man deprived of light. *Do I have dancers?*

Juradoc's chair sat between Morran and the plump Lord of Eldaban. The general finally moved into his seat, his robes creating a stir of air. A sweet stink quelled Morran's appetite. All Shades smelled as if they were rotting.

He pushed his plate aside.

"We can compare the dancers of your Great Temple with the

Kelthians once we reach Tymeera," Juradoc said, the violet pinpricks of his eyes glittering from the depths of his hood.

The statement was simple enough, but it sent a shock through Morran. *Are the Shades going to my home?* All at once, his limbs lost feeling, and he sank back into his chair. He ground his injured thumb against the wood, using the pain to focus his mind.

Was he panicking? Along with his memory, emotions blurred like colored inks in the rain. Joy, terror, anger—they had become one inarticulate shout in his soul.

He was going mad.

Thoughts of home slid away. Disappeared. All that remained was nameless anxiety.

What was I worried about? Uncertain, he schooled his features, keeping his indifferent expression in place.

The steady rhythm of the performers' feet was barely audible now. Magic crackled through the air, raising the fine hair on Morran's arms. Now he could hear music. It came from no instrument, but from the enchantment the dancers wove. A deep note pulsed like a heartbeat, guiding and pushing the swirling figures of the Kelthian fae. More voices rang above it, echoing in intervals so pure that the marble beneath Morran's feet shivered in response.

The notes rang in Morran's skull, clearing away the fog for a brilliant, amazing second.

He surged to his feet as if the motion would help him grasp the moment. His gaze was fixed on the woman with amber eyes, transfixed by the raw power shimmering around her. They were heatwaves, echoes of the sacred Flame, rising in a circle around the dancers. He could feel the forge-hot warmth against his face.

As the air rippled with heat, it became harder to see the writhing women. Their images melted as the elemental force that had birthed the fire fae took over. They became flames themselves, swirling and leaping to impossible heights. The wildness of it unlocked a raging hunger inside him, filling the emptiness in his soul.

The Flame knows me even if I do not.

The shimmering air gave way to pale tongues of yellow and orange. The fire roared to life around the dancers, licking the ceiling above in a chorus of unearthly music. A cry of wonder and dismay ripped from the spectators—some expecting to burn in their seats. But no scorch marks blackened the ceiling, nor did anything catch fire. This was a sacred blaze, meant to heal and warm.

And she—the dancer with the amber eyes—had summoned it. Any commander could tell she was the leader of the two. It was in the way she moved and the angle of her head. Now, she bowed over backward, a sinuous arc of blue dress and flaming locks. The move was an invitation—sexual and spiritual both. She might earn her bread from Lord Dorth, but she was utterly wild, a lioness of the Kelthian mountains.

With a kick, she straightened again, her hands held out in a plea. Flames licked at the ends of her fingers, promising pain and pleasure if only he would surrender. The keening of the spell grew sultry now, whispering an invitation. Cajoling. Begging.

Morran's mouth went dry. Flame save him, she was making him feel again, unleashing a tremor of fury in his limbs. Anger was a serpent forcing its way along every nerve.

He was beginning to remember who he was.

❦

LEENA SAW LITTLE THROUGH THE VEIL OF FIRE. THE DANCE HAD summoned the Flame, fulfilling Dorth's promise to the Shade general. All fae understood its sacred, elemental nature. The dance raised magic in its purest form.

Leena bent and twisted, sweat gleaming along her bare arms and plastering her dress to the small of her back. She slid past

Elodie, their flames flashing blue where they met, burning but never consuming their forms. When fire fae surrendered to their element, they could never be hurt.

Spinning, she turned again to the head table. Despite the leaping fire, Morran's form was clear. He stood with his weight slightly forward, as if he meant to spring over the banquet table to join her. Desire cracked his icy mask.

The emotion went far beyond physical need. Leena might be a humble priestess, but her magic spoke to a hunger inside him. The idea thrilled *and* appalled her. Morran was the powerful lord of Tymeera and all the sacred treasure it held. The Phoenix Palace—his palace—was the heart and hearth of the fire fae. Dared she hope he was not utterly lost to Faery and its people?

Leena reached out with her magic, seeking to touch Morran's spirit and find her answers. Instead, there was emptiness. She recoiled, losing her footing for a single beat. Something terrible had happened to the prince—something had ripped his soul apart.

Grief made her movements clumsy. Elodie covered her missteps, filling in until the dance swept Leena up once more. Tears stung her eyes, the fire drying them to salt before they fell. For a dizzying moment, she had hoped for salvation. She should have known better. Hope gave disappointment teeth.

A tug on the Flame brought Leena's attention back to the high table. Morran wasn't the only one on his feet now. Juradoc stood like a looming personification of Death.

To her astonishment, Death was eating. Nausea swept her like a tide of jellied rot.

Of course. She'd always wondered what Shades consumed. Now she knew—they ate the force of fae power itself. She'd seen them turn trees, animals, and even whole landscapes to ash, and this was how they did it—they sucked the life force dry.

The pull came again, as subtle as someone sipping from a glass. This was why Juradoc had wanted fire dancers—wanted her the moment he knew she was present. The dance summoned the mighty elemental force that had birthed the fire fae. Like a leech, the Shade was feeding on the Flame itself.

Furious, Leena lashed out with her magic, sending sparks flying in a shower of red and white. Juradoc jerked back as if stung. The Shade hadn't expected resistance.

His drain on the fire's energy left Leena lightheaded. As she moved, circling the floor once again, she narrowed the spell that fed magic to the dance, like pinching a hose. Juradoc fought back, struggling to take more, but Leena knew how to control the power. She spun, leaped, and swept the fire into a teasing dance, but she gave nothing away.

It was as dangerous as dangling meat before a tiger. Even Morran understood it, for she saw his eyes widen with apprehension. Leena leaned into the beat, swaying her hips as another rush of fire swept the circle. Darkness—Juradoc's Shade magic—roamed the edges of her spell, but she denied it entry. He got nothing she didn't give him.

She sank to one knee, suddenly short of breath from the effort. It wasn't fatigue in the normal sense, but spirit deep. It was then she caught Morran's gaze again. Without quite knowing how, she understood he'd seen her fight back. Like a man newly awakened, he regarded Leena afresh, frank admiration filling his expression. It was as if he saw the Flame inside her heart.

Perhaps there was something left of the Tymeeran lord after all.

Surging to her feet, Leena turned her back to the high table, facing Elodie. The two women mirrored each other in a complicated series of steps. Leena's limbs tingled with fresh energy despite the fatigue deep in her bones. She cast Morran a glance over her shoulder, sending her hair flaring around her frame. Daring. Enticing. Morran's regard was a second fire caressing her limbs.

And then, at a gesture from the Shade, Morran's face went

blank. He sank to his chair, his head in his hands. Disappoint-ment made Leena break her stride. She reached out again, hoping to call him back.

Her magic hit a wall of ice. Behind it, she glimpsed the cavernous dark of madness. For the second time, she veered away. The devouring abyss inside Morran would consume her in an instant, given a chance.

Leena's emotions had gone full circle. For an instant, Morran had sparked hope, but that was over. All that remained was to endure the performance and escape to safety.

Dread crawled through Leena, a living thing in her chest. She nearly missed Elodie's cry of dismay—a sharp, brief yelp that split the air. Leena skidded to a stop the instant before Elodie crumpled.

$$ \maltese \quad 3 \quad \maltese $$

"Elodie!" Leena cried.

Her friend sprawled, arms outflung and legs folded at an awkward angle. Bright copper curls pooled on the floor like a crazy halo. Leena stared, fear punching through her as the circle of Flame dimmed.

Leena had been able to resist the Shade. Elodie had, too, but barely. The struggle had wrung her dry.

A female diner screamed. The sound was like a knife on Leena's nerves, but it broke her paralysis. She sprang to Elodie's side. Her friend's face had gone a bloodless gray. When Leena clasped her hand, the skin was clammy and chill.

"Come back, Elodie," she whispered, her throat aching with panicked tears. "Think of your little one. Think of Riya."

Elodie's eyelids fluttered, but rather than waking, Leena felt her friend's spirit sinking out of reach. A tremor shook the other fae's body. Within seconds, Elodie's teeth chattered, back arching as the seizure pulled her from the floor with bone-cracking force.

Terror ripped through Leena. She needed to heal her friend, but her own power was almost exhausted. Leena ended the spell that fed the Flame, working too quickly for any kind of finesse.

Abruptly, the Flame's power catapulted free. The wrench of it made Leena reel, her vision lost in a burst of light.

The fire around them vanished, leaving the room ominously dark and silent. Only the torches along the walls shed light. The air seemed empty, devoid of warmth and comfort. Leena lifted her head, peering through the veil of her hair. Some healers could hear the Flame whisper the secret of a cure, but Leena had no such talents. Her skills lay with the dance alone.

Beneath Leena's hand, Elodie lay quiet. The shaking had stopped, but her pulse was fading.

Lord Dorth sprang to his feet and began to applaud, his round face beaming. "Spectacular finish! Such drama!"

There was a faint rustle as all heads turned his way, but no one spoke. His claps trailed off as his face fell in confusion. A moment later, he sat, face scarlet with embarrassment.

Juradoc had fallen to one knee, his black robes pooled around him. His gaze stung like twin points of ice. With crawling apprehension, she realized the backlash of the Flame's release had hit him, too.

"No one gave you permission to stop." The Shade rose after a long, terrible pause. "The promise was almost fulfilled."

Dorth had promised fae power to eat, but the words implied more. What was it? What drove the Shades to destroy everything in their path?

Leena rose, unsteady but still able to put herself between Juradoc and Elodie's still form. "Forgive me, my lord, but we could not continue. My friend is unwell."

Speaking was stupid. She was shaking herself now, certain she'd sealed her doom by slamming a door the Shades couldn't open by themselves. Only a priestess could call the Flame, and now the Shade doubted her cooperation.

A dangerous mistake.

Juradoc reached out his gloved hand, a ball of green light

forming a writhing spiderweb above his palm. Leena's stomach froze. Such magic had turned Morran's goblet to dust.

Leena willed her feet to move, but they remained cemented to the spot. Whether it was a Shade curse or simple fear, the result was the same. She couldn't see Juradoc's sharp smile, but she sensed it hiding beneath his hood, wickedly cruel.

She wondered if it would hurt to dissolve to ash.

"The wages of disobedience are final," he said as his weight shifted, ready to hurl the deadly magic.

The high table exploded in a crash of splintering wood. Leena sprang into the air like a startled cat, spinning to face the new threat. Lord Dorth shrieked and dove for safety as food and wine vaulted into the air.

With an angry roar, Morran tossed a platter through the air, scattering figs and sauce. It struck the floor with a loud clang, then bounced and spun on one edge before crashing to a stop. Morran towered over the other diners, a large man made gigantic with rage. Guests scrambled to their feet with cries of alarm, instinctively backing toward the far door.

One of Juradoc's guards rushed Morran, but the prince grabbed his attacker and hurled him from the dais. The man flew and tumbled as if he weighed no more than a feather pillow. He fell with a thud, limbs flopping as he rolled away.

Leena stared, her pulse racing with fresh alarm. The cold-eyed prince was utterly mad. As if acting out her thoughts, Morran clasped his hands in a double fist above his head, biceps flexing, and smashed what was left of the tabletop. The table's legs gave way with a deafening crack, and chairs toppled as it fell. A jeweled goblet rolled across the floor, bumping Leena's foot.

"Seize him," Juradoc ordered.

The guards hung back. Morran had picked up a carving knife.

Leena shrieked as a hand grasped her shoulder, but her voice was lost in the chaos. She wheeled to find Tovas at her side. He jerked a thumb toward the door, then scooped Elodie up with no more effort than if she were a toddler. The Master of Revels slid through the escaping crowd with surprising ease, Leena on his heels. He didn't stop until they reached the door she had entered earlier that night.

Remmik was still on duty. He began to salute, but he was interrupted by Tovas thrusting Elodie into his arms.

"Take them to the temple at once," Tovas ordered. "Don't stop for anyone."

Remmik wavered, but Tovas outranked him in the palace hierarchy. Leena cast a grateful look at the Master of Revels, who simply nodded. "I look after my children."

Leena kissed his warty cheek, ready to weep with gratitude and exhaustion. They weren't literal family, but the palace entertainers were close. He pushed the hair from her face with a fatherly gesture. "Go and be quick about it. I've heard the prince's rages don't last long. Eventually, the general will notice you're gone."

Leena was incredulous. "This has happened before? In front of Juradoc?"

"Morran's too valuable to kill, so the general puts up with it." Tovas gave her a gentle push to send her hurrying after Remmik.

Leena caught up, eager to get Elodie to the temple. The Mother of Flame—the high priestess of the temple—could heal such an injury if they got there in time. She hugged herself, willing Remmik to move faster.

Still, Leena missed her sandals—there had been no chance to gather her possessions, and her feet were bare. Even at the guardsman's quick pace, the temple was a twenty-minute walk away. The streets were bad enough near the banquet hall, where they had been paved for carriages. Once they'd entered the narrow, winding alleys of the old quarter, Leena had to step carefully to avoid filth and broken glass. Remmik asked no questions, but marched onward without so much as meeting Leena's eye.

"Do you need to rest?" Leena asked once, thinking Elodie

must be growing heavy in his arms. Dropping her wouldn't help anything.

Remmik cast a glance around the tall, narrow houses at the edge of the district where Leena lived. "No."

Leena didn't argue. He was an outsider in this neighborhood. Most buildings looked about to topple over, but every possible closet and cubby-hole was occupied by the Kelthians. With so many crowding in from the war-torn countryside, vacancies didn't exist.

The Temple of the Flame stood at the end of a narrow road. Once—before the Shades and long before Lord Dorth—it had been a grand civic building. Now the marble crumbled from its facade. Even so, the Kelthian tribes had turned it into their spiritual home.

The temple's healers were at the door before Remmik reached the porch steps. Leena guessed one of the temple cats swarming around their feet had seen them coming and run ahead to deliver the news. She climbed the steps, footsore and exhausted, but her heart rose as the Mother of Flame pushed through the crowd to greet them.

The Mother was tall and elegantly beautiful, with bright auburn hair pulled back to show the pointed tips of her ears. The long sleeves of her plain white gown were gathered into cuffs of copper engraved with intricate Kelthian knotwork. A matching torc circled her slender neck. She regarded Remmik with golden eyes slanted like a cat's.

"Greetings, Guardsman Remmik," she said. "We thank you for bringing our daughter home."

At her gesture, three of the women took Elodie from his arms and disappeared inside the temple. The guard flexed his arms, apparently relieved to be free of his burden. Then Remmik bowed, remembering his manners. "It was my duty. I wish her a quick recovery."

The Mother made a gesture, both an acknowledgment and a

blessing. "Your good wishes are appreciated. May you have a peaceful night."

Remmik departed at once, wasting no time to be free of the ramshackle neighborhood.

The Mother turned to Leena. "Come inside and tell me what befell you."

Leena followed the Mother through the ancient marble halls. The place felt spacious and orderly after the chaos of the banquet hall. The temple in Eldaban was a tiny satellite to the Great Temple near Tymeera, but it was no less solemn. In the central rotunda, steps rose in tiers around a stone basin where the sacred Flame always flickered.

Their footfalls echoed as they crossed the rotunda on their way to the infirmary. As they went, Leena recounted the night's events. She relaxed as she spoke, as if by sharing her story, she was healing herself.

She finished as they reached their destination. Through an open door, she saw Elodie at rest on one of the narrow beds, two of the healers bending over her. Leena's chest squeezed at the sight.

"Will she recover?" she asked.

The Mother drew a breath, but she held it for a long moment before she spoke. "I believe so. I hope so. Juradoc is a formidable foe. Elodie is not meant for such battles."

Leena gave a tight nod.

"Though you did well." The Mother touched Leena's cheek—a light, cool caress.

"Not well enough to help her," Leena murmured. "The Flame was silent to me. As always."

"You cannot force the Flame to speak. Humility and openness are required first. You must surrender."

As many times as Leena had heard that advice, she was still uncertain what it meant.

"You have done the best thing by bringing Elodie here," the

Mother said gently. "Go home and rest. You fought well and earned your weariness."

"I don't know if I will sleep. In my mind's eye, all I see is Juradoc."

The Mother's lips thinned. "Have you wondered why the general, in all his pride and fury, has not dared to attack the temple?"

"That is a good question." If Juradoc wished to access the Flame, why bother with a few dancers when the entire temple was nearby?

The Mother gave a chill smile. "He is a coward who prefers a fight he is sure to win. I embrace these streets like an eagle guarding her chicks. He will not attack the Kelthian tribe on my doorstep. Go to sleep knowing you are safe."

With that, she turned and entered the infirmary. Left alone, Leena retraced her steps through the temple, too tired for more than unthinking obedience. Still, she slowed as she crossed the rotunda, mesmerized by the flickering fire. She sank onto the steps, content to warm herself for a moment.

Kifi bumped against Leena's arm. Absently, she petted the cat, taking comfort from its soft fur. Here and there, other cats lazed on the steps, yellow eyes reflecting the fire. Most, but not all, were black like Kifi.

"I heard what you told the Mother," Kifi said. "You were lucky the prince interfered."

"I'm not sure he interfered on purpose," Leena said, lifting her arm so Kifi could crawl into her lap. "Who knows why he fell into a rage?"

Kifi's yellow gaze was steady. "Was he more terrifying than the Shade?"

"Violence is simpler than spells. I suppose that counts for something."

Kifi put a velvet paw against her chin. "I'm glad you're safe. No one else brings me treats from the palace."

"I'm afraid I had no time to steal any tidbits for you tonight."

Kifi sniffed delicately. "Perhaps I love you anyway."

They sat in silence long enough for Leena to start yawning. Kifi's purr was a comforting rumble against her lap.

"If Morran is so damaged, why not kill him?" Leena mused. "There's little of him left. It makes no sense."

"Does he have something the Shades want?"

"I overheard they're going to his palace at Tymeera."

Kifi raised her head. "The fabled city? The home of the Great Temple? That is where the first among the temple cats bowed to the Flame. To tread those sands would be the honor of a lifetime." The awe in Kifi's voice was plain.

"One which you are far too young to deserve," came a second feline voice. "A pilgrimage so rare is reserved for those with wisdom, not harum-scarum kittens."

A larger, fluffier cat sat nearby, her tail wrapped about her paws. Leena recognized her as a senior member of the temple's colony. The cats were the fire fae's memory, keeping the stories and wisdom that earth or air fae might write down in books. The language and meaning of the stars, the use of plants, the genealogy of kings—the cats of the fire fae remembered it all with perfect recall. What one cat learned, they all understood, though getting them to divulge the information was another matter.

Kifi sank deeper into Leena's lap at her elder's appearance, almost as if she hoped to disappear. Leena stroked Kifi's ears, but turned her attention to the senior feline. "What do you think of tonight's events, Grandmother?"

"Here is one fact," the senior cat said. "The enemy fed on the Flame. He demanded you to dance to summon it. Here is a second fact—the Phoenix Prince is the guardian of the Great Temple at Tymeera. The Shade holds Morran like a puppet on strings. Perhaps he is too valuable to kill."

"Why?"

A presence loomed behind Leena, and she craned her neck to

see the Mother on the step above, her white gown luminous in the firelight. The priestess settled at her side, quiet and graceful as a swan.

"How is Elodie?" Leena asked, abandoning her previous question.

"Better, but it will be far too dangerous for her to dance again anytime soon."

"I am glad she will be well. Her kin depend on her." Leena bowed her head, her stomach unknotting. Elodie would recover. Little Riya still had her mother.

"I give you my word that Elodie's family will be looked after until she is fully recovered."

"Thank you." Leena exhaled, unexpectedly lightheaded. The Mother's promise meant the world.

"You asked about the prince," the Mother said. "Understand that the Great Temple holds the core of the Flame. If Juradoc enjoyed a taste of elemental power during your dance, he will gorge himself once he reaches Morran's home. It is the difference between a glass of water and the entire lake. He will take what he can, even if that lake drowns him."

As horrible as the idea was, it made sense. "The Flame will only answer the summons of a fire fae."

"Precisely," the older cat said, arching her back in a long, thorough stretch before resettling herself on the step.

The Mother nodded. "Perhaps that is why Juradoc is taking Morran to the Great Temple. Only a royal fire fae can unlock the core of the Flame, but, after that, Juradoc could take his fill."

"What would happen then?" Leena asked, barely able to voice the question. "What would happen if the Shades devoured the Flame?"

"A world without heat or light? Faery would perish in an instant." The Mother bowed her head, the firelight gilding her even features. Her expression was unutterably sad. "The Shades have promised us destruction from the day they arrived. When they first attacked, many fae fled for the human realms. Others declared a war of resistance. There was a time we hoped Morran would be our champion."

"And now?" Leena asked softly.

"The Kelthian people have always been loyal to the prince, but he has lost his way."

"What can we do?"

The Mother stroked the senior cat. The feline's purr and the crackle of flames were a hypnotic duo.

"I dreamed a prophecy," the Mother said, her voice soft and low. "I dreamed of poison and the prince, of his fall into the Flame. You were part of the dream, sowing his ashes in a newly plowed field."

"I don't understand. What does the dream signify?" Leena waited, barely breathing.

The Mother rose in a rustle of robes. "Morran's death may be necessary to save us all."

﷽ 4 ﷽

"What?" Leena's voice faltered in surprise. "How?"

"That is yet undecided, though it is clear you might play a role in his end." With that, the Mother glided away, silent as the cats who followed in her wake.

Leena sprang to her feet, mute with shock. She was a penniless Kelthian. How could she possibly have anything to do with Morran, let alone his death? And when would that happen? Before he left for Tymeera?

She pressed her palms into her aching temples, struggling to think clearly.

It was far more likely the Mother would put Morran out of his misery. Her magic was subtle, and her reach went far—as she'd said, the temple protected the surrounding streets against all comers.

Still, Leena had experienced Juradoc's insistent power. After watching Elodie fall, nothing felt certain.

This was all beyond Leena's understanding. She sniffed, fighting back tears of exhaustion. Her dreams were about a home she could count on, a sound roof, and a full larder. She wanted nothing to do with the fate of princes.

Not even mad ones who saw the Flame inside her heart.

She was too exhausted to decide what was right or wrong. This night had broken her.

Leena left the womb-like warmth of the Temple, shivering as the night wind caught her bare skin. She still wore nothing more than her sleeveless silk gown—lovely for dancing but no protection from the rapidly cooling desert air. Her rooming house was close, so she pushed into a trot, limping a little as stones bruised her bare feet.

Lanterns of pierced metalwork hung in doorways and sat on windowsills, lighting the path as she threaded her way between buildings so close together that she could touch the walls on either side. The air in the narrow passage was heavy with the smell of garbage.

The door to her building was missing, torn from its hinges long ago. Leena entered, then climbed the three flights of stairs to her room. Her mind still swirled like a churning cauldron.

The memory of Morran's violence crawled through her, leaving her wounded and raw. His eyes had reminded her of the midnight desert—vast, dark, and alive with silent predators. He still had a hunter's instincts, whatever else had been stripped from his soul. She was no coward, but she quaked as she imagined his warrior's hands, large and strong, around her throat. He could snap her in two as easily as he could crush a gnat.

And yet, there was the shadow of a soul there, as subtle as a ghostly breath at the nape of her neck. A sentimental piece of her —the one that ached for wounded animals and lost causes— wished she could coax his spirit back to life. Such a leader must have been a formidable personality.

She stopped first at a small, splintering door on the landing below hers. Giving a quick knock, she walked in without waiting for a reply. This was Elodie's apartment, which she shared with her mother. There were two rooms, one with a fireplace the women used for cooking. The old lady was hunched on a stool before the fire, stirring a pot of soup that smelled of spice and onions. Leena's mouth watered, reminding her she was beyond hungry.

"Grandmother Vira," she said, raising her voice. The woman was slightly deaf.

Elodie's mother turned, her weathered face splitting into a gap-toothed grin. She'd borne a dozen children, although only three had survived to make the long march into Eldaban once their homeland fell. Elodie, a war widow and the youngest of Vira's brood, was the last survivor.

"Well, girl," Vira said, "have you come for a bite of supper?"

"No, thank you," Leena replied politely. There would be little enough food as it was. "I came to tell you that Elodie is at the temple. There was a bit of an accident, but she'll be fine."

Vira rose from the stool, the wooden spoon still in her hand. At the same moment, a girl, barely four years old, emerged from the other room. She was a miniature of Elodie, with bouncing curls and sun-browned limbs. She leaned against her grandmother's leg, her lower lip sucked in.

"Will she be back in the morning?" the old woman asked. The question was casual, but Leena heard the unspoken worries. *How bad is it? Will my daughter be able to dance? If she isn't, how can we afford to live?*

"The Mother of Flame has taken a personal interest in the healing. Elodie will be back before you know it." Leena forced a brave smile. "Will you be all right to look after Riya on your own tonight? I can stay and help."

Vira sniffed, visibly gathering her pride. "I can manage one little girl."

With that, she turned back to the soup and filled a small wooden bowl. She thrust it at Leena. "Here, take your dinner, girl. I can see you eyeing the pot like a starving dog."

Shamefaced, Leena accepted the soup from Vira's age-spotted hand. "Thank you, Grandmother."

Riya giggled. "You're not a dog."

"I don't know," Leena replied, bending to meet the girl's eyes. "Do I have a tail?"

Grandmother Vira flapped a dismissive hand. "Go home and wash your feet. You look like you walked the length of the riverbed, then dragged half of it onto my clean floor."

Obediently, Leena left, barely making it up the last flight of stairs to her room before she paused to sip soup from the bowl. It was tasty and surprisingly filling, with lentils and barley swimming in the broth. Vira could make a meal out of nothing.

Leena's room was smaller, with no fire. She had a washbasin, a small trunk, and a bedroll, but that was enough. She spent most of her time working, anyhow.

She finished her dinner and washed, changing from her dancing costume to a simple yellow shift. Once she was dressed, she pulled back the curtain of her single window to let in the night air. There were soldiers outside, bawling a drinking song at the top of their lungs. It broke off with a cheer and the sound of a smashing bottle.

She looked down into the street, spotting her younger brother among the handful of guardsmen. One man was telling a tale, and it must have been a good one, judging by the gales of laughter. Normally, the guards didn't stray this close to the Temple, but Fionn made friends everywhere.

Leena frowned, wishing her brother weren't quite so amiable, especially with Lord Dorth's guardsmen. They weren't on the same side—not really. With relief, she saw the guards finish their round of back-slapping and walk the other way, leaving Fionn standing alone.

As they turned, she saw their black-and-gold tabards. Leena's stomach dropped, threatening to dislodge the soup she'd just eaten. Cold crept from her core, raising gooseflesh on her arms. Those weren't Dorth's guardsmen, after all, but Juradoc's chosen men. Why was her brother with them?

"Fionn," she cried, leaning out the window to wave.

He looked up with what seemed like a guilty start. "Hello, Leena."

"Stay there," she ordered before turning back to her room. She pulled on her only other pair of sandals, struggling with the broken lace that wouldn't quite wrap around her ankle before racing down the stairs and into the street.

Fionn straightened from his slouch as she appeared, awarding her a bright smile. Tall and broad, with sandy curls and sky-blue eyes, he knew how to turn on the charm. Leena, however, was six years his senior and remembered wiping his runny nose.

"Hello, darling sister," he said with the confident cheer of the mildly drunk.

"You're keeping strange company." She tried her best to keep the accusation out of her voice, but it didn't quite work.

"I'm keeping pleasant company," he replied, making an obvious effort to remain calm.

A wave of exasperation swept over her. After the scene at the banquet hall and the race to the temple with Elodie, she had no patience for Fionn's recklessness. "They're not our friends."

He shrugged. "They have plans and ambitions. It's a nice change."

"From our own people?"

He shrugged. "The Kelthians lost the war. It's time to move on."

Leena's breath caught at his casual words. "Juradoc's men are the enemy."

"Only if we insist they are."

She tried to tell herself that he was too young to remember the carnage of battle. He was only eighteen now. "The general nearly killed Elodie tonight."

"These men didn't. They were with me," he retorted, barely registering the news about their friend. "I've been with the guards most nights this week."

His tone had an edge she hadn't heard before—more than defiance. It was almost fury. It was then she noticed he was clutching a bundle under his arm. She snatched it away, shaking out the cloth.

It was a gold-and-black tabard. The cold that had gripped her before solidified, freezing her limbs in place.

"You've joined them." She said it quietly, as if the words might shatter in her mouth.

Fionn sobered, the happy-go-lucky youth falling away. "I'll make enough to buy our way out of this slum. Then we can have a proper house, just like you dreamed about. You can have a dowry, so you don't have to dance for your supper anymore."

She crushed the tabard in her hands. Since when did dreams bite like angry serpents? "Don't do this for me."

"Think about it, sister. Think beyond the sad fiddle music and nostalgia for a place that doesn't exist anymore. Kelthia is history best forgotten."

"Fionn!"

"I need to earn my fortune with what I have. I'm not a servant of the temple like you are. I don't have any talent for magic. I'm good with a sword and not much else."

"What does that matter?"

"Do you really want to stay here forever?" He swept a hand around them, indicating the ramshackle streets. "You raised me to survive. Don't blame me for learning my lessons."

Leena's throat hurt, a sure sign she was near tears. "How long have you been thinking this way?"

"Always," he said. "Or as soon as I understood we were victims of the war. We are Kelthian fae, strong and fierce, but not strong and fierce enough. We won't survive by clinging to the same old tactics, and I, at least, want a future."

A mask had dropped, and her brother was gone. The strong young male looking back at her was a stranger.

"You must remember something of our home," she said in the

same strangled voice as before. "When our people refused to surrender, the Shades destroyed the very lands we stood on. They stripped our mountains bare, one after the other."

The magic had been cataclysmic, volcanic. The destruction had lasted years, turning the sky black and blood red as the forests burned peak by peak. Seas of lava had consumed the green valleys, leaving them rivers of stone. Savage rains and floods came next, destroying what was left of the herds and crops. Eventually, the remaining rubble turned to dust.

And then came starvation. In the end, it was simple hunger that won the war. The proud fire fae of the mountains had finally been driven to their knees.

All that was left of the southern mountains was a saw-toothed wasteland the minstrels called the Ravaged Lands. Its people fled to Eldaban—long columns of wounded and widows carrying their possessions on their backs. Leena had just turned ten, Fionn four. She'd held his hand as they'd trudged north.

"Oh, I remember," Fionn said, his tone gentler now. "That's why I've joined the winning side. They say I have a talent with people. Leadership quality. Someday, I could be a captain."

He reached out to touch her arm, but the betrayal was too much. Leena squirmed away, thrusting the tunic into his arms. Reflexively, he grasped it. As he did, the loose cuff of his linen shirt pulled up to show his muscled forearm.

Leena saw the mark. Grabbing his wrist, she pulled his arm toward her. The patch of darkened skin on the inside of his arm was no bigger than a coin, but it was already crusted with white scales. Horror twisted like a living thing inside her. She made a low, keening sound halfway to a sob.

"What?" He jerked his arm away. "What's the matter with you?"

She raised her eyes to meet his. His image blurred until she blinked hard. "How long have you had this?"

"A few days." For the first time, uncertainty dimmed his expression. "It itches a bit."

Leena fought to breathe, her panic turning it to a gasp. "You've had dealings with the Shades. Not just their fae flunkies, but the devils themselves."

Fionn took a step back, raising his chin. "The general appointed me to his personal guard. My company is escorting the Phoenix Prince to Tymeera. Imagine—me in the same place as Prince Morran, one of the greatest sorcerers and warlords of all time. Me, serving in General Juradoc's camp. I'm finally getting out of this place."

"Juradoc is evil, and Morran is a madman," she said flatly. "He tore the banquet room to pieces."

Her panic was gone, replaced by a strange emptiness. That emptiness echoed with screams, but they seemed oddly distant— as if she'd lost her heart down a well. Maybe it was shock. Perhaps she was going mad, too. After all, in the last few seconds, her life had shattered.

Her brother. Shades. Despair.

If she let the despair bubble to the surface, she'd lose her brother. Fionn couldn't abide high emotion. Somewhere deep inside, he was still a frightened child holding her hand.

"That's how it starts, you know," she said, still as frozen as the lava crusted over her childhood home. "That mark. Shade rot. They replace their numbers by infecting fae. If they choose you as their victim, you become one in time."

He made a noise of disgust. "It's a rash. Nothing more. Can't you just be happy for me? I'm good at what I do, and someone finally saw it."

"Happy for you? Fionn, you're sick. Everything you are is at risk. You might be able to recover if you get far enough away from Juradoc. The temple will know what to do."

But his expression had shuttered. "None of the others have turned into monsters."

"It doesn't happen to everyone. Just the ones the Shades pick. You said they singled you out."

"As a soldier. What else would they want from me?"

Leena couldn't answer that. She stammered something, but it made no sense.

"Leave me alone." He cursed and spun away, striding in the direction his new friends had gone. The light from a window fell over him, gilding his curls. For an instant, he was still the boy Leena remembered.

"Wait!" She bolted after him, needing to pull him into her arms.

He'd reached the street corner. Fionn glanced over his shoulder, not bothering to stop. The force of his glare made Leena skid to a halt. She'd never seen that look before.

"You're all that's left," she said, emotion leaking into her words until they barely made sense. She couldn't hold it back anymore. He was the last of her family.

He slung the tabard over his shoulder and kept walking. "You're resourceful."

Reason snapped. "Fionn son of Finra, you come back here this instant!"

Leena grasped her middle, panting. She couldn't stop her racing pulse. Fear made her lightheaded—for Fionn, for herself, of what this meant for her world. The enemy had crept in and snatched her happy-go-lucky brother, robbing everyone who knew him.

Fionn turned the corner without breaking stride. She stumbled forward a few steps, trying to keep him in sight, but the darkness swallowed his form. The finality of it was a drumbeat in her head. *Lost. Lost. Lost.*

Shade rot. Leena's knowledge of the infection was sketchy, but she knew the spreading mark mirrored a gradual corruption of mind and soul. No wonder he was acting strangely.

She couldn't force her imagination to go further than those

bare facts. Without thinking, she reversed direction and ran home, tears obscuring her sight. By the time she pounded up the stairs to her room, she was gasping for breath.

Fionn had been right about one thing—Morran had been a mighty general. While the Kelthian tribes held the southern mountains, Morran had defended the lands east of the Serpent River. Songs were sung of his deeds throughout Faery, recounting his armies' ferocity and the deadly elegance of his magic—magic strong enough to defeat the Shades. Between the Kelthians and the Phoenix Prince, the Shades had been caught in a tactical vice, and Morran had squeezed them without mercy.

Then something had happened, and Morran had vanished.

Her people had lost everything.

Leena closed the door of her room, then leaned her back against it. She was shaking now, the storm of her grief and rage finally finding a physical outlet. She slowly sank to the floor, legs refusing to hold her up any longer.

Fionn.

There was one other thing she knew about the rot. Whatever she'd told her brother, there was no cure, no medicine, nor any spell that left the patient alive. She'd seen the Mother treat such patients. Prayer and isolation could slow the disease, but life as a desert hermit was the best Fionn could hope for. Isolation would kill him as surely as the corruption.

Another wave of terror struck her, but this time her training took over. She stilled her mind, concentrating on the sounds of Eldaban's streets. Music. Voices. The clip-clop of horses as they passed. Slowly, her heartbeat returned to normal. Panic was the enemy of thought.

The temple—at least the temple in Eldaban—had no answers. There had to be a path forward, something she could try. Other experts. More power. A miracle.

She had to fix this.

Her brother had called Morran one of the greatest sorcerers

and warlords of all time. Maybe he had been before he'd begun smashing tables and roaring like a wounded tiger. All the same, the Great Temple was loyal to the Lord of Tymeera. If anyone could command a cure, it was the Phoenix Prince. His royal blood carried exceptional magic.

Or it had.

Now Morran was a madman. A dead man if the Mother's prophecy came true.

A lost cause—and yet she'd seen a flash of who he'd been, called forth by the Flame. Could she summon that spark long enough to save her brother?

Leena closed her eyes, willing her tears to stop. She wanted nothing to do with the fate of princes, but what if Morran held Fionn's future in his hands?

Was the Phoenix Prince a possibility—and a peril—she couldn't ignore?

"Lord Dorth is agitated," Juradoc observed as he leaned back against a pile of richly embroidered cushions. "You broke his high table."

"Do we care?" Morran asked.

They were no longer in the palace, but in an encampment outside Eldaban, among the fields of stunted grass. Juradoc's tent was the largest, appointed with the best of everything—from wine to Pomandine silks to silver dishes plundered from every corner of Faery. The slaves kneeling in the shadows were forest fae from Celador—small and pale green, with vines tangled in their long dark hair.

The carpet beneath their feet was worth a bag of gold— enough to buy a village—but the general thought nothing of tossing it on the bare dirt. *With all those black robes*, Morran mused, *the Shades must have a horror of dust*.

"We do not care about Dorth," Juradoc said. "However, it is expedient not to upset our allies more than necessary."

Morran's mind had wandered, and it took a moment to remember what they were talking about. The lord of Eldaban had wept over the destruction of his feast. Morran tried to feel sorry, but the fat little slug had sided with the enemy.

So what am I? Morran wondered, but, for once, he knew where he stood. He was a prisoner, for all that he was free of literal shackles. The chains that bound him were magic, not iron. But was he supposed to know that?

Anxiety stung like needles of ice piercing his mind, but he kept his features still. Juradoc was studying him, the violet glow of his eyes bright beneath his hood.

"It was a shame about the roast lamb," Morran said, feigning a casual shrug.

"Then consider the waste next time you drown the good and great of Faery in the main course." The general's tone was dry. "Wanton destruction always seems wrong coming from a guest."

"I thought that was the mark of a good party."

"The invitation specified formal wear. That does not include the condiments."

Morran laughed, but there was a thread of uneasiness in it. What was he doing in the Shade camp? Why did Juradoc keep him alive? Morran couldn't piece his circumstances together. Something told him if he regained his wits, the Shades would slaughter him in a heartbeat.

That meant the reason they kept him was important. Perhaps a potential weapon.

Weapons are good.

The silence in the tent had gone on a beat too long.

"There was enough food in that hall to feed the town for a week," Morran observed. "Eldaban must be a rich city."

"Dorth pays us to keep trade flowing."

"A time-honored arrangement."

"Lords paying thugs for protection?" Juradoc asked, a sneer in his words.

"Is that why we came here?" Morran asked, sounding bored. "To collect tribute?"

"Not entirely."

Then Morran recalled the general's words in the banquet hall. *You swore that ancient power would be ours for the taking.* The memory punched like a brawler's fist—hard and decisive. Somehow, it had stuck in his mind, unlike every other memory. *Why? Why remember those words in particular?*

The fire dancer.

There had been two, but only one had imprinted on Morran's shattered mind. She—or her kind, at least—was what Dorth had promised and Juradoc had claimed. Her ability to summon the Flame had been the price of Eldaban's safety.

And she was powerful. Though the Shades might not fully understand, the dance was a rite, a ceremony of healing. Ever since her performance, his head had been clearer.

That image—lithe limbs and fiery hair—brushed over him like something lush and ripe. She had lit his soul like a private sun, filling him with childlike wonder—though nowhere near so innocent. Her heat had reminded him that he was male and had been alone too long.

Out of her presence, he felt the creeping cold of darkness, as if the stars winked out one by one.

"I would like to see the dancer again." Morran kept his tone casual, settling back on the cushions. He waved a languid hand to one of the slaves, signaling for wine. A green-skinned youth rose at once to obey.

"Then we shall take one with us when we leave." Something in the general's tone said he'd already arranged it.

Morran nodded. There was only one dancer who mattered. "Where are we bound?"

"Tymeera." Juradoc spoke in patient tones. Given the state of Morran's memory, he had probably answered the question at least once before.

Why Tymeera? Morran turned the name over in his mind, his

breath quickening. It was a clue, a bread crumb in this hellish maze.

Another memory came, this time of smashing the banquet hall in his crude, inarticulate rage. Shame burned in his belly. Once, he'd been a fine, elegant swordsman, but none of that remained. Wanton destruction was the only weapon he had.

To do what? *Stop the enemy.* It was his old self who answered. A rusty voice, but recognizable.

Tension clawed through his neck and shoulders. He sensed Juradoc's eyes on him—those eerie, violet pinpricks probing his every change of expression.

The moment broke as the slave knelt before Morran, balancing a wine-filled goblet on a serving tray. Morran slowly sat forward to accept it, his eyes meeting the earth fae's deep brown gaze. The youth was terrified.

A memory emerged, shimmering into view for the first time in... Morran had no sense of time. All he knew was that it was brilliant and ephemeral like the lamplight caught on the surface of his wine.

Once, he'd been the sword of his people. He'd protected the vulnerable. He'd been filled with the fire of vengeance against the Shades. His knuckles grew white around the goblet's jeweled sides as a hunger of his own unfurled in his chest.

The Prince of Tymeera was shaking off his bonds.

LEENA STILL SAT WITH HER BACK AGAINST THE DOOR, HER thoughts pounding like a restless surf. The square of sky outside her window had turned the pearly gray of dawn, but she had no more answers than before. All she'd achieved for a night's misery was a numb backside.

The one concession she had made to the cool night air was wrapping herself in the shawl she used as a blanket. It was one of the very few things her mother had taken from their old home.

She shrugged it closer, digging her fingers into the thick, soft cloth, breathing in the faint scent of home.

The old woolen square carried burdens and gave comfort. Every Kelthian woman had one, using it as a baby sling, a market basket, or a shroud. The golden wool had come from the family herds, spun, dyed, and woven in a pattern common to her tribe. Just like the fate of her family, it was stained and threadbare.

She'd heard rumors that the fae—all fae, not just her people—were losing to the Shades. The high king's throne sat empty on the Wheel, the tall mountain at the heart of Faery. The great dragons were diminished. The king of the ocean deeps had lost his undersea palace and gone into hiding. The city called Pomandine had fallen into the sea.

But what mattered most to Leena was closer to home. Fionn was slipping away, and she had no idea how to save him. Worse, he was about to follow the enemy to a city far, far away.

Leena closed her eyes again. They were sandy with fatigue, but there was no chance of sleep. Not until she had some idea how to proceed.

A scrabbling sound on the window ledge made her jerk to attention. A black shape bounced through the opening before landing with a thump.

"I have news," Kifi said as she crawled into Leena's lap, pushing her whiskered nose close. "General Juradoc sent a messenger to the temple."

Leena sat up, wide awake now. "What for?"

"The general demanded that Elodie accompany the army to Tymeera."

Leena pushed the cat from her lap, then got to her feet. "Elodie is ill."

"Exactly. She is too weak to fight him. Perhaps that is why he chose her and not you."

Leena paced the small room, swearing under her breath.

"The Mother sent the messenger away," Kifi said with some

satisfaction. "She did not harm him—not in blood and flesh—but I do not think he will return."

Leena heard the Mother's voice in Kifi's words. As keepers of memory, the temple cats made excellent messengers—and reference books. "What do you know about Morran?"

"He is the Phoenix Prince."

"Which you neglected to tell me when he arrived at Lord Dorth's banquet."

Kifi gave a toothy yawn. "I didn't want to give you stage fright."

"Fine," Leena said with disgust. "What does the reference to the phoenix signify?"

"Ah," Kifi said, curling her tail around her paws. "His father was Prince Karth."

Even Leena had heard of him. "Karth threw himself off the palace roof. That was how Morran got the throne."

"Correct."

"And?" Leena prompted.

"Karth's difficulties were caused by what happened to his familiar."

"A phoenix? I thought they were a legend."

"Only rare. The Shades stole the bird to enslave it to fight the dragons." The cat licked a paw thoroughly before carrying on. "The enemy had never possessed a weapon against aerial attack, but a giant flaming raptor immune to dragon breath worked remarkably well."

"What happened to it?"

"A young dragon princess set it free. The bird flew off, never to return."

Leena was growing impatient. "So why is this relevant?"

"When the phoenix escaped, it did not go home. That's when Karth took his own life," Kifi replied. "It's not widely known, but the Phoenix Prince is not a shifter. He is two creatures in one— the lord and his familiar. Karth had been split in half, and the connection that made him one being was irreparably broken. He went mad as a result."

Leena stared out her window, seeing and not seeing the silent, early morning street. There was an odd parallel between her longing for the home she'd lost and the old prince mourning his missing soul. "And Morran?"

"He bonded at birth with his own familiar. One, it seems, no one has seen for an awfully long time."

Leena turned to face Kifi. "You think they've done the same thing to Morran."

"It's a theory much discussed among the cats," Kifi said with a flip of her tail. "The phoenix is said to grant the prince untold magic, which would explain his earlier victories."

"Where is the bird now?"

"Who knows?"

"And the Shades are on their way to the Great Temple and Tymeera."

"The Queen of Cats is there," Kifi said gravely. "So is the source of the Flame. Morran's madness puts them all at risk."

Leena crossed to her bed and sat, putting her head in her hands. "If that's their end game, why bother asking Elodie and me to dance?"

Kifi jumped up beside her, a warm, soft presence. "The cats have one or two memories of Shades attempting to feed on fae elemental power, but not with any great success."

"Juradoc is definitely hungry. I felt it during the dance. He would have sucked us dry if he could have."

The cat's ears flattened with anger. "Perhaps Juradoc was testing his method of feeding. It would make sense to start small. If he intends to taste the Flame at its source, he'll need to practice."

"Whatever the reason, he won't test his theories on Elodie again. Riya had lost one parent already. I won't allow her to lose another."

Leena fell silent for a long moment. Kifi put a paw on her arm. "There is more you aren't telling me."

Leena let out a breath that might have been a sob. "Fionn. He has attracted the general's attention and earned a place in his guard. He's on the road to Tymeera, too."

Kifi's yellow eyes grew sharp. "Has he sickened? The rot is usually how the enemy shows preference."

Leena met the cat's gaze. Her chin trembled, but she stiffened it against oncoming tears. "Do the cats know how to save him?"

Kifi rubbed her chin against Leena's hand in a gesture of sympathy. "Only extraordinary magic will work."

"Like Morran's?"

Kifi sagged despondently. "Maybe once upon a time."

Leena's throat squeezed. She had to save Fionn somehow.

"If the Shades are expecting a dancer," Leena began, "we can give them a dancer."

Kifi hissed in dismay. "You would go in Elodie's place?"

"Yes." The more Leena thought about it, the more sense it made. She could keep an eye on Fionn. She could save Elodie. Plus, she could find out what power Morran actually had—hopefully before the Mother's prophecy of death came to pass.

That assumed Morran could be reasoned with. She'd seen the madness in his eyes as he'd destroyed Lord Dorth's feast hall, tossing guards across the room like napkins. She might be risking her life for nothing.

Leena bent and scooped Kifi into her arms, kissing the cat on the nose. "Thank you for everything. I'm going to miss you terribly."

"I will miss you, Leena of the Temple." Kifi regarded her with large eyes. "I will give your farewells to the Mother."

A sudden ache lodged in Leena's throat. "Please understand that I'm desperate."

"The army is camped at the east gate," Kifi said quickly, as if afraid to prolong the goodbye. "They will leave at first light, so you need to hurry."

With that, the cat leaped free, bounded to the windowsill, and vanished.

Leena swallowed hard. The task she'd set herself was simple. All she had to do was leave everything she had ever known to walk into impossible danger—and beg a doomed prince for his help.

There was every chance this would be a one-way trip.

＊ 6 ＊

Dawn lit the horizon as Leena reached the east gate. At this hour, it was unlikely she'd meet anyone she knew, but there was still a risk of recognition and questions would slow her down. Accordingly, Leena wore her long cloak and used both the hood and a scarf to veil her features. She carried her few belongings bundled in her shawl beneath the cloak.

A stone's throw beyond the gate, a row of spears was thrust butt-first into the dirt. This marked the camp's outskirts. She had arrived just in time, judging by the bustle of soldiers. Tents collapsed one by one in a flutter of silks, reminding her of landing birds. Horses stood patiently as waggoners fastened their jingling harness. From somewhere to the right, she caught the scent of wood smoke and frying meat. All at once, she felt her long night and empty stomach.

A guard stepped in her path before she'd crossed the space to the army's domain. He was a tall, rangy earth fae with skin the color of an old oak.

"State your business," he said. The accent was from Kyleen.

"I was summoned from the temple to dance for the general and his guest, Prince Morran."

"Your name?"

"Elodie, daughter of Vira and dancer of the Flame." She gave a demure curtsey as she said it. Her height and build were nothing like her friend's, but the guard wouldn't know that.

"Right you are, miss," he said, standing a little straighter and giving her a broad smile. "I was told you would be coming. Follow me."

Leena exhaled in relief. Apparently, news of the Mother's refusal to send Elodie hadn't made it back to the camp—or at least not to the patrol at the gate. So far, everything was falling into place.

The guard shouted at another soldier to relieve him. Then he led Leena across the camp. The dry ground had been churned to dust by thousands of feet and hooves. Everywhere, figures in black and gold strode past.

At the sight, Leena's plan lost much of its shine. Some of the soldiers were fae, but more were Shades. A sense of danger settled over her like a heavy cloak.

Fionn was nowhere in sight. She was both relieved and worried—if her brother recognized her too soon, the game was up. If she could get him alone first, she could explain why she'd come in Elodie's place. Surely, he'd go along with the deception until it was too late to send her home. But what would she do when Juradoc realized there had been a switch? Leena's stomach flipped uneasily. Risking the Shade's temper was a terrible gamble, but she'd take that chance for the sake of her friend and, most of all, her brother.

Their destination was the largest pavilion in view. It was at least as large as the cottage Leena had been born in and a thousand times fancier. The white pointed roof was luminous in the swelling light of dawn, and, as they approached, she saw the door panels were pinned back to reveal luxurious sleeping quarters. Morran was inside, pulling on his boots. Servants were on their way out after clearing away the remnants of breakfast.

Leena and her escort stopped outside the entrance, and the guard gave a smart salute to someone she guessed was a junior officer. She waited as they established General Juradoc was not on hand, and they weren't sure what to do with her until he returned.

Tovas would have boxed their ears for treating his prized performer like a misplaced delivery. She had a queasy feeling it would be a long time before anyone cared for her so well as the Master of Revels.

Morran approached the entry to the pavilion. "Is there some difficulty?"

"Greetings, my lord." Both guards regarded him with wary respect, as if he were their master's expensive but unpredictable pet.

Curious, Leena looked on. Morran's words were cool but courteous, not at all like those of a man who had recently dismantled Lord Dorth's hall.

"This is the entertainer General Juradoc requested," said the senior of the two. "But the general is not here."

Morran cocked an eyebrow. "No, he is not. You can go."

The guards saluted before turning to obey. Leena moved to follow.

"Not you." Morran's voice cut from the gloom of the tent. There was command in his tone.

She froze, watching helplessly as her escort left. Although she had hoped to speak to Morran, nerves suddenly overtook her. He was like a tiger—large, potentially deadly, and impossible to fathom. There was no telling when he might bite.

She turned gradually, the air heavy with her apprehension.

"Come here." Morran withdrew deeper into the gloom, not looking back. He expected obedience.

Reluctantly, Leena gathered her courage and entered the shadowy pavilion.

He remained standing, towering over her by at least a head. As her eyes adjusted to the gloom, she saw he was freshly shaven and wearing a spotless tunic. She bowed low, careful to keep her veil in place.

"What is your name, dancer?" he asked, running a hand through the black waves of his hair.

"Elodie, daughter of Vira," she said for the second time.

"You may rise." His chin lifted in an expression that reminded her of a displeased schoolmaster. "I am still enough of a sorcerer to know you just lied."

Leena said nothing, keeping her eyes downcast. Silence gathered around them like a heavy mist.

"You are not the one who was summoned," he added slowly. "Juradoc asked for your friend."

She dared to look up through the gauze of her veil. "My name is Leena."

"Leena." The briefest of smiles crossed his face, crinkling the corners of his dark eyes before it vanished. "I will keep your secret safe as long as you do not lie to me again."

"Why would you do that?"

"Why not? I live by a minimum of rules. Honesty is the first."

With that, he reached down and hooked a finger over the end of the scarf that hid her features. His grasp was light but certain as he pulled the veil away. Leena gasped, and the sudden breath of free air was intoxicating.

So was the slight widening of his pupils. He could hide much, but not that rapt male attention. Leena drew back a step, color rising to her cheeks. He'd seen her face before, yet it felt as if she'd just been exposed. The feeling went deeper than her disguise.

"You were the defiant one last night," he mused. "A dangerous course, given your audience."

"I got away."

"So why risk coming now?"

Leena considered her answer. "Elodie isn't well. She would not have danced to your satisfaction."

"Honest, but incomplete," he replied. "What do you know of my interest or my satisfaction?"

He lingered suggestively on the last word.

Anger pricked her. "I am a priestess of the temple."

He drew closer, looming now. "Have I offended your modesty?"

It was a clear attempt to unsettle her, perhaps trick her into revealing more secrets. She refused to rise to the bait. "The Flame touched you when I danced."

His brows drew together. "And what does the Flame know of my desires? Did it tell you?"

No, the Flame never spoke to her. Not directly. She would have been a better healer if it did. Mounting tension made her muscles ache. "No. I mean...it knows you. Whatever happened, you are still a child of the Flame."

"Whatever happened," he murmured, but there was fury in his words. This time, he pulled away, putting space between them. "What else did it have to say? What did you learn in your dance?"

Slowly, Leena shook her head, unsure how to reply. This was why he'd chosen to speak to her. He knew they'd shared something significant, and he wanted answers as much as she did. But what to say? If Kifi had guessed right, Morran had been irrevocably broken. Telling him that served no purpose, especially right now, when she needed his help.

When she didn't answer, he shifted impatiently. "Well?"

"Flame recognizes desire, rage, lust, heroism, love, compassion." She spoke each word quietly, forcing him to bend slightly to listen. "The Flame saw the places inside you where those fires have been."

"You mean it saw the desolate ashes of my soul."

This was dangerous territory, inappropriate between a servant and lord, much less two strangers. Still, Leena didn't falter. This was the sorcerer who might save her brother. "Ashes or embers, that is not for me to say. I'm just a dancer."

He laughed then, a soft chuckle that was both bitter and genuinely amused. The sound slid over her skin like warm fur. "Fire dancers are healers, and I thank you for what you did. Last night, I recovered a scrap of who I was. I wonder if you could give me more."

Sudden wariness made Leena grow still. She hadn't expected gratitude.

"I can't restore your familiar," she said.

Puzzlement spread across his features. "I don't understand."

Her breath caught as she glimpsed the extent of his inner wound. *He doesn't even know.* "Then it does not matter."

He began a slow circle around her, studying her from every side. From beyond the silk walls came the squeak and rumble of the heavy wagons, the sound of shouting soldiers, and the stomp of hooves. The camp was mobilizing. She was running out of time.

The light suddenly dimmed. Leena spun to see that Morran had let down the silk panels forming the space's entrance. No one could observe them now.

She was alone with him.

He walked toward her. No, he prowled, a stray shaft of morning sunlight highlighting the hard lines of his warrior's body. Leena swallowed, suddenly aware of her heating flesh. Whatever crippling wounds he might bear, they weren't physical.

Morran came to a stop, clasping his hands behind his back like a general reviewing the troops. His forehead furrowed in concentration, the corners of his lips turning down. Leena was grateful for the cloak that still hid most of her form. She needed a barrier between them.

"I require your healing power," he said in a voice pitched for their ears alone. "But first I require the complete truth. Why did you really come in your friend's stead? You might care for her, but no one walks into the lion's den for one reason alone."

Something within Leena cracked—whether it was her reserve

or her resolve, she wasn't sure. She'd expected to study Morran from afar, to choose her moment, to slide her plea into a conversation like a magician pulling a coin from thin air. Instead, he'd pinned her inside of a minute.

His gaze held hers, patient and unblinking. Her mouth went utterly dry.

"My brother is here, among the guards. I'm afraid for him."

"Ah. So you should be." For the first time, there was a softer edge in his voice. "There is no return from serving with the Shades."

Leena flinched, pressing a hand to her stomach as if he'd struck her. "If you know that, why are you here?"

Her pulse drummed in her ears. She'd spoken without thinking, without regard for rank or courtesy—or the mad fury she'd seen at the banquet. Though Morran's expression was carefully blank, she could still see the tension around his eyes. Her knees trembled, wondering what would come next.

It wasn't what she expected.

"Do you hope I might save your wayward brother?"

"Yes." Surprise robbed the word of strength.

His face changed for an instant, giving her a glimpse of a different Morran—one who was wry, wise, and sympathetic. "Have you come to save me in return?"

Leena's breath stopped. She hadn't imagined it was a possibility.

"You need someone with more skill than me," she replied, her voice thick with regret.

He nodded, not meeting her eyes.

The Mother prophesied his death, Leena thought. Her gut twisted. Morran was unpredictable, dangerous. He was also a victim.

"But I'll try." Giddiness swept her, as if she'd stepped off a cliff.

"You're speaking the truth." It wasn't a question.

"I am."

Instinct made her reach out. She brushed her fingertips against the dark indigo of his sleeve. He didn't withdraw, but he was gone again, fallen back into that careful blankness. All that was left was the cool-eyed prince she'd seen at Juradoc's side.

Had she revealed too much? Had she been tricked?

Then he released his hands from behind his back, raising the arm she touched. Without warning, his long fingers traced the line of her cheek, gently and with a connoisseur's precision. Leena froze in place. His hand was warm, calloused by the sword, but as elegantly formed as any fae's. He repeated the gesture, cupping her chin in his palm. His touch was considering, as if she were an artwork he wished to study, though with one word or look, it could become a lover's exploration.

"As I said before," he murmured, "you have power, Leena of the Flame."

His gaze said a thousand things more.

Temple dancers—both male and female—received their share of attention, but she wasn't prepared for this side of the Phoenix Prince. The urge to run was strong.

But then he leaned in, almost magically drawing her to him at the same time. Leena had no intention of moving, but found she'd risen on her toes so that her lips met his. She leaned in for balance. The sudden intimacy seemed the most natural thing in the world.

Do I want this? she wondered, but the thought didn't survive long. This was a matter of heart and blood, not of the mind.

His were not the soft lips of a youth. They were firm, almost hard, and there was no hesitation. This was the kiss of a man who knew how to offer himself to a mate. He nipped at the corner of her mouth, then the fullness of her lower lip. Deep in her belly, the Flame stirred, sending sparks of pleasure through every limb.

Leena tilted her head, seeking a better angle. She'd dallied with the young swains of Eldaban, but this was a warrior in his prime. The Flame approved her choice with a surge of heat in her core. Her tongue sought entrance to his mouth. It found an answering warmth as he deepened the kiss, taking what she allowed.

Her cloak fell to the floor. A moment later, his hands found her waist, tracing the curve of her spine and hip. In response, her fingers gripped the fabric of his tunic, wanting to tear it from his body. At the last instant, reason fumbled for some wisp of control.

She broke the kiss, pushing him away until she could see his face. The softer Morran she'd glimpsed a moment ago was back, a sly smile on his lips. It was the look of someone who knew they'd hit the mark. It slid away in seconds, but not before she understood she was one of the things he desired—and meant to have.

But for how long? Morran was no Kelthian shepherd boy begging for her favor. No, the moment he was whole, he'd slip through her fingers like the desert sand.

A phoenix rose from the ashes to fly free. It did not sing sweet songs from a cage.

Leena stepped away from Morran, welcoming the space between them. She could give him her strength as an ally and her compassion as a healer, but that was all.

Her heart wasn't part of their bargain.

$$\text{❈} \quad 7 \quad \text{❈}$$

The camp mobilized, pushing Leena's scheme past the point of no return.

Morran ordered that she be assigned a small wagon to herself. While there were no other living occupants, the inside was piled with sacks of grain, reducing the available space by half. She made a nest in one corner, then arranged her belongings to form a more or less comfortable bed. The day passed against a backdrop of heat, dust, and the rumble of wheels.

Sunlight filtered through the canvas stretched over the wagon's arched iron frame, baking the air inside. When Leena woke from a nap, groggy with heat, she struggled to her knees and pulled a corner of the canvas aside to look out. With nothing to do, she'd been dozing on and off for hours. By the angle of the sun in the cloudless sky, it was late afternoon. A sea of parched scrubland stretched to the horizon, with no other life in sight.

Where were they? If they'd been following the Heartrun River to the coast, there would be crops and flocks of seabirds. The absence of anything but scrub and dust meant they were traveling to Tymeera overland. There would be nothing but desert for hundreds of miles.

Leaning out, she caught a glimpse of the piebald horse pulling her wagon, its feathered hooves maintaining a slow trudge in the dust. The driver, or what little she could see of him, had the stocky build of a human. Every army employed mortals in such roles, but only the most desperate worked for the Shades.

Her wagon—one of many—was somewhere near the end of a long column of cavalry and foot soldiers. When she tried to guess the total number of soldiers, she failed. The line of moving bodies snaked out of sight. Most were Shades, their hooded cloaks wrapped tightly around them. They could move in daylight, but only with discomfort. If Juradoc was marching his army this hard, he had plans.

Leena pulled her head inside, dizzy with panic. She was alone in the enemy's army with Morran—a prisoner and madman—as her only ally. How long he would help her was unknown. Until he lost the thread of his reason? Until he realized she couldn't cure him? Or would Juradoc destroy her first?

And every Shade was, by definition, a killer of fae. She was a scrap of meat among a starving pack of wolves. Yet, if she ran, the chances of surviving the wastelands were painfully slim.

She was an idiot to come here.

I did this for Fionn, she reminded herself. *For Elodie*. Terror chittered in the back of her mind. Her brother's future depended on Morran—assuming she could find a way to restore the prince. She was gambling everything on healing him, though she had little information to work with.

The one good thing was that thinking about Morran steadied her nerves. Despite everything, he was a reassuring presence—and an intriguing one. Leena fanned her face, not sure how much heat was due to the memory of Morran's mouth on hers. That couldn't happen again.

She slumped down, unscrewing the top of her flask to take a swallow of water. It was warm, but it cleared the dust from her burning throat. As she fastened the top again, she considered what step to take first. Her biggest problem—Shades aside—was a scarcity of facts about Morran's condition. Every patient had a history, which played a vital role in diagnosis, which led to a cure. Until she knew the details of his story, she was fencing in the dark.

And the next time they spoke, she would stay on topic. No kissing. No losing herself in the sensation of those huge arms around her body.

A small black head poked out from between the grain sacks. "You're finally awake."

Leena squeaked in fright. "Kifi!"

Terror gutted her. One of the guards could squash the kitten in one hand—but common sense had never clouded Kifi's personal sky. Ever.

Annoyance swiftly followed. "What are you doing here?"

"Aren't you glad to see me?" Kifi asked, hopping onto Leena's lap.

"Idiot." Overcome, Leena scooped Kifi up and pushed her face into her soft black fur. She must have squeezed a little too hard because Kifi mewed in protest.

"Why aren't you at the temple?" Leena demanded.

Kifi struggled out of her grasp, landing in her lap. "Upon reflection, I could not refuse this opportunity for adventure."

"You're still a kitten. Travel is forbidden."

"This is my chance to see the Queen of Cats," Kifi said without apology. "How can I not take that up as my mission? Such an opportunity may never come again in my lifetime."

"It's a risk."

"What in Faery is not these days?"

The feline had a point. "I might not make it to Tymeera."

The two stared at one another for a moment, the cat's golden eyes meeting Leena's. Silently, Leena poured water from her flask into the bowl that had held her dinner of rice and beans. She pushed the bowl Kifi's way. Immediately, Kifi lapped noisily until the water was gone and then lifted her head. "Your chances are greatly improved if I am with you."

"I'll worry about you the entire time," Leena protested.

Kifi gave a bone-cracking stretch before flopping into an elegant sprawl. "I'm a friend. I think you need one."

An ache formed in Leena's throat. "How can a junior temple cat help me battle the Shades?"

"Your prince is missing his bird. Cats are all about catching birds."

"I spoke to him. He knows nothing about the phoenix. Maybe you're wrong."

"Unlikely," Kifi sniffed.

"You said this one was as big as a dragon and spouting flames. Remembering it would hardly be an issue."

"Not necessarily."

"Explain."

"Memory, stories, and history itself are all surprisingly fragile." Kifi's scholarly tone said this was the collective wisdom of the temple cats. "A severe wound often erases a patient's recollection of events."

As a healer, Leena was well aware of that. "But other people remind them of important facts, like big burning birds."

"Morran is isolated from his own soldiers. He could be manipulated."

"Maybe, but..."

"Familiars often carry the memory of their masters. They're typically more objective observers."

"But where did the familiar go?" Leena asked in frustration. "If it flew away, how do we get it back?"

"Catching a phoenix won't be simple," Kifi said with a flick of the tail. "Mice are a matter of patience. With birds, technique is everything."

The conversation ended as the wagon jolted to a halt. Kifi sat up, ears cocked forward and whiskers at attention.

Leena listened. Sergeants shouted orders up and down the line, growing easier to hear as the creak of wheels and clomping of feet gradually stilled. She pushed the canvas apart just far enough to peer out. A wave of cooler air caressed her face. The angle of the sun was dropping, indicating that dusk wasn't far behind.

Someone in a black-and-gold uniform was walking beside the wagon train, clearly on a mission. Leena dropped the canvas, then shrank back inside the wagon. She had no illusions of safety. To a large extent, survival would depend on staying out of sight.

Footfalls approached, sand and gravel crunching beneath leather soles. Then they stopped. The canvas cover wavered as someone searched for the opening.

Kifi dove for cover, her dark fur vanishing in a shadowy corner of the wagon. Pulse pounding, Leena grabbed the scarf she'd been wearing, draping the painted silk around her like a veil. Then she shrugged on her shawl to hide her form. Her palms were slippery with sweat as she searched for her belt knife.

Gloved hands parted the fabric. Feet scuffled, and the head and shoulders of a guard pushed through the opening. Leena glimpsed Fionn's profile and quickly turned away, pretending to hunt for something in her bundle of belongings. Why was he at her wagon?

More importantly, why was every instinct telling her to hide from her brother? Hadn't she come here to rescue him?

Her mind swung back to their last encounter, so full of anger. Now that he was here, doubt froze her tongue. This would have been easier if she already had a cure in hand.

"We're setting up for tonight," Fionn said. "The general orders you to dance."

Although it was Fionn's voice, the harsh, abrupt tone didn't sound like him. It chilled Leena, but she remained where she was, her back to him. Her only response was a graceful nod.

"Look at me when I speak," Fionn ordered. "Demonstrate some respect."

Slowly, Leena turned toward him, mind racing.

"Show your face," he snapped.

"I am a dancer of the Flame, here for the general," she said in an icy tone that usually worked on troublesome clients. "I will not subject myself to the common gaze."

He gave a bark of laughter that held no warmth. "Then avoid the looking glass, sister."

Leena's breath caught. The game was up.

Fionn climbed in, letting the canvas drop behind him. He was as handsome as ever, but he seemed older, the lines of his face harder. Pulling aside her veil, Leena took in the black-and-gold tabard he wore over a long-sleeved black tunic. A longsword was strapped to his back, along with an expensive-looking knife at his belt. Fionn could never have afforded the weapons or uniform on his own, which meant someone with money had sponsored him. Someone had turned him into a traitor. Had it been Juradoc himself?

He crouched in front of Leena, absently scratching his arm. "What are you doing here?"

"I could ask the same of you."

"Answer me." He gripped her upper arms, giving her a none-too-gentle shake. He was hurting her, his fingers digging into her flesh.

"The infection is spreading, isn't it?" she asked softly.

He pushed her away, sending her sprawling against the sacks of grain. Leena fell with a grunt, more from surprise than pain. Fionn had never been rough with her, even as a child.

Angry yellow eyes flashed in the shadows. *Kifi.*

"Ouch!" Leena said loudly, desperate to keep Fionn's attention fixed on her and not the cat. "What do you think you're doing, Fionn?"

He sat on the heels of his new black boots, heaving a pointed sigh. "I know it should be Elodie sitting here. I should turn you in to the general."

"Elodie couldn't even walk after the performance in the banquet hall. She wouldn't have survived this journey, and then where would her family be?"

Fionn sat, bracing one arm over his knee. His mouth worked, biting down on angry words. "You're forcing me to choose between duty and family."

"Is that a real choice, brother? You know Elodie. You know me. We are your people."

He gave her a baleful glare. "You were. I'm part of something larger now. Whatever you're thinking, I'm not going back to Eldaban."

Leena's vision blurred. "You're still my brother, whatever you say."

"Don't start. Weeping won't change my mind."

"You *have* to see sense."

"We've had that conversation. I'm not going through it again."

Leena met his gaze, then averted her eyes, her throat burning with tears. She wasn't going to win him over through simple argument—nor was he offering to get her to safety, out of danger of the Shades. He *had* changed.

He grimaced. "If General Juradoc thinks I've had anything to do with this, I'll lose everything. He'll probably kill me."

"I'm sorry I put you in a difficult position." She almost meant it. "I'll be careful, but I couldn't live with myself if they'd dragged Elodie from her bed."

Fionn's head suddenly jerked up, and his gaze swept the far end of the wagon.

"What is it?" Leena asked, forcing her voice to sound calm. *Be still, Kifi.*

"I saw something move," Fionn replied in a tight voice.

"I don't think so," she said. "I've been in here for hours. There's no one here but you and me."

Fionn grunted. "If you say so."

Leena's stomach dropped. For the first time ever, she'd lied to her brother. "Are you going to turn me in?"

He cast her a sidelong look. "You're brave, Leena. I'll give you that much, but be careful. Your kind of magic won't stop a blade."

The words were reasonable, but his voice was as cold as dank, foul water.

"That's not an answer." It slowly dawned on Leena that she was growing afraid of him. The idea made her sick to her stomach.

He made a derisive sound. "You're safe enough for the moment. One of the slaves will bring you dinner. Someone will summon you to dance after nightfall. I was sent to warn you to be ready."

He gathered himself to leave.

"Can't you stay to talk for a while?" Leena reached out to touch his arm, but he'd already risen.

"I have duties," he said. "There's extra work I must do."

Disappointment twisted in her chest. She wanted to keep him a moment longer, to remind him of who he was.

"What extra work is that?" Leena heard the plea in her voice.

Fionn smiled, but it was a cruel thing, as if he enjoyed keeping her in the dark. "I've been chosen for a special mission. That's all you need to know."

8

Now that Morran's memory lasted longer than a moment, it was impossible to ignore Juradoc's ongoing monologue about his epically evil plans. For an entity of darkness, the Shade did love to hear himself talk.

By the time the moon rose over that night's camp, Morran had discovered it was possible to be anxious and bored at the same time. Bored because, well, who wouldn't be? Anxious because Juradoc never actually revealed any actionable information. The Shade was arrogant, not stupid.

"We've tracked the Shades' fiercest enemy to the human world," Juradoc said, continuing his one-sided conversation. "He's traveled between realms more times than I can count, and we lost sight of him altogether after the affair with the Sea King."

Morran searched his memory, but, as usual, it failed him. "Which affair was that?"

Juradoc seemed to ignore the question for a moment, but then answered. "The ocean fae were getting uppity. As usual, John Barleycorn stirred the pot."

The name lingered in the air, inviting Morran to recognize it. He did, almost. Not quite.

"And this enemy of yours went through a portal to the human realm? He left Faery?"

Juradoc's black hood nodded. "Most inconvenient. He is a collector of objects of great power. In particular, he has a tool that would guarantee the success of my plans."

Morran waited as questions fell like snow in his mind, eddying and drifting, while Juradoc watched his face. It was a game of cat and mouse, where the mouse's only hope was to play dead. If he revealed that his mental powers were coming back, he might find himself in chains—or worse.

"And you, my friend," the general said with oily satisfaction. "You have your role to play in this as well. We are nearing the critical time."

Morran nearly twitched. What *exactly* did Juradoc need him to do? But he knew better than to ask, and the Shade's spate of words resumed.

Morran's mind drifted. He sat inside the pavilion, chair angled so he could see the camp through the open doorway. Moonlight hinted at the endless open scrub of the surrounding landscape. More interesting by far was the trickle of peasants bringing tribute from nearby villages. These were the same earth fae as in Eldaban, dark-haired and solidly built, but he still found himself searching for fiery red hair. Since meeting Leena, he looked for her everywhere, whether or not it made sense.

A random image flooded Morran's mind—thousands of fae fleeing through portals they called the Shimmer. The Shades had brought portal magic with them when they invaded, but a handful of fae sorcerers had stolen the technique. Mostly, they'd used it to evacuate cities threatened by the Shades.

Morran's kin had stayed to fight. So had the dragons. And John Barleycorn's name was linked with those days as well. He was one of Faery's defenders. Morran fervently wished he remembered more.

"Barleycorn was earth fae, wasn't he?" Morran asked, breaking into Juradoc's story. He realized his mistake at once.

The Shade's posture registered surprise. "You're asking a lot of questions today."

Morran forced himself to remain perfectly still. "Your conversation inspires me."

Juradoc's features were invisible, but his voice grew smug. "It's endearing that you try to keep up."

The Shade rose, then crossed to a small trunk he kept among his personal possessions. There, he extracted a round, flat object that at first appeared to be a carved plaque. Only when the general turned it over did Morran see it was a mirror in an ornate rosewood frame. Morran sat straighter as tension crept up his spine. Shades were masters of mirror magic—that was how they cast a Shimmer.

Juradoc pulled his chair near Morran's before resuming his seat. "Our operatives have located one of Barleycorn's flunkies."

He held up the mirror, which was the size of a man's outspread hand. The reflection was perfectly ordinary, showing the inside of the tent. Then Juradoc passed a gloved hand over the mirror's surface, as if wiping away steam. The image blurred, grew cloudy, and reformed into something new.

A woman dressed in an unfamiliar style sat cross-legged on a bed. She held an object Morran did not recognize. It reminded him of a writing slate, but she tapped it with her fingers for no purpose he understood.

Juradoc spoke a word, and the image closed in on the female. She was a fae of the woods, tall and lean with almond eyes and slightly pointed ears. Her brown hair hung in a braid down her back.

Morran wanted to ask who she was, but he feared rousing suspicions with yet another question. Instead, he waited until Juradoc missed the sound of his own voice.

"She appears and disappears from our surveillance. It's plain she does not understand how to maintain a reliable cloaking shield," Juradoc mused. "Then again, what does one expect from an untutored exile? It's probably all she can do to disguise her fae heritage from the humans around her."

Morran waited again. His questions weren't a snowfall now, but a blizzard.

"We think she knows where Barleycorn is," Juradoc added. "She might even be his student. What do you think of that, prince?"

Morran caught the general's sarcastic tone, but he stifled any reaction. "What are you going to do?"

"I have plans." Juradoc rose, then put the mirror away. "Just wait and see."

Frustration gnawed at Morran's gut. As always, the Shade shared just enough to intrigue. What exactly had Morran learned? Evil plot. Ticking clock. Hapless student. Nothing of immediate use—unless one counted Juradoc's love of drama.

Something far more interesting pushed that thought aside. Leena was approaching. She was veiled from head to foot, but he knew her lithe figure and the graceful sway of her walk.

They had parted with a bargain—if she could heal him, he would do what he could to save her brother. It was what he needed, but not all that he wanted. He hadn't realized how much he missed a lovely female to touch and hold. Not until he'd kissed her.

But she'd walked away, ending matters after that single embrace. There had been no invitation for more, and Morran was not so mad that he'd failed to notice that clear boundary. Predictably, denial inflamed desire.

Morran's magic stirred, surprising him. He'd all but forgotten the tug of his power growing alert—and then quickly reined it in before Juradoc noticed it.

In the next moment, he sensed Juradoc sitting forward, hunger in every line of his body. Leena would dance again, and the

Shade would steal the energy if he could. That was how the other dancer, Leena's friend, had been hurt. A jolt of protective instinct nearly sent Morran leaping from his chair.

Careful. Leena had managed the Shade before. She was strong. And yet, Juradoc's greedy hunger vibrated in the air like a plucked string. And the more the Shade consumed, the stronger he would become.

How could anyone survive that? Her light would be inexorably crushed.

Slowly, the abyss of despair began to rupture once more inside Morran's mind.

❧

Leena approached the center of the camp, her heart thundering with apprehension. The moon lit the white silk of the pavilion, sharpening its outline against the night. Framed by standing torches, Morran and Juradoc sat side by side in the pavilion's entrance. In its own way, the scene was every bit as formal as Dorth's banquet hall.

Before them, a large circle had been raked clear of stones. It was preferable to have her dance here, outside, where there was plenty of space. Above, the stars were a scatter of white points in a clear indigo sky, and a cool, sage-scented wind tugged at her skirts. An illusion of liberty lifted her heart, but it didn't last.

There was too much to fear. Shades gathered at a distance from the circle's periphery, their dark robes making them all but invisible. A hundred pairs of glowing violet eyes reminded Leena of a distant storm, remote but seething with menace. Instinct clawed at her to back away.

Think of Fionn. Perhaps you can still save him.

Now that she was closer, she saw fae guards among the Shades, cloaked like their masters. And yes, Fionn was there, too, his hood pulled up to match the rest of the crowd. When he refused to meet her eyes, fear heated to anger, carrying her the last few steps.

Leena paused at the edge of the circle, bowing toward Juradoc and Morran. She was veiled, but the general might realize she was not the dancer he expected. Her pulse raced as if she'd been running, but when Juradoc looked her way, he said nothing.

Morran's expression was as perfectly controlled as a monument of marble. There was nothing of the man who had slipped past her defenses to deliver a scorching kiss. And yet, though distance obscured detail, Leena knew when her gaze found his. From the angle of his head, she guessed he was asking himself a question.

Was it the same one she'd been pondering since they'd last met? Whether, despite her refusal, the connection between them was real? Or, had it been a fleeting attraction, duly indulged and dismissed?

It seemed like a foolish concern now, when she was surrounded by deadly enemies and battling for her brother's soul. Morran himself was on a precipice.

There was little room for hope—and yet his dark eyes held her gaze.

Her train of thought broke as the general stood, raising his hands to still the crowd's shuffling.

"We are at a crossroads, a milestone," he said in a voice that carried over the crowd. "Soon, I will have achieved our ultimate goal. We have taken many realms during our conquest, but it has always been my belief that Faery holds the most promise."

His words snagged Leena's attention. She'd never thought of the Shades as having a goal beyond malicious destruction.

"Mine has not always been a popular opinion among the Shades. My ways are not always understood. I have been accused of extravagance with our lives and power."

A mutter ran through the crowd.

"But I promise you final mastery," Juradoc continued, opening his arms in a gesture that embraced the whole camp. "We shall be what we once were, our glory plain for all to see. I, Juradoc, shall deliver this to you."

A throaty roar rose from the crowd, sending gooseflesh down Leena's limbs. Juradoc was a general, not the supreme commander of the Shades. And yet, he was talking as if *he* were in charge. What did that mean for Faery?

"Do you desire proof?" Juradoc demanded. "Do you wish to see how I have bent the power of this land to serve our cause?"

He pointed a gloved hand Leena's way. "Witness how the servants of the Flame perform my bidding. Feel its mighty power."

Then the general leaned forward a little, as if imparting a secret. "See how I consume and bend its magic to my own ends."

❊ 9 ❊

Juradoc's words chilled Leena. Her earlier guess had been right. This was a demonstration of how the Shades could devour fae power, undoubtedly preparing for an assault on the Great Temple and the Flame.

By the time she could draw breath again, fear had rendered her numb. She could not let Juradoc succeed, but the general would never allow her to run. He had too much to prove.

Her gaze went to Fionn, but he had not moved. She looked at Morran, knowing this might be her only chance to heal him. But how to raise the Flame's power without losing it to Juradoc's hunger? This would be a battle of wills more brutal than the last.

In her mind's eye, every Shade was a carrion crow willing to devour her alive. All it would take was one wrong move, and she would be ash and bones.

Panting with fear, Leena stepped into the center of carefully cleared space. She'd performed this dance a thousand times before, and long practice saved her. She immediately cast her consciousness to the circle's edge, claiming it as her own. Next came a series of mental wards, simple but enough to hold Juradoc off for a while.

She whispered a prayer to summon the Flame, drawing it around her like a cloak. She felt its heat, but the sensation was not painful. Another might have said it was like the gentle pressure of rain or the caress of hot wind. Neither was completely accurate in Leena's mind. There were no words for its touch.

It gave her the courage to move her feet and to lean into their rhythm. Once her limbs had found the pulse, she wove the dance, summoning the beat and spinning it the way an acrobat balances on a ball. The Flame moved with her, flowing into the night like the mane of a wild mare.

The power of the Flame grew and grew, building in her like a shout. Surely, she would suffocate unless she gave it voice. Yes, some claimed to hear the Flame speak, but they were in the safety of the temple, not encircled by enemies. This was not the place for surrender, for absolute trust. Leena held the power with an iron hand, balancing its wildness with protective caution.

Her magic reached out to Morran, connecting with him almost without effort. He was a fire fae like her, and their shared nature made it simple. From there, the healing was natural. It flowed with the beat of the dance, with her heart and bones and her quickening blood. She moved to that song, to the wordless lyrics of the Flame, and Morran's shattered power came with her.

This time, she glimpsed more of his mind, of the raw wound that gaped like a severed limb. Distress. Fury. Dread. Despair.

She closed her inner eye to the flood of images that streamed from his mind through hers. Healing was more intimate than any kiss, taking her deep into another's soul. It was her job to unlock memories, to restore them—not to indulge her curiosity. The tiny fractures in his mind began to close and seal over.

Like a battering ram, Juradoc crashed through the swards and was there, grabbing for the power she'd extended to Morran. Leena wrestled with him, aware that if she unclenched her mental fist, he would drain her to a husk.

She succeeded—not easily, but well enough to take care of

Morran at the same time. Searing pain shot through her head, numbing her grip on the Flame's power. She barely kept it from slipping away, but she held on, lashing out with her own mental fire.

Her mistake was getting distracted. Juradoc nearly slipped inside her guard, but she closed her mind just in time. It worked, but frustration seared Leena. It was impossible to heal with her defenses up so high.

I know you. You are the dancer who battled me before. The whisper slithered through her thoughts, spreading terror like trickling acid.

So much for pretending to be Elodie.

Twice you have defied me. I could destroy you in an instant. We both know that.

You won't, Leena replied. *I am your key to the Flame. I'm the only one here who can summon it.*

Not forever. There will be much bigger game once we reach Tymeera.

Then she would die. There was no need for him to say it.

Time passed—how much was unclear—in that tug of war. Juradoc's hunger gathered like a condensing mist. Despite her best efforts, tendrils of power wormed their way past Leena's shields. She kept healing, giving of herself along with the sacred fire, but her efforts dwindled as exhaustion won. The dance flagged, the earth gradually weighing on her limbs.

Alarm seeped through her like poison. Juradoc was gathering his power for another attack. This time, she would not have the strength to hold him back. He would tear the Flame from her protection and control.

Leena stumbled to one knee, her sudden fear bright as the fire itself.

Morran exploded from his chair with a roar, snatching up one of the torches that had been thrust into the sandy earth and brandishing it like a spear. The bond of magic he'd shared with Leena snapped like a frayed rope, hurling her to the ground.

Unmoored power rolled outward from the circle in a punishing wave, flattening Shades and soldiers like corn in a gale. Tents collapsed. Mules and horses bolted. Morran hurled the spear, skewering a Shade.

Juradoc screamed in frustration.

Rough hands hauled Leena to her feet. It was Fionn.

"Run," he said. "Go back to your wagon and stay there. You'll be safer there than anyplace else."

"What about you?" she asked.

Fionn shrugged. He looked more like himself, as if the Flame had restored him a little, too. "There's nothing you can do. I'll be safer if you're out of the way."

Leena took one glance back. Morran was hurling his chair at the Shades, big muscles straining as the wood shattered in his hands. With a yell, he smashed Juradoc's chair, too.

He was out of control, filled with unfocused, destructive rage. She could feel its echoes through the remnants of their bond. It was a repeat of the scene in the banquet hall.

"Go," Fionn repeated, sounding less friendly now.

Leena's legs didn't want to move, but she forced herself into a run, roots and rocks bruising her bare soles.

She'd tried. She'd given everything to the ritual, yet Morran had sunk back into mindless violence. A hope she'd barely acknowledged died within her. That kiss would never be anything more.

When she reached her wagon, she scrambled inside, pulling the canvas flaps closed behind her. Leena shut her eyes, too tired to even summon tears. Failure clung to her spirit like sticky slime.

Kifi slunk out of the darkness. "What happened?"

"Nothing good," Leena replied, scooping the cat into her arms. She sank her fingers into the warm fur, grateful for the small, solid body. An aftershock of emotion passed through her, making her tremble hard enough that her teeth chattered. "I can't see a way forward. Not with the magic I've got."

"What will you do?"

"We could run." But where to? She would need supplies and a plan before crossing the desert alone.

"The general will expect panic. Don't give it to him. Brazen this out like a cat."

"What do you think he'll consider a fitting punishment for defiance? A whipping? Utter annihilation?"

Kifi put a paw against her cheek, the pads soft and cool. "Perhaps it's time to bring stronger players to the game."

The cat was right. Though it was a long shot because of the great distance, she should contact the Mother.

It took several hours for the camp to quiet, but no one came to her wagon. When it finally seemed safe, Leena dug in her bundle to find the objects she required. Fatigue and reluctance made her fingers clumsy, but she soon had everything assembled —a small brass bowl, a tiny box of incense, and her mother's chatelaine.

The last was her most prized possession. A central ring was meant to hang on a chain or belt, and from that were strung keys and small useful objects a housewife might require. Leena picked it up, taking comfort in the familiar sound of the metal objects clinking together. There were no locks for the keys anymore, but she kept them as a reminder of where her family had been. Besides the keys, there was a spoon for medicines, a flint, and a tiny baby rattle for the grandchildren her mother would never see. There was a vial of holy oil so the Flame would never lack fuel at their hearth. Finally, there was a second vial no bigger than her smallest fingernail, sealed with wax. Leena had never opened it, but she knew it contained a deadly poison in powdered form. It was the last weapon, and the final escape, in a world overrun by the likes of Juradoc.

Kifi finished the remains of Leena's dinner, thoroughly cleaning the chicken from her whiskers. She hopped down from her perch on the grain sacks, then began batting the container of incense to and fro like a toy.

"Stop that," Leena said, snatching up the box and unscrewing the lid. She dropped a tiny pinch of incense into the brass bowl.

"You are taking your time," Kifi observed. "Are you stalling?"

"Perhaps I'm afraid I won't like the Mother's answer."

And maybe she was afraid of the Shades catching her in the act, although her spell was quiet magic, barely more than a prayer. Still, her message might be powerful enough to reach its destination—and she sorely wanted the Mother's comforting touch.

Leena drew a shape in the air with her fingers, then let that shape catch fire. She dropped it into the bowl, the incense igniting with a hiss and a plume of smoke. The glowing sigil rose, spinning in slow revolutions before Leena's eyes.

"Temple Mother," Leena whispered, "I am far away from your gentle guidance. Answer this plea and tell me what to do."

She sent a silent message, capturing all that she had done and the results of her efforts. When she had finished, she dispersed the swirling smoke with a puff of her breath, sending her questions home.

Then she sat back to await answers. Kifi crawled into her lap, curling up to sleep. As the scent of the incense faded, Leena's eyelids grew heavy. She was tired, and the effort required for the spell had all but exhausted her.

When the answer returned, it came scratchy and faint, as if the magic that powered it was encountering resistance. "I wondered where you went. Tovas is beside himself with worry."

Leena winced, regretting she'd upset the kind Master of Revels. And yet, she'd expected worse from both Tovas and the Mother for leaving without permission.

The Mother continued, leaving her no time to reply. "You cannot balance your personal quest with guarding the source of the Flame."

"Fionn's future depends on me," Leena whispered. "Tell me what else I might do to heal Morran."

"That will not save the Great Temple."

"But if I heal Morran, I can do both."

"What you have told me leads in a different direction, my child. Sometimes, a blighted plant must be culled to save a garden." The words broke, tangled with regret. "Destroy Morran before he destroys us all. Everything depends on you."

"I'm a healer."

"Yes, one who understands the mixing of medicines."

Horror prickled over Leena's skin. Her mind flashed to the poison in her chatelaine, then veered away just as quickly. "I can't do it, not even if that's what the prophecy means."

Leena was arguing with the Mother, and disobedience was treason, but poisoning Morran was murder. The miles between them crackled with ponderous silence.

"Ah, yes, the prophecy," the Mother finally said. "You are the hand destined to strike the necessary blow."

The connection broke with an almost audible snap, the Mother's voice vanishing from her mind.

❧ 10 ❧

Leena's thoughts refused to quiet. As the night crawled on and the wagon grew cold, she cleared away the evidence of her spell and settled down to rest her body, if not her mind.

If the Mother asked her to strike the blow against Morran, that meant the temple's enchantments couldn't do the job. It was too far, or the Shades created magical interference. Perhaps, like everything else in Faery, the Mother's power was fading. Leena went over the conversation time and again, weighing each word.

Kifi curled into the hollow between her ear and her shoulder, purring softly to give comfort. The temple cat had overheard what the Mother had said, and she seemed equally troubled.

"For a moment, Morran's mind was as clear as my own," Leena murmured. "Doesn't that mean he might be helped?"

But that made his explosion of temper a shock.

Her healing efforts hadn't been enough.

She hadn't been enough.

"I'm not a killer. Not like that."

Kifi didn't reply. The cat had drifted off to sleep.

Leena stared at the ceiling of the wagon, absently petting Kifi.

Wasteful though it was, she'd left the stump of her candle burning. The wavering light fluttered and bobbed, the living flame her only shield against darkness.

Sadly, the Mother's fears were understandable. Morran's unpredictability was a wild card—a dangerous trait when he could unlock the heart of the sacred fire. If he fell prey to Juradoc's manipulation and allowed the Shades to plunder the Great Temple, Faery would fall into darkness and death.

Dread had her in pincers—fear of what she must do and fear of failure. Her breath came unsteadily, as if the smallest motion might send her tumbling off a cliff. She wasn't made for this. She wasn't a soldier like Fionn.

A rustle outside made Leena sit bolt upright. Dislodged, Kifi gave a cranky mew.

Was it the guardsmen, come for her at last? Leena scrabbled for a weapon, finding only the small knife she used to cut her meat. She parted the canvas with her fingertips, peering through the crack.

She caught an impression of movement in the dark before the cloth was snatched from her hand.

Leena gasped in surprise as Morran crawled into the tent, bending low to navigate the small space. Thankfully, Kifi had vanished.

Spotting the knife, the prince grabbed her wrist. Leena shrank back, but there was too little room to effectively twist away.

"Why the knife?" Morran demanded.

"I thought you were the general's men come to punish me."

"Definitely not."

"Aren't you under guard yourself?"

He flashed a narrow grin. "So they imagine. I gave them the slip."

She stopped struggling, trying to assess that quicksilver expression, so unlike anything she'd seen from him before. "The general should be more careful after you broke his nice chairs."

"I'm lucky he still needs me. I'll pay for that eventually."

Her thoughts scrambled in all directions like startled mice. "I don't understand."

Releasing her, he raised his hands, palms out in a gesture of peace. "I am here for two reasons. First, I came to apologize if I caused you any distress. Creating a distraction was the only way to stop Juradoc tonight."

She blinked. "You *meant* to do that?"

His expression darkened. "I could feel him through the bond of your healing magic. He was hurting you."

"He was." Leena sifted through those moments. Morran had slipped away from her, as if his mind had vanished into a yawning pit. Volcanic rage had come back out.

"Perhaps a little of the madness was on purpose." His words were so mild that she had an irrational urge to laugh.

And then cry. "I regret my healing was cut short."

His fingers brushed her cheek so lightly it was little more than imagination. "You helped me. I've lost myself before, but, this time, I went of my own accord. More than that, I knew I would return to sanity."

He repeated the gesture, this time pushing a strand of hair from her eyes. "You cast me a line so that I would not drown. There is no treasure equal to that, Leena of the Flame."

His praise sank deep, tangled as it was with his nearness and the Mother's bleak orders. She fell back on her healing role, needing distance. "Are you able to remember anything more?"

"A jumble."

"That's normal. It may take time to make sense."

"How much did you see of my thoughts?"

"We learn not to look."

He was too close, his dark eyes searching her face. She could feel the pulse beat at the base of her throat.

He met her gaze again, but there was fury in every line of his face. "I remember my magic. I remember the phoenix."

Leena's lips parted, but she had no words.

"If only I could remember how it happened, it might be undone," he said, and it was barely more than a growl. "If I remembered who did it, I could exact revenge."

Silence pulsed around them as those final words filled the small wagon. She could see the strain of his self-control in the faint lines bracketing his mouth.

She'd stolen his oblivion. "I'm sorry the price of memory is sometimes grief."

He took her hand in his, his palm hot as it touched her skin. "It's still a gift."

He lifted her hand to his lips, a dark lock of hair falling over his brow. The combination of his banked anger and graciousness was like strong liquor, and Leena felt it going to her head. There had to be one more step to take, another avenue to explore—anything except the path the Mother had set before her.

"Can you sense the phoenix at all?" she asked.

"No."

The single word held so much loneliness, it was impossible not to feel it, too. Leena put a hand on his shoulder, tentative at first, but then easing into his arms. All she had left to offer was the comfort of touch.

His mouth found the curve of her shoulder, his lips hot and hungry on her skin. She slid closer, daring to slip her hands beneath the fabric of his tunic. In the heat of their embrace, the grim future became a dark phantasm she chose to banish.

Leena found the arch of his spine and the hard muscles that flared outward to his shoulders. Her pulse galloped, suddenly out of control. Their lips met, tasting, questing, seeking life and courage.

The bond they'd shared in the dance sparked to life. As Morran said, he was far better than before, yet there were jagged edges where something essential—his other half—had been torn away. Her chest ached, as if she shared his ceaseless psychic pain.

Fae did not fade and die as humans did, but no one could survive that much heartbreak forever.

Sadness brought her back to the here and now. She pulled out of his arms, trying not to see the confusion in his eyes.

"What is it?" Morran asked, his breath warm upon her cheek.

A shout came from outside the wagon, rescuing her from the need for an explanation. They both froze like guilty youths caught in their embrace. Morran pushed the flap of the canvas aside to peer out. Pale dawn leaked through the opening. Against all odds, the dreadful night was over.

Leena crouched to look over his shoulder. A dozen yards from her wagon, a clutch of peasants from a nearby settlement was lined up before a handful of guards. Behind the visitors was a sorry-looking mule pulling a cart. The bed of the cart was piled high with baskets of bread. The Shades might not eat, but the rest of Juradoc's forces had to be fed, and the general commandeered supplies wherever he went.

"We demanded sixty loaves, and you have brought us barely half that number," barked the guard in charge.

The man holding the mule's bridle visibly flinched, making the animal bray. The second peasant, a girl, vanished behind the cart, clearly intending to hide. The third was a graybeard, possibly the father of the other two. He fell to his knees, pressing his forehead to the dirt. He had the wiry muscles of someone used to hard work.

"Forgive us," he said. "We only had enough grain in the whole village to make what we brought. There was no time to get more."

Another figure approached, this one wearing the cloak of a Shade. He turned to the guard who had spoken before, inclining his hood in a nod. Leena saw with a shock the newcomer was Fionn. He stood without expression, the perfect picture of obedience.

"Punish the peasant," the Shade said.

Fionn did not hesitate. He kicked the graybeard hard enough to send him sprawling into the dirt.

Leena recoiled with a gasp, nausea rolling through her. That was not her brother—or not who he'd used to be. Fionn had seemed better last night—why was he slipping so fast into the Shades' power?

Morran gathered himself to spring from the wagon and intervene. Leena grabbed his shoulder. "Don't. Giving yourself away won't help."

A tremor passed through him, but he let the canvas drop and turned to her.

"That was vile."

"That was my brother."

"Ah." His eyes narrowed in understanding. "The one you desire me to save."

"Yes. His name is Fionn. He is—" She broke off, unable to keep going. "He wasn't like that."

"They never are. Not before they are chosen to become the tool of their new masters." Morran paused. "Does he know you're here?"

"Yes. He found me out right away."

Morran cursed under his breath. "I said I came for two reasons. My apology and thanks were but one."

"And the other?"

"Now that you've restored my ability to think clearly, the other is obvious. I beg you to leave."

"But we had a bargain." And their embrace still lingered in her pulse, warming her to the core.

"And I will honor it, but you do not need to be present. If you stay, your brother will betray you." Morran took her hand, pressing it between his. "I'm sorry."

"He's all the family I have left." Her tone was defiant. "We were children when we made the march from the mountains to Eldaban. I'm not abandoning him now."

"Family doesn't matter once the infection begins." Morran's features tensed, as if he were in sudden pain. "I've seen it time and again. Unless the victim is born with strong magic, there is little hope."

And Fionn had no magic of his own. "Can you heal him?"

"In time, but I'm not strong enough. Not yet."

Not until Morran was completely whole again, and that was beyond her abilities. Tears slid down Leena's cheeks. Morran brushed them away with his fingers, his face set in granite lines.

"I will stay here," he said. "I will do what I can to foil Juradoc's plans. In my current state, it's my only means of striking a blow for the fae. And I promise to help your brother if I am able."

"Tell me one thing," she said.

"Anything I can."

"Fionn said he was being sent on a special mission. Do you know what that is?"

Morran released his breath. "Juradoc was rambling about finding a fae named Barleycorn, but I do not know all the details."

"Fionn is no spy. What could he possibly do?"

"The Shades corrupt their victims to make them ruthless, obedient soldiers. You just saw the evidence of that."

Leena didn't want to believe it. "I can be just as ruthless if it brings him back to me."

Morran gave a low laugh. "I've heard tales of the fearsome Kelthian women."

"I do not jest."

He grew serious. "I believe you. You are a daughter of your tribe, with your magic and your medicines." He waved a hand toward the scatter of possessions littering the wagon's floor. "You honor who you are with every choice. That's what brought you here to save him. And me."

"Absolutely," she said with a lift of her chin.

He gripped her shoulders. "That's why the Shades win. They use our love and our hope against us. If you stay for your brother, Juradoc will find a way to twist both of you to his ends."

His words frightened Leena, and that made her angry. She shook him off. "I'm stronger than that."

"Are you? Fionn will betray you. Blood and thunder, so could I. If you fall to Juradoc, so falls the Flame. Run while you can."

She stiffened her spine. "No, I don't run."

Morran cupped her face in his hands, his eyes soft with grief. "You've shown me great compassion and care. You deserve the same. Live, Leena. Faery needs your light."

She couldn't move except to fold her hands over his. "Don't you and Fionn need it, too?"

"The risk is too great. We will be coming to an oasis soon. From there, you could make it to the Serpent River and the safety of Kyleen. I'll help you get away."

Leena's skin crawled hot with foreboding. "But can't you let me heal you as much as I am able? You might get more memories back."

"I'd rather you were safely out of Juradoc's reach." Morran's expression darkened. "There is a reason he didn't send guards to drag you away."

She froze. "What?"

"He has no appetite for ordinary punishment. He will demand you dance again tonight. This time, it will be a battle to the end."

They made plans before Morran slipped away. Then Leena sharpened her knife and hid it in her dancing costume. After that, she wound her mother's chatelaine inside the length of fabric she used as a belt.

Morran's visit had given her time to consider the Mother's orders. Leena' decided those orders were delivered without a full understanding of the situation. Morran had improved, and no healer destroyed where there was a possibility of a cure—even if that instinct led to bold disobedience. The Mother had trained her priestesses to trust a healer's intuition above all else. Leena embraced that wisdom.

But she would keep the poison with her. There was no telling when any weapon might come in handy.

"I agree with allowing the prince to live if you're uncertain," Kifi announced. "It's hard to change one's mind later."

"I'm glad you approve." It was impossible not to sound a tiny bit sarcastic. Fretting about the matter had given Leena a stomachache.

"I am less pleased that you intend to run and take me with

you," Kifi said with a disapproving glare. "My quest is to stand in the presence of the Mother of Cats. This is my pilgrimage."

"We can still go to Tymeera. In fact, we should go to the temple to warn them."

The feline's whiskers twitched. "Very well. That would be an acceptable outcome."

Leena hated leaving Fionn. She'd come to save her brother, only to find the situation was far worse than she'd expected. Unfortunately, she didn't have the tools to help him. Not until she could beat Juradoc. Even then, ordinary healing magic couldn't cure the Shade rot that was quickly taking him over. She needed better answers. Hopefully, those could be found at the Great Temple.

She lay in the wagon, staring at the dirty canvas that closed her in. Fear crawled over her like a swarm of ants—fear for Fionn, for the Flame, and for everyone she loved. Beneath it all was a gut-twisting terror for her own survival. That kind of heroism wasn't at all the life she'd trained for.

Kifi slept or chased flies. The cat smelled fresh water long before they saw it. Evening brought them to a blessedly green space—the oasis. From here, they could make it to the Serpent River and safety.

The sudden abundance of life bewitched Leena. Palm trees surrounded a pool fed by an underground spring. Bird song filled the purpling dusk, the piping calls lifting her mood. Even the air smelled sweet after days marching in choking dust.

She knew the reprieve wouldn't last. Now was the time to make her move.

As soon as the column stopped to set up camp, Leena hopped down from her wagon to look around, leaving Kifi and her bundle of possessions inside. As soon as she saw the ground was covered in lush grass, she stripped off her sandals and threw them into the wagon. The feel of the soft, cool green beneath her toes was heaven.

Through the light silk of her veils, she scanned the chaos of milling soldiers for Morran. He'd promised to help her escape the camp once it was dark.

A sudden, putrid smell made her jump, banging her shoulder blades against the wagon. Shades circled her, cutting off every avenue of escape. They stood shoulder to shoulder, their black cloaks blocking the light.

"General Juradoc summons you," one said, fixing her with his flickering violet gaze.

Leena's stomach dropped. She felt poleaxed, unable to move. Where was Morran?

"Do you require us to carry you?" the Shade asked, lifting a gloved hand.

The threat of their touch shocked her back to life.

"N-no." She shook her head. "No, thank you."

The Shade laughed, sweeping a mocking hand toward the heart of the camp. "Then, if my lady would care to follow."

Leena obeyed, though it felt surreal as a dream. Shades surrounded her as they walked, giving her no chance to lag behind. It took the distance to the general's tent to fully grasp what had happened. She'd lost her chance to get away.

Now, the fight of her life was about to begin.

The scene that greeted her was familiar. Again, a black-cloaked crowd had gathered and Morran sat beside Juradoc in the pavilion's doorway. But the similarities to the last command performance ended there. The chairs were sturdier, and there was no carefully prepared ground for her to dance on.

Morran didn't meet her gaze. He slumped low in his chair, eyes glazed and dull. Leena's steps faltered, earning her a shove from the guard who dogged her steps.

What had happened? Had Juradoc caught Morran slipping away?

As she drew near, the violet pinpricks that were Juradoc's eyes watched her every move. It was difficult to read his expression, but she sensed a sneer.

"As I said before, I know you are not the dancer I asked for," the general began. "But now I have the full story. You came in place of your sickly friend as a selfless gesture of compassion. At least, that is the story you gave your brother."

Fionn had betrayed her. Leena stiffened.

"In truth, I suspect you came to save him from our clutches."

Juradoc waved a hand toward the crowd, where her brother stood. Fionn stared straight ahead, oblivious to her presence. The sight of him was a twist of the knife.

The general folded his gloved hands across his middle. "I am also aware that you've been entertaining the prince. While I have no aversion to showing our royal guest every comfort, this was not authorized."

Just like Fionn, Morran did not look her way. He did not even blink.

The Shade had him under complete control. No wonder her escape plans had turned to dust.

Morran had warned her about betrayal.

Rising anger unlocked Leena's tongue. She bowed low. "Forgive me, General, but who am I to refuse a prince?"

Juradoc laughed, and it was not a pleasant sound. It left Leena helpless with revulsion.

"Lord Bird has proven troublesome of late." Juradoc kicked Morran's chair, getting no response. "His usefulness is drawing to a close. Once I get what I need, all that will remain is choosing the most amusing method of his disposal."

A niggle of disquiet sparked in the back of her mind, but it vanished in a tide of choking panic. Morran was beyond her help, completely at Juradoc's mercy.

"Of course, that leaves you and me to finish our business," he continued with the same false good humor. "Twice, our gallant prince interrupted your dance with his tantrums. It won't happen a third time."

Leena forced a breath past the iron bands of terror squeezing her ribs. "Understood."

"A showman to the last," Juradoc replied. "You honor your kin."

Despite herself, Leena glanced at Fionn, betrayal ripping at her guts. Too late, she realized her pain was exactly what the Shade wanted.

"And since he is present for your final performance, it is only fitting that you are here for his grand triumph. You shall witness the fulfillment of your brother's dreams." With a flick of his gloved hand, Juradoc beckoned Fionn forward.

Her brother approached, moving like a sleepwalker.

"No," Leena murmured. Fionn had fallen so quickly, so completely.

For every step her brother took, Leena backed away. Animal instinct made her put distance between them, and no one stopped her until one of the fae guards caught her from behind, gripping her arms.

Fionn stopped a respectful distance from the general's chair, bowing deeply. Juradoc rose from his seat, then crossed to where Fionn stood. As he walked, he slowly pulled off his right glove, loosening one finger at a time. The fine black leather came loose with the sound of something sticky peeling away. When the glove finally came off, Leena gagged at the rotting stench, though they stood a dozen feet apart.

Juradoc's hand was a mere claw, blackened and bony with mottled grey talons. With an almost paternal gentleness, he pushed back Fionn's hood and pressed his palm against her brother's forehead. It looked as if he were delivering a benediction.

Fionn gave a violent jerk. Leena's first instinct was to leap forward and pull her brother away, but the guard holding her closed his grip like a vice. She struggled, but not for long. Bone deep, she knew there was nothing she could do.

Greenish light spilled from Juradoc's hand and over Fionn's face and the russet curls of his hair, then dripped down his body like a thick syrup. No murmur, no whisper came from the rapt onlookers, as if the moment were holy. Seconds passed, each surely lasting an hour.

Leena's knees faltered. She was caught in a nightmare, waiting, wondering, dreading what horror would come next. By making her watch this, the Shade was torturing her, robbing her of the will to fight and survive.

As she watched, a gray sheen spread out and clung to Fionn, coating him like a cloud of mist and then seeping into his skin. By the time it had been absorbed, corruption covered his entire body in patches of dark, scaly gray. His eyes flashed violet before closing. He stood immobile, not breathing, as still as a corpse.

Leena cried out—or tried to. The sound choked and died in her throat.

Her brother had become a Shade. A collective sigh gusted through the crowd as they all fell to their knees in worshipful awe.

Leena's guard released her. What could she do now?

The sound that escaped her hung between a curse and a whimper.

"And now," Juradoc announced, returning to his chair, "our chosen warrior will begin his special mission."

The general picked up an object that sat between his chair and Morran's. He turned it over, setting it on the dirt where they all could see it. Leena took one shaky step forward, hardly believing her eyes. A small mirror rested on the ground, emitting a soft, shifting glow.

A whisper of anticipation rustled through the crowd. Juradoc was creating a portal—perhaps to another part of Faery, or even to another world. Leena had never seen a Shimmer, but she'd heard of the Shade's mirror magic.

A bright pinprick of light appeared above the glass at about eye level. It swirled like a child's pinwheel, expanding slowly as it spun. The air grew heavy with static, like the moments before a storm.

From the corner of her eye, Leena saw a shadow move beneath the general's chair. With a stab of dismay, she saw it was Kifi, watching the spinning light with wide, fascinated eyes. It was the look the cat got right before she hurled herself at a bug to catch it with her paws. Leena closed her eyes, spirit reeling under one more blow. Tears spilled down her numb cheeks, but they relieved nothing.

No. The one word was all the prayer she had. She couldn't bear to lose another friend.

But she would lose and lose, just as she had lost her home and family and everything familiar on the long march to Eldaban. It was happening again—unless she did something to strike back.

Yes, she'd wrest something from this situation. Save an innocent. Hurt the enemy. She wasn't strong, but she was smart. Picking her moment was the key.

Leena compressed her grief into fury, needing that hot energy. She shot Kifi a quelling look, but the cat merely flicked her tail.

Oblivious, the general turned to Fionn. "You have been given your instructions. Do not fail and do not suffer anyone to stand in your way."

The Shimmer had grown to the height of a man. It was more or less round and filled with a silvery cloud, like a mirror coated with steam. From where Leena stood, she saw that the Shimmer had no real depth, measuring only an inch or two in thickness. She took another step toward the chairs so she could view the front of it, horrified and fascinated at once.

Morran rose as well, as if there was still a sliver of curiosity buried beneath the Shade's controlling spell. He stood transfixed, a frown of concentration on his handsome face.

The mist in the Shimmer began to clear, showing a confusion

of buildings and people. The strangely dressed figures hurried past, oblivious to the fact that they were being watched. The buildings were taller than any Leena had ever seen, some stretching halfway to the clouds. She drifted another step toward Morran, which brought her close enough to see the entire image. It struck her that the passersby were all human—not a pointed ear in sight.

Her concentration sharpened, shaking off some of the shock. Exiled fae hid in the human realms. Morran had mentioned the Shades were searching for someone named Barleycorn. Was he there?

She cast a sideways glance toward Morran, checking his reaction to the scene. The prince stood a few steps away from her, close enough to read his expression, but the only sign of life was the slow rise and fall of his chest.

"Come," Juradoc ordered, beckoning with his bare, clawed fingers. Fionn crossed to stand before the Shimmer, his movements more like a puppet than a living creature.

The portal hung in the air like a bizarre painting, disjointed from the backdrop of the desert sky. The Shade pointed at the scene. "Fulfill your mission. Find John Barleycorn and bring him to me. He will join the Phoenix Prince as my guest until he gives me what I need."

So this was to be a kidnapping, with the victim ending up a prisoner. Would his mind be shipwrecked as well? Leena uttered a soft moan as Fionn took a step toward the Shimmer. This was the worst of it—that Fionn would be responsible for a dreadful crime. Was he even her brother anymore?

Fionn stepped into the portal.

Leena's hands made fists at her side as her muscles gathered to...

Kifi leaped forward, scampering between Juradoc's feet and swiping the mirror with her paw. It spun, rocking on the uneven dirt. The image in the Shimmer cycled as well, the buildings going by in a blur. Fionn was already halfway through, only his back and one leg still visible. The rest had disappeared into the whirling image.

The general's outraged shriek split the night, promising murder.

There was no time to think. Leena scooped up Kifi, gasping a little as the cat dug in her claws. Then she bounded to her right, and, with her free hand, grabbed Morran's wrist.

He didn't move, standing like an oak rooted deep in the earth.

"Please," she cried, tugging hard.

All around them, black cloaks swirled in an angry cloud. Desperate, Leena yanked on Morran's arm, and he lurched into motion.

Before Juradoc's shout was over, they'd stumbled through the Shimmer into an unknown world.

Stepping through the Shimmer was not like passing through a door. One moment, Leena was racing for freedom, and the next, she was suspended in frozen, airless dark. This was not the dark of midnight, with starlight to break the obsidian sky. It was utter, absolute nothing. Her only sense of physical being was the solid bones of Morran's wrist and the prick of Kifi's claws.

Then, after a weightless pause, she dropped. The fall was only about a foot, but it was unexpected. Leena stumbled, releasing Morran but keeping Kifi close. She caught herself before she fell headlong, but not before stubbing her bare toes on the hard ground.

For a moment, everything was eye-watering pain. Her head whirled, as if the spinning mirror had spun her in turn. Nausea lurked at the back of her throat.

"Why did you do that to the mirror?" she asked Kifi.

"Because it was shiny," the cat answered. Clearly, that much was obvious. "Also, I thought it might stop your brother. It didn't work."

As Leena's senses recovered, she grew aware of the chaos

around her. A glance told her they were standing on a square of grass beside a broad roadway. Morran was regarding the traffic with his arms folded, where strange vehicles streamed by at the speed of dragons. Leena fell back a step, putting more distance between herself and the road. The air was dusty and foul.

She looked around, turning in a circle with Kifi still wide-eyed in her arms. There were many-storied structures on every side, looking even taller now that she was in their midst. After every street and building, there were more streets and buildings with no relief in sight. It was almost like being lost in a maze of canyons. There were trees, but they looked like twigs straining for the sun.

And they weren't alone, not by far. Every city in Faery had its share of mortals, but humans were everywhere here, standing in groups or hurrying down the sidewalks.

Fae were as varied as a garden of flowers—large and small, round and wand-thin, winged, horned, and in every color of the rainbow. Humans, by contrast, varied far less—and that meant Leena's party stood out.

Where had she brought them? Had it been a mistake? She looked back, but the Shimmer was gone. The spell had been meant for one traveler, not four, and they'd probably used up its capacity. However, Juradoc could make another portal soon enough, so vacating the area would be smart.

Someone leaned out of a passing vehicle, whistled, and pointed at them as the red contraption rumbled past. It was impossible to tell if it was her dancing costume or Morran's muscular frame that had attracted notice, and she didn't care. It was time to find cover.

"You're a temple cat," she murmured to Kifi. "Where does the Flame bid us to go?"

"Unclear," the cat replied, "but lore recommends we avoid the cars. They do not always pause for my kind."

"Cars?" Leena understood Kifi meant the vehicles, but she'd

not heard the word used quite that way. "Have temple cats come here?"

"Where the fae go, we go." Kifi snuggled closer. "We have mixed our blood with the mortal felines of this place."

While that was interesting, it wasn't helping Leena plan. Morran hadn't budged, still glowering at his surroundings. She looked the other way to see Fionn slowly approaching, his hood drawn low over his face.

"Fionn?" she called, keeping her voice gentle despite a thrill of horror at seeing her brother as a Shade.

He stopped an arm's length away. "You interfered."

It was hard to hear his words over the traffic, but they were clear enough. The accusation raked her. "I came to save you. I won't give up on you, no matter what."

He reached down to his belt, then slowly drew his knife. With the horrible clarity, she noticed the bone handle and the long, double-edged blade.

"What are you going to do?" Her voice was lost in the chaos of sound.

Fionn lunged. Kifi sprang from her arms, her claws aimed for Fionn's face. He ducked, his attack spoiled, and the cat landed on the grass unhurt.

Then the knife slashed again. Leena spun away, using her dancer's speed. "Please, Fionn, no!"

She held up her hands just in time for the next slice to score her palm. She snatched her hand back, vision blurring with tears. She fell to one knee, scrabbling for a rock to use as a weapon. All she managed to do was throw a fistful of dirt in his face. He swept the grains away, as if they barely deserved attention.

Kifi lunged, biting his boot to no avail. Fionn struck again. She dodged, falling into a roll, but Fionn stomped on the hem of her gown, pinning it to the earth. Leena jerked to a stop, the strong silk refusing to tear.

One of the vehicles on the road honked, indicating someone

had noticed the fight, but Leena had no attention to spare. She snatched at the knife handle, but Fionn grabbed her wrist. His flesh felt wrong—cold and clammy, almost slippery. Her revulsion rose like an irresistible pressure. She drew breath to scream.

"You should not try to stop me," Fionn said, his voice dropped to a growl.

"Please, I'm your sister. I love you."

"Then you should have listened."

The knife caught the sun as Fionn fell to one knee to deliver the killing blow. Leena finally let loose a wail, sure she was about to die.

As if in answer, white lightning filled the cloudless sky, sheets of brilliance flaring until the heavens lost their daylight hue. Startled, Fionn looked up.

Suddenly, Morran grabbed Fionn by the back of his robe, hauling him to his feet so hard his boots left the ground. Leena scrambled to her feet and grabbed the knife from her brother's hand, throwing it as far into the chaos of the street as she could. That was an instant improvement.

Thunder crashed, making them all jump. Fae magic hung in the air, indicating it was no natural storm. Leena looked wildly around for more fae, but saw only a clutch of startled humans. A few had been running their way, hoping to stop the fight, but they had other distractions now.

What came next was pure earth magic. A tremor vibrated through the soles of her feet, making her stagger. Leena had grown up in the mountains, and she recognized it was an earthquake. A sandwich board at the end of the block fell over with a clatter. Alarms sounded. Excited voices rose to compete with the complaints of the gulls and pigeons taking flight. Kifi crouched, her ears back and tail lashing.

A split second later, the cat sprinted away.

"Kifi!" Leena cried.

The shaking abruptly stopped. The cat didn't.

Fionn picked that moment to attempt an escape. Morran gave him a savage shake before tossing him to the ground. Leena lunged toward him, but Fionn rolled and scrambled upright without losing momentum. Lunging into the street, he snatched up the knife Leena had thrown. Then he bolted through the traffic, weaving between moving cars like a madman. Morran sprang after him, light as one of the temple cats despite his size. Neither man seemed afraid of the hurtling cars.

Leena ran parallel to the traffic, trying to keep up while watching in all directions for Kifi. The chaos of buildings and people seemed muted now. A strange quiet had followed the terror, thick with anticipation for an aftershock.

The peace was broken by the roar of thunder. Morran's back vanished from view, drawing every curse from Leena's vocabulary. She had speed and endurance, but she was too cautious of the cars. And now her bare feet ached from running on the smooth walkway. Leena slowed and finally stopped, ablaze with frustration.

What was she supposed to do now? And how had they all become separated so quickly? She bent to catch her breath, feeling the start of bruises where Fionn had knocked her to the ground.

As she moved, she felt the hard form of the small knife she'd hidden in her clothes. She'd forgotten about it—hadn't even thought to use it against her own brother. Not even to save her life.

Leena looked at her hand, smeared with blood from the slash of Fionn's blade. She couldn't afford to hold back again. She had to start thinking like a warrior.

Her eyes burned with tears, but there was no time to grieve. Her immediate problem was finding her friends and keeping them whole.

A familiar, imperious mew said Kifi had been calling her for some time. Leena straightened to see the cat crouched in the mouth of an alley to her left. Heart leaping with relief, Leena started toward her, but the ripple of an aftershock rattled the windows in the buildings above. Kifi scampered deeper into the shadows.

"Come back here," Leena called. "You're safer with me."

Kifi stopped and spun, her golden eyes huge in her tiny face. For all her talents, Kifi was still a spooked kitten. Chasing her wasn't the answer.

Leena skidded to a halt, gasping again. She normally could have run forever, but the air smelled bad here, and it hurt her lungs. A second or two passed before Kifi crept up to Leena, tail down, and brushed against her several times. Then she put her front paws against Leena's knee in a familiar request to be picked up.

Leena complied, pressing her cheek to Kifi's soft black fur. Thunder growled above, still fueled by unexplained magic. The cat shivered for a moment before relaxing into her arms.

"I'm so, so glad you're okay," Leena murmured. "I've lost Morran and Fionn."

"It can't be too hard to find two armed fae in a sea of humans." Kifi began cleaning her whiskers. "They smell entirely different."

"I can't follow their scent."

"Then be glad you have me on this adventure."

"You took a terrible risk when you interfered with the mirror."

"It pained me to think the general would get his way," Kifi grumbled. "That stinky creature is far too smug."

"Oh, my girl. I don't know what I'd do without you." Hysterical laughter bubbled inside Leena. Her nerves were shredding to pieces as they spoke. She set the squirming cat back on the ground.

The feline gave the briefest of purrs, but she stopped abruptly when she saw another cat coming down the alley. It was small and white with a blotch over one ear, but the newcomer was eyeing them with clear suspicion.

Kifi hissed, putting herself between the cat and Leena. "This is my charge. She is under my protection."

The white cat gave a small growl. At the signal, more cats appeared, creeping up stairwells and slinking out from behind garbage bins. At first, Leena had been amused, but the number of felines kept multiplying. There were five, then twenty, then a sea of fur and tails. Kifi began to tremble, but didn't move a whisker.

Leena moved to pick her up, but then stopped. She would do nothing to undermine Kifi's authority among the cats. Faced with so many beasts, their lives might depend on it.

These cats did not speak in the language of the fae, but, judging by the growls and hisses, they were trading insults. Kifi gave as good as she got, tail lashing.

Lightning flashed, followed by a rumble.

As the sudden brightness faded, a large ginger tom arrived, his tail held high over his head. The cats fell silent and stepped aside, allowing him to stalk through their midst until he was nose to nose with Kifi. She was a third of his size, but she puffed up until she resembled a shiny black ball. The tom sat on his haunches, his green eyes narrowed to slits.

"Fire burns the sky, and the earth shakes in warning," he said in a voice that matched his impressive size. "Your arrival awakens powerful magic. Why are you in my city?"

Leena opened her mouth but faltered, astonished this cat of the human realms could speak, but it was Kifi who answered. "Our apologies, my lord. It was not our intent to cause a disturbance."

The tom looked up at Leena, eyes filled with an intelligence more wizard than alley cat. Leena's neck prickled in warning.

"Regardless of your intent, you brought the tainted enemy to our streets," the tom said.

Leena's breath caught. He meant Fionn.

The orange cat rose, ears flattening against his huge head. "We shall not forgive that trespass."

❧   13   ❧

Morran hurled himself through the traffic after Fionn. He'd battled trolls with nothing but a broom handle and a bad temper, but the streets of the city held a new level of chaos. A thread of clarity had returned since his arrival, but the noise and stink weren't helping. Nor was the thunder still prowling the sky.

Wavering at the edge of the road, he studied the flow of speeding vehicles, each one promising to crush him. They ripped by with grumbling howls, suggesting there were demons trapped inside the gleaming shells. Huge birds flew overhead like dragons. Everywhere was hard, dead stone. The only thing that seemed to thrive here were humans—thousands and thousands.

But, at that moment, he had only one point of focus. *Stop Leena's brother.*

Fionn was a dozen yards ahead, dodging through the lanes of traffic with a sense of purpose. Perhaps the Shades had provided a destination, or the unfortunate lad was following the source of the quake. How—Morran could not say. This unfamiliar realm had jumbled his usual sensitivity to natural power.

All the more reason not to lose Fionn. Morran leaped into the traffic, earning a furious blare from one of the hurtling demons. He ignored it. A swirl of dark robes disappeared between the careening vehicles ahead. He set off at a run, leaping aside as one of the monsters all but clipped him. He jumped over the next, feeling as if he'd joined a bizarre type of chariot race. In the frenzy, he lost sight of Fionn.

Lightning flashed. Thunder boomed.

Before he'd crossed the next lane, the vehicles inexplicably came to a halt. Morran seized the opportunity to vault onto a large blue specimen and use the height to find his quarry. *There.* Afraid to lose him again, Morran jumped from car to car. That raised a blaring ruckus akin to startled sea monsters.

He barely made it to the other side without losing sight of Fionn. As he leaped off the last vehicle and onto the sidewalk, the black cape swirled around a corner. Morran bolted after him. Humans shouted in protest as the two runners pushed past, sending bystanders reeling.

Fionn was unnaturally fast, no doubt a result of the Shades' magic. Morran turned down the alley where he'd last seen him, then skidded to a halt. It was a dead end, and it was empty. Cursing, he leaned against the brick wall, coughing as the city's air burned his throat. He must have made a wrong turn, and his prey was getting away.

Doubt skittered through his mind, followed by an acidic wave of loss. *You're half of what you used to be.*

A faint tremor rippled under his feet, shaking the small rocks and bits of detritus coating the alley's ground. Thunder growled again, as if chiding him for wasting time.

Frustration jittered through Morran as he caught his breath. He'd have to retrace his steps and try again, but time was running out. Soon, more problems would emerge—notably an absence of money and local knowledge, compounded by the suspicions of this world's occupants. Fae kept themselves hidden in the human realm, and Morran stood out. It wasn't just his height and not-quite-human features—he moved like a warrior who'd trained with a sword since he could walk. Even humans sensed that kind of difference, and it made them afraid.

Afraid.

The word unleashed an avalanche of memories—Leena's two-edged gift to him. They infiltrated his mind's eye, obscuring the world around him.

Morran as a child, following his father through the palace like a faithful puppy.

Terror and revulsion during his first command against a cohort of corrupted fae.

His ascension to the throne of Tymeera, still clad in mourning for his father.

One more image—he sat on horseback at the head of his army. There were so many dead—fae, human, and Shade. Most numerous were dozens of enemy sorcerers sucked dry of their power. Juradoc had squandered his people rather than admit defeat.

The Shades had been trapped between Morran's forces and the Kelthian tribes for years. Juradoc's solution had been to tear all life from the southern mountains, one by one, leaving nothing but ash and the rocks beneath. They called that place the Ravaged Lands now. Nothing would grow there—not a single blade of grass.

The fierce, loyal, and utterly wild Kelthian tribes had been forced to flee, losing everything. Morran's memories stopped there, but one terrible truth was clear—he hadn't been able to stop the carnage.

Why not? What happened? There were heavy losses, but I had Juradoc on the run.

Then again, maybe he did understand after all.

Behind it all, behind every remembered image, had been the fleeting impression of flight and fire, of the wild, fierce joy of air. *The phoenix.* Once upon a time, he'd been that wild creature, filled with crackling power and the drive to hunt. Together, they had been invincible—and then there was nothingness.

He had woken to the vision of Leena dancing. She had been his candle in the night, leading him home.

Memories retreated slowly as Morran came back to himself. He'd caught glimpses of his past before this, but never so much at once.

Thunder rumbled, but it was growing fainter now as the magic that fueled it ran its course.

He slumped against the wall, narrowly avoiding the questionable muck sticking to its surface. His head pounded, vague nausea making his mouth water. He was healing, but it was exhausting. Slowly, he straightened, refusing to compound his failure to catch Fionn with public vomiting.

The glass towers piercing the sky glared like accusing eyes. Rivulets of sweat trickled down his temples. He had to pull himself together and act like a prince, a leader of men. Morran sucked in a deep breath, steeling himself for whatever came next.

Something bumped his foot. He looked down into a black, whiskered face. He vaguely recalled Leena grabbing a feline as they'd jumped through the Shimmer, but he'd dismissed it as a particularly odd hallucination.

"What do you want?" Morran asked somewhat gruffly. He'd never been a cat person.

The animal put one dainty paw on his foot. "You shouldn't have run off like that."

He was being scolded by a creature no higher than his boot top. There was only so much indignity one man could accept.

Then he noticed the notch in the cat's ear, the missing tufts of fur, and the long, bloody scratch that barely missed her right eye. He'd seen that expression on many a swordsman. The cat had fought and won, but at a price. He'd bet good silver the other cat had been a bruiser.

He sank to his haunches to meet her eye to eye. "Did you leave your opponent standing?"

"More or less." The cat sat stiffly, as if moving hurt. "But I made him offer his throat."

Although he was well aware of the temple cats, he'd had few dealings with them. Perhaps they weren't the spoiled, lazy beasts he'd imagined. "I hope you exacted a price for his life."

She slitted her eyes. "I made him send his minions to find you."

Automatically, Morran scanned his surroundings, searching for whiskers.

"You won't see them," the cat replied. "I might have defeated the local cat king, but he's good at his job."

There was a flurry of veils at the alley's mouth. "Kifi!"

Leena hurried toward them, her hands raised in an exasperated gesture. "Stop making me run after you. Both of you." She shot Morran a glance filled with worry.

Morran stood, his chest suddenly hollowed at the sight of her. Her long, fiery hair and floating silks were like bright plumage against the alley's brick. Before he realized it, he'd moved to her side. She drew him in like warmth.

"Are you well?" she asked, a thousand questions packed into those three words.

"Better. Juradoc discovered I was working free of his enchantments. He strengthened his hold over my mind, but his spell is fading."

"Because we are far away?" she asked.

"And because you've healed me. I am able to fight back."

Leena's shoulders sagged in relief, but Morran could see her moving onto the next worry without a pause. He took her hands in his, uncurling her fingers so they relaxed between his palms.

He had held her far more intimately than this, but something in the moment felt new. Perhaps it was because they'd shared danger and cared enough to ensure the other was safe. There was a difference between simple attraction and affection born from respect.

She felt it, too, because a flustered blush spread over her cheeks. No one with that shade of hair could hide it. He kept his calm façade, but he grinned inside his heart.

"Your berserker found me," he quipped, nodding to the cat.

Her lips twitched, almost forming a smile, but not quite. "I owe a great deal to Kifi's prowess in battle."

He returned the half-smile, but then their situation pressed in on him once more. "I am deeply sorry I lost your brother. I thought he came down this alley, but I was mistaken."

"Not necessarily," the cat piped up.

Kifi, he reminded himself. Her name was Kifi. "How so?" he asked.

The feline turned to look at the brick wall that formed the dead end. "Behold."

As if by magic, a large orange tabby appeared from nowhere, seeming to emerge from the solid wall.

"According to the locals, there are hidden passages in these alleys," Kifi explained. "The fae who live here frequent this part of town."

The tom cat cautiously approached, giving Kifi a wide berth until he hunkered down a respectful distance away. Kifi pointedly ignored him.

"How did Fionn know where to go?" Leena wondered.

Morran shook his head. "He might be following the source of the lightning and tremors."

"Why that?"

"They are caused by magic, and his quarry is a powerful earth fae."

Leena's look said he was explaining the obvious. "Yes, but why is the storm happening?"

"Our passage here triggered something—a Shimmer is powerful, even with one person crossing through. Four individuals and a mirror spinning hard enough to form a magical cyclone are bound to trip any alarms."

Leena looked at him quizzically. "And those alarms are enough of a beacon to lead Fionn to his victim?"

"It's a theory. Our best lead is to follow the same path."

Leena pulled her hands from his. "Can we find the source of the storm?"

"Of course," Kifi replied.

As if summoned, the orange tabby got to his feet.

"This is the leader of the local colony," Kifi said. "His name is Fang of Deadly Retribution. His humans call him Mo."

Kifi gave the animal a nod. Mo flicked his ears, then began trotting toward the street.

"Wait," Morran said. "Fionn didn't go this way. I would have seen him."

"Do you really wish to squeeze through hidden passages and leap from roof to roof?" Kifi asked. "I promise the destination will be the same."

"No more leaping today." Leena carefully lifted the battered feline into her arms.

With that, they fell into step behind Mo. It felt good to be moving with purpose again, and with fellow warriors—even if two of them were cats. The Shades had taken this from Morran, too— the simple bond of a common purpose.

He would never take agency or companionship for granted again. Now that his past and memories were coming back, he could look to the future. The idea was new and raw, and he left it alone for the moment. Some matters needed immediate attention.

Surviving this world was a good beginning. Morran soon found he wanted to be on all sides of Leena at once. Too many men regarded her with interest, eyeing her revealing silks with no respect for their ritual purpose. Morran glowered at each reckless fool, noting with satisfaction how quickly they backed away. In between scaring the leering buffoons, he searched every shadow for signs of a threat.

The tomcat, Mo, led them onto a smaller street lined with more modest structures. The crowd thinned considerably, and the buildings had a different feel, as if these places were for living in rather than for businesses. Most had wide porches with a flight of steps down to the street.

He saw a figure descending from one such building, her hand skimming the iron handrail as she ran down the stairs. She was obviously in a hurry, her brown braid swinging behind her. Morran stopped dead, taking a second look. She had cast a glamor over her appearance, but it didn't hide her lean form and almond eyes.

This was the woman he'd seen in Juradoc's mirror—the one who knew where Barleycorn was. Sooner rather than later, that was where they'd find Fionn.

Leena stopped and turned. "Morran?"

He debated a moment. No doubt, the cats could identify the origin of the fae spell that had shaken the earth, but that would provide limited information. According to Juradoc, this woman could lead him to Barleycorn. Her cooperation would ensure success.

"Morran?" Leena repeated.

His mind might be damaged, but his gut knew which decision was right.

"Change of plans," he said, estimating the number of humans on the street. There were a few, but any bystanders were some distance away. There was no chance they'd be overheard.

As she reached the bottom of the stairs, the woman glanced up to see two fae and two cats just paces away and staring directly at her. Her eyes went wide.

"Who are you?" she demanded in a low-pitched, slightly husky voice. While the fae had spells to help them understand foreign speech, she spoke in the language of Faery. She might not know their names, but she knew exactly *what* they were.

Morran took a step toward her. "We are the friends you were not expecting."

"Oh, yeah?"

He tried to smile, hoping to appear helpful. "There is trouble here, and we've come to stop it."

Her eyes darted to his belt knife, then to his face. She shifted her weight, getting ready to fight. "You'll get nothing from me."

Satisfaction speared Morran. She knew something. Yes, his instincts were working again.

Her fist shot out, unnaturally fast.

Morran danced back, cheek tingling with the rush of displaced air. The woman was tall and had a long reach.

Adrenaline surged, awakening long-forgotten instincts. Morran raised his guard, almost eager for more. She recovered and jabbed again, but he was ready—a good thing. She was strong, trained, and knew enough to fight foul, especially with her knees and feet. If he planned to father children, he'd need to end this quickly.

He slid under her guard, using his height and weight to push her into the iron stair rail. Once she was trapped, he was able to pin her arms—barely. Sometimes, it was possible to tangle an opponent in their clothes, but she wore leggings and a short-sleeved tunic that showed tanned, muscular arms. He held her wrists, crossing them at the level of her waist and using his weight to keep her trapped against the handrail. They might have looked like reunited lovers stealing a kiss, though she was obviously willing to bite.

From the corner of his eye, Morran saw Leena put Kifi down. After a brief hesitation, she drew her belt knife. She ran up the stairs with the cats at her heels. The three circled the woman, screening her from the view of potential observers.

The woman clearly understood what was happening. Morran saw her faint frown and the widening of her eyes. Then she opened her mouth to scream.

Leena slid an arm behind the woman in a friendly embrace, except the small knife was in her hand. She pressed the blade against the woman's spine.

"Do you feel that?" Leena asked. "I'm a temple healer, trained in the mysteries of flesh and bone. My knifework is swift and accurate, so I advise you to cooperate."

That earned her a glare filled with venom.

"Just so we are entirely clear, if I cut right there, you will never walk again." Leena's voice was calm and sweet, as if handing out a tincture for a cough. "A bit higher, and you're bedridden. Above that, and I won't guarantee your ability to breathe."

A chill coursed down Morran's back and shoulders, lingering at every point Leena mentioned. Her face had drained of color, showing how much this display cost her. He was almost certain Leena was bluffing. Almost.

As the seconds passed, he studied the hard set of her jaw. A man could go far with a woman that determined at his back. The idea prowled through his mind.

The woman finally heaved a sigh of resignation. "What do you want from me?"

"It would be best to continue this conversation in private," Morran said. "Do you live here?"

"My home is off-limits," the woman all but snarled.

She was an earth fae, Morran guessed, probably one of the forest dwellers who shapeshifted into an animal. It would explain the territoriality.

Leena slid the strap of the woman's bag from her shoulder before dropping it on the ground. "Kifi, check for keys."

Immediately, the two cats scrabbled through the bag's

contents. A moment later, Kifi had a ring of keys between her paws. Morran scooped them up, nodding his thanks to the felines. "Shall we see if there is a door that matches?"

"Fine," the woman said, snatching the keys from his hand. "Follow me."

Since Leena was doing an excellent job with her knife, Morran let her take point. He gathered up the strewn contents of the bag and followed, the cats in his wake. The place looked respectable, if plain, and the layout was not unlike the multi-family dwellings in Tymeera.

They climbed two flights of stairs before going down a long corridor to a door marked with "301" in gold letters. It opened into a room with wooden floors and large windows. Two overstuffed couches flanked a low table covered with books and papers. A few pictures hung crooked, possibly a result of the tremor.

Once the door shut behind them, the woman jerked away from Leena. "Time to talk. Who are you?"

Unfazed, Leena shifted her grip on the knife. "My name is Leena. That's Kifi, and that's, um, Fang. Or Mo. Now it's your turn."

The woman's brow furrowed. "I'm Anna. If you don't know that, why jump me on the front stairs?"

"We owe you an explanation," Morran replied. "One thing at a time."

"And you are?" Anna prompted.

"Morran of Tymeera."

"Ah." Anna abruptly sat on one of the couches. Her expression cycled through disbelief, exhilaration, and fear. "The Phoenix Prince. You're the weapon the Shades fear the most. And you're in my apartment. Yay."

Morran knew dry sarcasm when he heard it. "It is not my intention to put you in danger."

Leena sat opposite Anna, her silks vibrant against the pale, nubby fabric. She fixed Anna with a distrustful glare.

The other woman flicked her gaze from Leena to Kifi. "If you are a healer, perhaps you should tend to your injured companion. There's a first aid kit under the sink."

A flash of guilt crossed Leena's face. "My healing magic is not working as it should."

"It takes a while to adapt to a different realm," Anna said. "I feel it every time I cross the Shimmer."

Leena gripped her knife harder. "I'm not so easily dismissed, especially when we have little time."

She cast Morran a glance filled with questions, primarily about why they were there.

"I'll watch our hostess," Morran said.

To underscore his point, he unsheathed his own knife. Like Leena's, it was a small blade meant to cut meat at dinner—so commonplace, Juradoc had allowed him to keep it. This said more about the Shade's overconfidence than anything else. Any blade was deadly in the right hands.

"This won't take long," he added.

Nodding, Leena rose with a rustle of fabric, followed by the cats. She probably didn't know what a first aid kit was any more than Morran did, but she'd figure it out.

He turned to Anna then, weighing his next move. He had much to say about Fionn and Barleycorn, but not before he knew if she was friend or foe.

"You know my name," he said lightly. "My fame precedes me, even here."

"Not in a way you'd like," Anna replied, sitting back as casually as if he were a guest. "Most consider you a puppet of the Shades, even here among the exiles. Few of us know what really happened."

That was unsurprising, given Morran wasn't sure himself. "And what do you think that is?"

"You lost your bird." For once, the sarcasm was gone. "My sympathies. I understand what it is to have a dual nature. My wolf is who I am."

So he'd guessed right about her lineage. "Have you ever heard news of my other half?"

Her eyebrows rose. "Only that the Shades are furious because it's nowhere to be found."

His heart leaped, but he pushed down the surge of emotion. Hope could be treacherous. "Are they?"

"There's chatter, and it makes sense. If they had a phoenix under their spell, they'd be using it in the war."

As they had his father's phoenix. "Go on."

"I don't know much more than that. Essentially, they screwed up." She shrugged. "It's not hard to see how. Catching a burning raptor big enough to fight and kill a dragon—failure is a possibility."

He sat back, matching her casual posture. This Anna, whoever she was, had to be a spy. How else could she know so much?

"If the Shades wanted the phoenix as a weapon," he said, "what possible use does Juradoc have for me?"

Her smile was sharp. "Why do you think I know?"

"Maybe you don't."

"He wants power."

"Don't we all?"

She gave a low laugh. "When the Shades failed to capture the phoenix and make it a weapon, they planned to execute you. Juradoc took you prisoner instead."

"Why?"

"He wants free access to the Flame at the Great Temple, and you're the key to that. Anyone studying the war has figured that out."

"Except I have no idea how to unlock the Flame or how to render it safe enough for the Shades to access its power."

"Not without the bird."

"Not without the bird," he agreed. "And you're giving me answers rather easily. Aren't you afraid I'm here to harm you?"

"You've already guessed these answers. You're just looking for confirmation."

That was true.

"What's more, you came with a temple cat. I would know, animal to animal, if she had been forced or corrupted." She gave another sharp smile, "Her presence says you're here of your own free will."

Morran decided he might be a cat person after all. "Then tell me this. How does Juradoc think I will summon the phoenix?"

"Who knows?" Anna sat forward, warming to the discussion. "My best guess is Juradoc believes your death will summon the bird. He's kept you alive until the time is right."

Was that why Juradoc had kept Morran deliberately addled? So the summoning would wait until they reached the Great Temple, and then Juradoc would order his execution?

The delay also gave the general a chance to perfect his power-draining techniques. It was why he'd been interested in the fire dancers. They didn't provide ultimate access to the Flame, but what they summoned was more manageable. As evil plans went, it was well strategized.

"What do the other Shades think?" he asked.

"They think Juradoc's a fruitcake. Even if the Shades could access pure elemental magic, it's deadly to consume right from the source. Otherwise, they would have done it before. He says he has a plan, but untried theories are a good way to die."

"And yet they leave him in command of a large army."

"He's just dangerous enough that they're reluctant to cross him. Rumor has it he's a deadly enemy even to his own kind."

Her words made sense to Morran, like bricks forming a neat row. "How did you become so well informed?"

She sat back, wary again. "Because I'm no stranger to Faery. I keep my ear to the ground."

"Let's be plain. You're an intelligence agent. Who do you work for?"

Morran waited, letting silence fall. Most people would eventually feel the urge to fill it. A long pause followed.

"I have to say," Anna said in a bland tone, "you must be strong to have survived this long in Juradoc's camp. Stronger still to find a way out and go looking for answers."

"I had help."

At that moment, Leena returned with Kifi and Mo at her heels. The blood and scratches on the cats had been cleaned up.

"Unusual help, from what I see," Anna observed.

"I have an unusual problem," Morran replied.

Anna gave them all a cool smile. "I heard a news bulletin about cosplayers disturbing traffic along the highway. Don't do that again. And don't go flashing those knives in public. Human authorities get nervous."

Morran decided she'd changed the subject long enough. "You asked why we were here. Juradoc has sent an agent after John Barleycorn. He intends to take him prisoner."

Anna sprang to her feet. "What?"

The sudden move startled Leena, who grabbed for her knife. Morran put out his hands in a calming gesture. Anna's sudden reaction confirmed one thing. Juradoc's information was good. She did indeed know Barleycorn.

"I heard this from the general's lips, assuming he has any," Morran continued. "He believes you are the key to locating him."

Anna swallowed, her features drawing tight. "Oh?"

"He's been watching you in a mirror. Evidently, your concealment spells aren't consistent."

She flushed. "I never worried too hard about this place. I'm hardly ever here."

Morran fervently hoped Juradoc wasn't checking the mirror now. "Your one advantage is that I don't think he knows your name."

Anna released her breath in a rush. "Then how did you know where to find me?"

"We found you by chance," Leena said, speaking up for the first time since she'd rejoined the group. "Or perhaps it wasn't chance at all. The agent we're searching for is my brother. He's under Juradoc's control."

Anna's brow gathered in a frown. "You mean, he has the rot?"

Leena nodded, her misery plain.

"Then we had better move. If the Shades find us, we're all as good as dead."

⚘ 15 ⚘

"Understand three things," Anna said. "First, you do not fit in here, so keep your mouths shut and follow my lead."

"Happily," Leena said. She still didn't trust the woman, but she recognized her efficiency.

They were on foot, moving at a pace just short of a run. Anna had quickly found clothes for them. She'd given Leena black leggings, a cotton jacket, and a stretchy top patterned with running wolves. Most welcome were the lace-up canvas shoes. They were a size too large, but thick socks helped.

Morran's boots and leggings were plain enough to escape notice. Now he wore a long-sleeved shirt advertising beer that belonged to one of Anna's friends—someone named Burtock.

"Second, I'm only letting you come because your brother is involved. I understand what it is to lose family, and you might be helpful if we find him—if he's not too far gone."

Leena nodded, suddenly unable to find her voice.

"Third, know that I have a pack at my command. These aren't your latte-drinking, poetry night kinda wolves. If you've misled me or mess with us in any way, you will regret your actions."

"Understood," Morran replied, sounding a touch impatient.

Anna led them across a street. Almost at once, a hospital came into view.

Apparently, Barleycorn had been there, unconscious, for some time. The pack members were his security guards. As their leader, Anna had taken the nearby apartment for convenience.

The coma had been unexpected news. Whether the Shades knew about it was a good question.

Anna slowed when they got close enough to see the building in detail. The afternoon was fading into dusk, washing the streets in shadowy blues. Leena studied the place, mentally contrasting it to her own healing temple. Her place desperately needed repair and supplies, but still managed to serve everyone—even the lowliest beggars.

This hospital was an ornate stone building four stories high, topped with a peaked copper roof. It was set far back from the road, surrounded by grass and trees. A wrought-iron fence circled the perimeter of the property, adding to the stately look of the place. This, Leena guessed, was no hospital for the poor.

"Plenty of opportunity for concealment on the grounds," Morran muttered.

Anna grunted her agreement. "It's an old place, not built with security in mind. Multiple entries, windows that open. That's one reason the pack provides added security. I was on my way here to take my turn on guard when you stopped me."

She pointed toward the grounds. "And this was definitely the source of the quake. Look, I think the power is out. Those must be emergency workers if they're on the job after hours."

They were walking beside the grounds now. Inside the fence, men with tool belts were milling back and forth, pointing to a pole strung with cables. A few examined the building's foundations, no doubt looking for obvious structural damage.

Kifi poked her head out of the backpack Leena now carried, straining to get a view of the place. Mo, though now sworn to his new mistress's service, had refused any form of transportation beyond his own four paws. He strutted beside Morran, a male among males.

"This is a good place," Kifi said, pulling herself up onto Leena's shoulder.

"Why do you say that?" Leena asked, wincing as whiskers tickled her ear.

"The other cats know there are many women here, and they have gentle faces."

"You can share memories with the local cats, too?"

"Many here are descended from temple cats. They have some gifts."

"Are you their leader now?"

"For now," Kifi said with evident satisfaction. "I journey to meet the Queen of Cats, and do not aspire to rule this kingdom."

"No?"

"This is not my home. Still, I was victorious, and it's wise to celebrate victories as they come. Finding the wolf was a win."

"Very true." Leena wondered how much of a win it truly was. Finding Anna had eliminated much guesswork, but they were still a long way off from curing Fionn.

Anna led them through the back gate, where there was less commotion. Despite her dance training, Leena was slightly out of breath after the brisk pace.

"Make yourselves scarce," Anna said to the cats. "Animals aren't allowed inside."

Offended, Kifi crawled back into the pack, which Leena partially closed. When she straightened, adjusting the straps of the pack on her shoulders, she noticed a figure dart from the trees to the foot of the building. A sick sense of urgency assaulted her. She elbowed Morran, pointing to the shadowy junction where two walls met. A black-cloaked figure scaled the stonework, almost invisible in the dusk.

Anna followed their gaze and swore. "Barleycorn's on the top floor. That's where he's headed."

"You know the hospital," Morran said. "Take the inside route. I'll try to stop him from here."

For a fleeting moment, Anna balked, as if she had no intention of taking orders. Then she gave a quick nod before sprinting for the door. Morran pulled Leena out of sight behind a stand of oak trees, crouching low.

"Wait here," he said, then he was gone.

Leena watched him ghost across the lawn, resentful at being left behind. Kifi shifted inside the backpack, poking a paw into her kidneys. Mo sat beside her, his ginger fur dulled by the fading light.

"Uh-oh," he said. "Hard hats at three o'clock."

Workmen rounded the corner, continuing their check of the building and grounds. Within seconds, they were going to cross paths with Morran.

"That's my cue," Mo said, then he, too, bounded across the grass. Suddenly, the tomcat was between the workmen's feet, arching his back to be petted.

"Whoa there, boy," one of the men said, reaching down to stroke the thick orange fur. "Watch where you're putting your paws. There's broken glass around."

Mo bumped his head against the man's hand, asking for more attention. Morran ascended the wall unseen. Leena decided she wasn't about to wait where she was, and quickly but calmly entered the way Anna had.

Once inside the doors, Leena was swallowed by bedlam. Staff scurried to and fro in carefully controlled chaos. Leena took her time crossing the entry, listening carefully to the conversation of the locals. Her powers were recovering from crossing the Shimmer, and the spell that enabled her to understand the human language was slowly starting to work. By the time she found the stairs, she'd learned the power outage had the staff working double time. Leena sympathized—she'd felt the same when fever had struck Eldaban and sent half the city to the temple doors.

There was light in the stairs, but not much. Leena summoned a flame, letting it hover over the palm of her hand, then climbed until she reached the fourth floor. Then she pushed through the door to the ward.

A paw poked her in the back. "Put me down." Kifi's muffled voice emerged from the pack.

"I thought you liked to be carried."

"I did. Now I don't."

It was a cat's answer. Leena unzipped the pack and let her out. "Just stay out of sight."

Kifi didn't answer, but moved like a black phantom at her side, tail puffed. The place was deserted, dark, and eerily silent. An unnatural scent hung in the air. Leena moved as silently as she could, listening intently for the usual restless moans and rustles of the sick ward. None came. There seemed to be no patients here.

For a disorienting instant, Leena wondered if she were caught in a bad dream. She'd left everything behind except the small bundle she'd carried to Juradoc's camp. Then she'd come here with only the clothes she wore—and now she didn't even have those. Only her knife and chatelaine were stuffed in the pockets of her borrowed jacket. She was in a hospital that had no patients, searching for a brother who wasn't Fionn anymore. What was she doing here?

Kifi meowed, but the sound was coming from someplace ahead. The cat had run off while she brooded. When the sound came again, Leena ran toward it, her shoes skating on the slick floor. She slid around the corner to find Kifi crouched in the middle of the hallway, her ears flat. A few feet ahead, her brother stood with his back against the wall. Morran had his forearm pressed to Fionn's throat. Fionn gripped Morran's wrist, struggling to push him away.

She'd come here to find her brother, but the sight of him still sent a zing of shock through her core. "No, wait. Please don't hurt him."

Neither man replied. For a heartbeat, she wondered which one she meant.

"Please!"

She might have been speaking to herself. Fionn didn't so much as blink. The struggle went on, each straining until their muscles corded. Then Fionn suddenly jerked aside. Morran's feet slipped on the polished floor, and Fionn ducked free.

Morran dove after him, teeth bared. Fionn sped down the hall, grabbing a flimsy chair set outside one of the rooms. He flung it at Morran, who leaped aside as it crashed and bounced, narrowly missing Kifi. Fionn made a right turn down another corridor. Leena rounded the corner just in time to see Fionn burst through a door, followed shortly by Morran. A soft light fanned into the corridor, showing this room, at least, had an occupant.

Leena reached it just in time to see Fionn towering over the room's only bed, where a figure lay motionless on his back. Leena lunged forward with a cry. At the sound, Fionn pulled a long-bladed knife from his belt—the same one he'd used against her before.

Morran grabbed Fionn, forcing him face-down on the bed. Kifi sprang onto the covers. The cat dug her claws into Fionn's hand, giving an eerie yowl. The blade dropped, and Leena snatched the knife away.

It was only then she saw Anna on the floor, bleeding from her forehead. Anna got to her knees, shook herself, and then drew a weapon from her shoulder bag. She pointed it at Fionn's head. Leena only knew guns by reputation, and it was far smaller than she'd imagined.

Still, she knew what it did. "No!"

Morran looked up at her cry. It was all the opening Fionn needed. He twisted aside, creating just enough room to bring up his foot and kick Morran away. Anna fired, but Fionn was already in motion, sprinting from the room.

Leena was in his path. He drove his elbow into her ribs, knocking her into the doorframe. Her head smacked into the wood, and her vision went white. Fionn bolted past with Anna following a bit behind.

Morran's hand was on her arm. "Are you all right?"

She squinted, groggily bringing him into view. Her ribs were on fire from Fionn's blow, making it painful to breathe. "Yes, I'll be fine."

He squeezed her gently and was gone, racing after Anna. Leena sagged against the wall, still holding the knife. She took a step, hoping to follow them, but a wave of nausea rolled up from her gut. Suddenly, she needed to sit down.

"They won't catch him," Kifi said. She was still crouched on top of the sleeping man. "Sadly, that's not a good thing."

Leena had no words to answer the cat's declaration. She sank into the chair by the bed, then set the knife on the nightstand beside it. Bending forward, she buried her face in her hands. Her body ached, every heartbeat pumping fresh exhaustion into her veins.

Yet, one thing had gone right. They'd stopped Fionn before he could kidnap Barleycorn. It wasn't a complete victory, but it wasn't a failure, either. If they could catch him, there still might be hope for a cure.

She raised her head and drew in a deep breath, fixing her eyes on the sleeping man's face. To the humans, he would appear to be somewhere in his thirties. Dark-haired and clean-shaven, he had pleasant features, handsome even, but it wasn't a remarkable face. He had the perfect looks for someone working in the shadows—and if he worked with Anna, chances were high that he was some kind of spy.

"Well, John Barleycorn," she said to the still figure, "why are you in this adventure?"

MORRAN reached for the third-floor door when ANNA grabbed his shoulder.

"Don't," she warned. "He didn't go there."

He turned, frowning. They'd chased Fionn into the stairwell. Since there were no steps up, descending was the only option. "Why not?"

Anna had already crossed the landing. She leaned out the window. "This was open. Besides, there are people on the other floors. Someone would have set off the security alarm if a cloaked villain had dropped by."

Morran leaned over her shoulder, impatience ripping at his nerves. Now that it was full dark, the grounds were deserted. "Can you spot him?"

"No. We could ask the power guys working out front, but I doubt any humans saw him. A Shade in stealth mode is hard enough for the fae to detect." Anna shut the window, then locked it.

"The orange cat remained outside to patrol the perimeter."

"If there is anything to report, he'll let us know. The cats are the best eyes and ears around," Anna said. "We're better off staying on the fourth floor. Eventually, he'll be back to finish the job."

They began mounting the stairs. "Tell me," Morran began, "why is your friend the only patient on the top floor?"

"He was easier to guard that way. Fewer comings and goings. Less collateral damage if something like this happened. We were just lucky he had the money to secure a whole hospital floor for himself."

The explanation only increased Morran's puzzlement. "Who is Barleycorn, and why does he interest the Shades?"

"He's well-known among the fae exiles—many business interests, pillar of the community, occasional faery godfather. That sort of thing."

"Not the usual way to inspire enemies."

"I don't know everything about him, though I've worked for him for years. "

Morran raised a brow. "How did he end up here?"

Anna pulled open the stairwell door onto the fourth floor. "He had me working at this professional diving business, mostly to keep an eye on one of the employees there. To make a long story short, she got into trouble and he played detective. A fight with some deep-sea fae put him in a coma. I got the task of looking after him until he wakes up again."

"What are the odds of recovery?"

"Hard to say. He's healthy enough, for all that his test results confuse the human doctors. In fact, I'm almost certain that earthquake came from him."

"Why?"

"Whatever else John Barleycorn is, he's an earth mage. I think your arrival disturbed his sleep."

Morran pondered that a moment before asking, "So what's Juradoc's interest in Barleycorn?"

She slowed her pace, turning to regard Morran. She held a device—a flashlight, she'd called it—in her left hand, and she switched it on and off, on and off. A nervous habit. Morran was tempted to take it away. "I don't know. Not for certain."

"Guess."

"Not many people know this, but he collects artifacts—old scrolls and obscure maps from forgotten realms. Along the way, he's studied the Shades more than anyone I know. He's tracked the other realms they've destroyed, searching for some way to unravel their power. Maybe they've noticed. Maybe he has something they want."

She started walking again. Morran kept pace, curiosity burning. "Do you know what he's found out?"

"Nothing we haven't already discussed." Anna shrugged her head. "He might have said other stuff, but it went over my head."

Morran wasn't sure he believed her last statement, but they were already back in the room. As they entered, Leena was sitting by the bed, her eyes ringed with dark circles of fatigue.

"I'm going to make some calls," Anna announced, taking a second chair that sat in the far corner. "There were supposed to be pack members guarding the room until I arrived today. Someone clocked off early."

"We need more sentries on the grounds," Morran said.

"You bet." Anna pulled a device from her shoulder bag. "And I also bet you're hungry. I'll get them to bring pizza."

"Bring what?" Morran asked.

"Pizza. You'll love it."

Morran was more restless than hungry. Now that his mind was healing, the yawning absence inside him was growing worse. He noticed it less during a chase or fight, but any moment of quietude was pure misery.

The phoenix was a dream, a grief, and a prayer scorched into his spirit. Those who knew no better referred to it as a familiar, but it was no mere magical assistant. It was fully half of who he was.

Its—his—name was Arlanoth. The knowledge broke through him like a storm.

"I'm going outside," Morran said, aware he sounded abrupt. He couldn't help it, nor could he face the questioning glances of the others.

He'd recovered the name. *Arlanoth*. He whispered it like a prayer as he crept out the window the same way Fionn had gone. He needed the freedom of the open sky and stars. He wasn't meant to be earthbound, much less domesticated. He was the Phoenix Prince and meant to fly.

It struck him, with the bloody sharpness of a spear, that he finally understood his father's death.

$\maltese$ 16 $\maltese$

"You don't trust me," Anna said once Morran had left the room.

Leena looked up. She'd been staring at nothing, lost in a haze of pain and fatigue. "My brother has been infected in body and soul. I'm trying to save him. Forgive me, but everything is subject to that one concern."

Anna shrugged, fiddling with the light in her hand. There was one panel of soft light overhead—enough to see by—but Anna's device cast sharp, dramatic shadows. "I get it. Just remember that I am a friend, not an enemy."

"Noted." Leena shifted, wincing when her ribs complained. "Fionn is all the family I have left. I don't want to lose him."

"Sadly, the fae are good at losing things," Anna said softly. "I just lost my friend, Burtock, to a mission."

Leena remembered the shirt Morran had borrowed. This friend was close enough to leave his laundry behind.

Anna's lips twitched, evidently reading her face. It wasn't quite a smile, but it softened her lean features. "It's not like that. He's looked after me from the time I was a child, more a father than my own was. But now, he's off with the dragons on a wild goose chase in a far-off realm. He's left me here to deal with this." She nodded her chin toward the patient on the bed.

"That is a great deal of responsibility," Leena said.

"I don't mind providing security, but the city is not my favorite place. I'm not an urban wolf."

"Then why stay?"

"Burtock taught me loyalty to the cause of Faery. Or perhaps hatred of the Shades who killed my family. Sometimes, it's hard to tell the difference."

Leena understood that far more than she cared to say. "And so, you keep fighting."

"There's a point where it becomes impossible to stop." Anna rubbed her forehead. There was blood where she'd cut it earlier, and a bruise was forming around the wound. "I've given too much to walk away, so I keep going and pray it wasn't a bad investment."

Her words described so many Kelthians that Leena knew— angry, proud, lost, desperate people. She rose, every joint stiff. "Let me clean your injury."

"I'm fine. It's nothing."

A shapeshifter could heal by transforming to another form, but that took energy Anna probably didn't have at the moment.

"Be still." Leena went to the room's tiny sink. While Anna remained sitting, Leena did what she could with water and paper towels, and then a simple healing spell.

"What lies in Barleycorn's vault?" Kifi asked. The cat had been so quiet that Leena had almost forgotten her.

Anna looked up sharply, ending Leena's examination of her handiwork. "How do you know about that, feline?"

"Temple cats know much," Kifi replied, her back arching in a stretch. "Is there something there General Juradoc wants?"

"As I told Morran, I'm not certain. I've seen some of his collection, but most are just relics of sentimental value. Broken crowns, famous swords, that sort of thing. Mind you, there are a thousand places he could hide something. John is clever."

There was a wistfulness in her tone that struck Leena. She looked at the man on the bed again, wondering what he was like when he was moving, laughing, and—if she read things right—being an object of fascination to Anna. He must have enjoyed fine things, for his nightclothes were made of ink-black silk and he wore a heavy neck chain and golden pendant. The robe hanging on the back of the door was soft, dark velvet. Even sick and in bed, there was no question of his status. "He's a bit mysterious, isn't he?"

Anna gave a soft laugh. "He's the definition of it, but he has to be. If anyone is going to break the Shades, it will be him. He's spent centuries researching their kind, searching for a weakness."

"And you've been working at his side," Leena added.

"For a little while. Enough to feel the heady excitement of being around that much intelligence and charisma." There was that wistful voice again, that hint of a bruised heart.

"Morran is a little like that," Leena ventured. "I can't imagine what he was like...before."

"Be careful around him," Anna said, serious again. "I saw Prince Karth's phoenix. It was under the power of the Shades, webbed in dark magic, but it was still a fearsome creature. It killed a full-grown dragon. Their flames meant nothing to it."

"Morran wouldn't burn anyone but the enemy," Leena replied.

"That's not the point. A phoenix has more power than you or I could understand, and it's dwelling inside another person. Binding with a creature like that makes Morran different from ordinary fae." Anna shook her head. "He would never hurt you intentionally."

"But?"

"We can't understand what it must feel like to have that much power, much less lose it. He's got to be messed up."

"Maybe," Leena said reluctantly. "It would make an ordinary life difficult."

Anna shrugged. "Even with regular folk, some people can't

give a mate what he or she needs. It's not personal. They're just not built that way."

How much was Anna talking about Barleycorn? It didn't matter. Leena already feared much of what she said was true about Morran.

He was a prince, and she was a temple dancer—that was mismatched enough, but it was just the beginning of the gulf between them. He had commanded vast armies, enormous wealth, and unimaginable power. If healed, he would be the next thing to a god. After all, he'd held the south against the Shades for a hundred and fifty years before suffering defeat.

She was saved from her thoughts by a knock on the door. It was a male dressed in boots and leathers, holding two large, flat boxes.

"Pizza's here," Anna said. "This is Edgar. Edgar, Leena."

Edgar nodded, giving Anna a cautious look. There was no debate about who had alpha-wolf status.

"Surrender the pizza," Anna said, "and get out there on perimeter patrol."

"I got cat food, too, like you asked," he said, pulling two tins from his pocket before vanishing out the door.

"Doesn't he get any food?" Leena asked.

"Don't worry about Edgar," Anna grumbled. "He probably ate a whole pie on the way here—that he charged to my account."

Leena's mouth watered at the savory scent, but she controlled herself long enough to ensure Kifi was fed first. The cat fell on the food with gusto.

"This pizza is for meat lovers," Anna said, opening the box on top. "The other is vegetarian with extra cheese. No olives or pineapple. I have standards."

Leena bit into a hot, spicy slice. Cheese, peppers, and basil danced on her tongue. "How did this recipe never arrive in Faery?"

"Probably because it never tastes the same when you make it at home."

Leena took two more bites, not caring if she looked greedy. The last time she'd had a satisfying meal was before Lord Dorth's banquet. She finished her slice within a minute, then loaded two of the meaty triangles onto a paper towel. "I'll take these to Morran. He won't have gone far."

Kifi was starting on seconds and Anna was chewing, so Leena left, her own second slice in her free hand. It was hard not to fantasize about arranging inter-dimensional delivery service. The people of Eldaban, high and low alike, would adore this pizza concoction. If she survived this adventure, it might be a lucrative business venture.

Her thoughts turned serious again when she stepped outside. The heat of the day was fading. She caught the scent of a sea breeze, suggesting this crowded city must be near the coast.

She set out cautiously. It was dark, and they hadn't caught Fionn. She couldn't let her guard down for an instant.

Happily, she hadn't gone two steps before she saw Morran sitting under the stand of oak trees. He wasn't looking her way, so she took the opportunity to study his still form. The shirt Anna had supplied should have given him a more casual air, but nothing hid his nature. His tall warrior's body was poised ready to burst into motion. He was strength and potential—the very essence of the Flame.

Morran got to his feet as she approached. She handed him the food.

"What is this?" he said, taking a bite.

"Pizza."

"Ambrosia," he countered, closing his eyes. "Food of the gods. I was hungrier than I thought."

"There's more where that came from." She took a bite of her own slice.

Somewhere outside the fence, one of the workmen shouted.

All at once, the block was flooded with light, as if a thousand captive suns had been released. Leena blinked at the sudden brightness flooding from the city's thousand windows and street-lights. A cheer went up from inside the hospital.

"The horizon looks like a glittering crown," she said, inching a little deeper into the oak tree's shadow. The light made it easier to see, but also to be seen.

Morran made a contemplative sound, his expression remote. Leena chose not to interrupt his thoughts, but instead scanned the grounds for Fionn. Her brother's presence was a worrying shadow, never quite seen and never quite forgotten.

"I'm remembering more," Morran said without warning.

"You are?" Leena finished her last bite of crust, then wiped her hands on the paper towel.

"Yes. Scraps and details of the war. I came across a crown, once, trampled into the mud. A petty king running from the Shades."

"People take their treasures when they flee," Leena said. "They soon toss most aside. It's like leaving pieces of who you once were, but your past won't help you survive."

"What does?" he asked, his voice tight.

She took his hand, squeezing it. In his own way, he was just as displaced as the Kelthians. "Everyone's answer is different. My reason to fight was my family. Almost all are gone now."

Morran's expression softened. "What exactly happened?"

"Juradoc's sorcerers attacked." Leena turned her face away, hiding her emotions. "It began when the birds flew away. Great flocks left the mountains, already aware of what was coming. I stood in our doorway, holding Fionn's hand, and watched them pass overhead. The sound of it was like a rushing surf."

"And then?"

"My mother grabbed whatever she could, and we made for the road." She paused to clear her throat. "One step behind us, the stones turned to sand, draining down the mountainside. Then the cottages and trees slid away because there was nothing to hold them in place. We ran fast—literally ran—because those who lagged behind were buried alive."

Leena had never returned, but she'd heard the traveler's tales. All that was left was bare rock without enough soil to support life. She sucked in a shaking breath, cutting it short when her sore ribs protested. Morran lifted their joined hands, kissing hers.

"Thank you for telling me," he said softly.

He bent his head, kissing her as he pulled them both into deeper shadows. Above, the oak leaves rustled encouragement. Leena had been bruised that day, both in heart and body. Telling that story had pushed her over the emotional edge. She had no boundaries left, only the need for comfort. Morran seemed to sense it, and he gathered her close.

She bit at his lips, boldly teasing him. Slowly, he ran his hands down the curve of her back and over her hip. He was stroking her as if she were a cat, and she arched against his hand. Desire rose, catching at her magic, and then at the answering flame in him. In her fae sight—the one that saw beyond hard fact and into magic—a faint flicker of flames surrounded them both.

Morran kissed her more deeply still, and she opened to his caress. He tasted like masculine heat and savory food—a perfect mix of comfort and temptation. But even as she sailed on their cresting need, part of her cried out for control. Anna was right— Leena needed assurances, some indication the hope she felt for him was justified.

She broke the kiss, leaning into his chest instead. It cooled the moment to a safer level.

"I've told you my reason to fight," she said. "What's yours? Is there someone you love back in Tymeera?"

"My family is gone," he said. "Maybe that was for the best."

"But Tymeera has never been conquered. Others dear to you might still be alive."

"Juradoc would use me to conquer the city. That can never happen."

His words echoed the Mother's fears. For an instant, Leena thought about the capsule of poison dangling from her chatelaine, which was currently tucked in the pocket of her jacket.

"You see, I remember now how they severed me from my familiar," he said, his voice carefully controlled. "It requires a death spell. Nothing else has sufficient power."

He stopped speaking. Leena waited, her hand tingling where it touched his. Whatever came next would not be pleasant to hear.

"As ever, I was at war against Juradoc's army. We were camped west of the Serpent River, far from home. To my delight, my lover arrived one night, surprising me in my tent. I trusted Paya completely. I'd planned to someday make her my wife."

Leena's mouth went dry.

"The curse that sunders the phoenix comes in the form of a poison. The black spell itself is bound into a potion that weakens its victim in body and magical essence. Such forbidden magic is known only in the darkest circles. How Juradoc obtained the knowledge is a mystery that will eventually end in dire retribution."

Gently, he pulled his hand from hers, his fingers curling into a fist. "It was Paya who poisoned my wine. It turns out the Shades had her family—parents, sisters, and her sisters' children. She sacrificed me to save them. I can't blame her for that."

"By the Flame," Leena whispered.

"She carried out her mission as she did everything, with utmost grace and consideration. She watched and waited as I drank the wine, then she kissed me until my drugged sleep crept close. And then, with no warning at all, she cut her own throat."

"Oh, no." Leena's heart seized, mired in pity and hatred.

"The deed was done," he said, features twisting with pain. "I was sure Arlanoth—the phoenix—could never be taken from me. I was sure Paya could be trusted."

He looked up at the night sky of the human world, the stars dulled by thousands of lights. "It turns out that I am sure of nothing and no one. I won't be ever again."

The words were like a door closing.

"Are you certain you won't find another love to rebuild your hearth and home?" Leena held very still, careful not to give herself away.

He brushed her hair aside with his fingers. "I'm broken, Leena. You know that better than anyone."

Disappointment pushed through her like a ravenous, burrowing thing. She nodded, not trusting herself to speak.

He'd told her everything she needed to know.

❧ 17 ☙

Morran watched Leena walk away, transfixed by the sway of her spine and hips. She rolled her shoulders, shrugging off the lingering sensation of his touch. Morran released a frustrated breath.

He'd hurt her. He'd said the wrong thing. Except he'd spoken the truth, which was worth more than pretty phrases. Wasn't it?

He leaned against the oak, grateful for its solidity. On the street, the workmen loaded up their vehicle so they could finally go home. Traffic and voices increased as the city's confidence returned with the streetlights. If only his own case was as easy to resolve.

Oblivion had been simple. His past was not.

After such a long lapse in memory, it seemed the terrible night of betrayal had only just happened. The nightmare memories were too fresh, too raw not to be all-consuming. He'd been betrayed, but so had Paya. *Poor, lovely, lost Paya.* Shock froze pieces of his soul, leaving him to fumble with the aftermath.

Lady Paya of Alkamen had been the daughter of an influential lord. Their relationship had been typical of the Tymeeran nobility—a complicated web of lust and opportunism—but there had been real affection, too. He would carry the guilt of her death to his grave. She'd died because he was the Phoenix Prince.

But beneath that guilt was an unforgivable wound. She'd violated the man she'd professed to love in the one way that could not heal. When she'd offered him that cup of poison, she'd known what it would do.

The night air chilled his face. When he rubbed at his cheeks, they were wet. An odd pain twisted in his chest. He'd not had the chance to mourn until now—not for her, himself, or their broken faith.

Even now, there wasn't the luxury of time. He swallowed hard, concentrating on what lay ahead and how to get there.

He started toward the building entrance, allowing his mind to roam. One day, he would stand on the balcony of his palace and greet his people with the news that Juradoc and his foul army were destroyed, and the south was safe again. And maybe he would say that Leena's brother had been saved, and the Kelthian tribes could rebuild their mountain homes in peace. His bargain with Leena would be complete.

Morran's step hitched at the idea of Leena gazing up at him from Tymeera's courtyard, eyes shining with slavish gratitude. The image was wrong. Despite their mutual attraction, Morran formed no part of Leena's goals, except when it came to saving her brother. Even then, she would be grateful, but never subservient.

No, he was a fellow traveler, not the destination. She'd stand beside him on that balcony, taking her own bows. Faery would not be saved by one person, not even the Phoenix Prince. Morran was broken and far less trusting, but maybe he was smarter, too.

He was almost at the hospital entrance when the orange tomcat emerged from the shadows, tail puffed. "Hey, bird boy."

Morran stopped with a grimace. "Are felines devoid of respect?"

Mo's ears went flat. "No time for it. I've been on sentry duty as commanded by my queen."

"Then deliver your report, soldier."

"I've seen your quarry," Mo added with a growl. "The smelly thing in the cape is inside the building."

⚜

BROKEN. LEENA CURSED UNDER HER BREATH AS SHE WALKED away from Morran. *Broken* was hardly an original excuse for emotional retreat. Who in Faery hadn't been shattered by the war? Who hadn't fought for survival, jostling like cattle around a shrinking water hole?

And trust? Trust had become increasingly conditional as conflict with the Shades dragged on. Today, the Kelthians were trusted—or at least tolerated—by the citizens of Eldaban. Tomorrow, if food became scarce, their welcome would end. That was just how things were.

Leena crossed the lawn at a ferocious pace, her feet swishing in the grass. She ranted inside her own head, not quite making sense. But his words stung more than they had a right to, slicing right through to her core. She put a hand to her waist, half expecting blood.

Morran had no business kissing her if he couldn't see a future with hearth and home—with *her*—in it.

Leena stopped, her hand on the entry door. If she turned around, he would still be brooding beneath the oak tree. She could see him in her mind's eye—a strong, tall warrior. She liked him better in the clothes of this world, with no hint of his princely rank. It put them on an equal footing.

Heat crept up her cheeks. Anger was making her unjust—at him, but also at herself for playing the fool. She'd made herself vulnerable, and she was blaming him for her stupidity. Morran *was* truly broken—Leena knew that was far more than an excuse—but not so broken that he had to stoop to loving a temple dancer. If she'd believed that, she was the one with a poor grasp on sanity.

Ah, yes, for an instant, she'd thought there had been room for something between them—despite the Mother's warnings, despite Anna's logic, and despite her own misgivings. *Foolish, foolish girl.* The most she could hope for was a brief flare of passion, take it or leave it.

But without trust, there could be no meaningful connection between them. She would not settle for less.

She pulled open the door, refusing to glance back.

With the newly restored lighting, it wasn't as easy to travel the hospital unseen, and she had to resort to a distraction charm. It wasn't as strong as a true invisibility spell, but it was enough to make humans look the other way. She found her way back to the top floor without incident.

When she turned the corner into the corridor to Barleycorn's room, a sound made her stop. She looked around, a bit disoriented by the bright overhead lights. Everything appeared different in the glare.

The sound had come from somewhere ahead. She started forward again.

There was little to block her view of the hall—a few chairs. and a rolling cot pushed against the wall. The cot was empty, but there was something—someone—beneath it. Leena ran a few steps, then stopped, afraid to approach. She circled the prone figure, staying out of reach. Predators could play dead if that brought their prey within easy reach.

The figure was male, wearing boots and leathers. Nothing about him jogged her memory until she saw his face, which was turned her way. The eyes were closed, but she recognized the wolf who had brought pizza. What was his name?

Edgar. That was it.

With his features slack, he seemed painfully young. Leena swallowed hard, her misgivings surging like a rogue tide. She knelt beside him, noticing for the first time that there was blood pooling beneath him. Lots of blood once she let herself look. She could smell it now, coppery and rich.

The scent triggered her years of training, turning off her emotions as her thoughts grew sharp and clear. She glanced back where she'd been, noting there were no obvious signs of violence in the corridor. Yet, Edgar had crawled beneath the cot like a wounded dog. A knife wound to the belly perhaps? If the blade was still in it, the bleed might be slow.

She checked for a pulse, finding nothing though his skin was still warm. Then she used her healer's senses, digging deeper. He was dead, but only just. The sound she'd heard might have been his last breath.

She could turn the body to search for the wound and the weapon that caused it. Moving Edgar wouldn't hurt him now, and curiosity urged her to investigate further. But whoever had killed him wouldn't be far.

Leena got to her feet. As a dancer, she could move with perfect silence. She used that skill as she glided toward Barleycorn's room. Now that she was searching for them, she saw drops of blood on the patterned tile of the floor ahead. By the wide spacing, Edgar had been running—running and hiding for his life.

Her knife was in her hand, although she didn't remember reaching for it. She was three doors away from her destination, then two. Light spilled into the hall in a narrow sliver, indicating that Barleycorn's door was partially open.

Leena stopped, senses straining for information. Her pulse pounded so hard that all she could hear was her heartbeat. She took a breath, letting it out slowly. That should have calmed her, but she was too frightened for her ribs to move. Still, she caught enough air to taste the permeating rot. *Fionn.*

A low, grumbling yowl came from the room. It sounded like every imp from the demon dimensions had assembled behind that door. It trailed off into a bone-chilling hiss.

"Kifi," Leena murmured, an icy tide filling her veins. The cat was fierce, but she was no match for a Shade.

The urge to protect carried Leena the last few steps to the door. She peered through the opening, shielding herself from sight. Her heart plunged.

Fionn stood by the bed, his right side to Leena. His hood had fallen back, showing the full devastation of Juradoc's spell. His skin clung loosely to his skull, the flesh beneath melting away. His sandy curls had fallen out in clumps, leaving patches of gray-blue scalp behind.

Anna struggled in his arms, but he had a knife to her throat. Blood spattered his clothes, though only a thin trickle was coursing down her neck. The rest may well have come from Edgar. Kifi was on the bed, legs splayed in a protective crouch over the unconscious Barleycorn. The cat's ears were back, her lips lifted in a muttering growl.

"I called the pack," Anna said, her tone defiant. "They'll come at any moment."

"Then they'll die like the other one," Fionn replied, pressing the blade into her throat.

Anna drew in a rattling breath, the blade clearly hurting her. Leena felt a pulse of magic against her face—ice and stone and the smell of moss.

"Don't," Fionn ordered. "If you try to shift, I'll slit your throat."

Leena's throat ached, pity and terror congealing inside her chest. This wasn't her brother, yet there had to be something of him still there. A shred she could reason with, even now.

She stepped into the room, then circled to where Fionn could see her. Kifi's growl cut off with a hiss.

Anna's eyes went huge. "Don't be an idiot. Run."

But Leena looked past Anna, staring straight at Fionn instead. His sky-blue eyes were violet now, but she caught and held his gaze. Images of blood, of Edgar's still face, ghosted through her mind.

"Hello, brother."

"You never knew when to leave things alone." His lip curled, showing rotten stumps of teeth.

Horror rocked Leena, weakening her knees so she swayed where she stood. He was so far gone, the decay advancing since they'd come to this realm. Still, she kept her voice even and light. "What do you want, Fionn?"

He flung out his free hand toward the bed. The cat lashed at it, but her efforts weren't needed. Blue-green lightning crackled and arced over the bed, striking his hand away. Kifi's fur puffed with static, but she didn't budge from her post.

"You know he's my mission," Fionn said. "This she-wolf won't remove that spell."

The knife tip pricked a fresh gash in Anna's throat.

"I don't know how," Anna ground out through clenched teeth. "I didn't put it there."

"It wasn't there earlier today."

"I know."

"Do you expect me to believe an unconscious man cast it on himself?"

Leena listened to the exchange, her mind churning. Earthquake and lightning—powerful earth magic—had come to life when they'd arrived, perhaps in response to the Shimmer. Now, Barleycorn was warded. Sometimes, a threat could activate latent spells, but it was more likely that he was waking up. Even in a semi-conscious state, some fae could use magic for self-protection.

If he woke up right now, it went without saying there would be a fight.

"Fionn," she said. "Let Anna go."

The room went deadly quiet for a split second. Traffic rumbled in the street outside, louder than before. Leena recognized the brash sound of the transports Anna had called motorcycles. The wolf's eyes turned to the window without moving her head, as if she knew who was pulling up to the hospital's gate. *Her pack*, Leena thought. Yet more opportunity for chaos.

"Let Anna go, Fionn," Leena said again, pleading now. "She's not your enemy. None of us are."

Fionn exploded, eyes blazing. "Don't you think I know that?" he howled.

Leena fell back a step. "What?"

"I know, I know, but it's gone too deep." Suddenly, he was weeping, dark tears staining his ruined cheeks. "I can't stop. I don't have a choice anymore."

"Fionn?" Leena whispered, her voice too pinched to speak.

He broke into sobs. "It hurts, Leelee. Make it stop. Please, make it stop."

She made a noise, almost a whimper. He'd used her childhood name. Tears blurred her vision. This was a wound she couldn't bind and kiss better. "Put the knife down, Fionn. I beg you. The only way to help yourself is to stop."

He sucked in a gulping sob. "I can't. They know where I am. They know I've failed. I'm being called back."

He was right. A pinprick glow spiraled to life in front of the window. Someone was opening a Shimmer.

There were only so many things that could happen next, especially when Fionn was still holding Anna at knifepoint. Morran had spoken of Juradoc's interest in the woman. If Fionn couldn't touch Barleycorn, he might take her instead.

Leena drew closer, wondering how best to snatch Anna away.

"*Don't*," Kifi cried.

The door banged fully open as Morran plunged into the room, followed by a blur of orange fur. The tomcat landed on the bed beside Kifi, fangs bared at the enemy.

Morran vaulted over the end of the bed to grab at Fionn. The prince landed neatly, skidding to a stop, but Leena was already there. Her hand brushed Anna's sleeve, but Fionn lashed out, knocking Leena away.

The force of his blow sent her reeling into Morran. Leena bounced off the hard wall of his chest and stumbled against the window, banging her elbow on the frame. Morran caught her, but it was too late.

Fionn dragged Anna through the Shimmer to almost certain death.

❧ 18 ❧

"No!" Leena plunged toward the Shimmer, but the silvery light swallowed Fionn and Anna, leaving nothing but a ripple behind. A cry ripped from her throat, half frustration and half a moan of loss.

"Wait." Morran gripped her arm. "We can't leave Barleycorn undefended."

Leena whirled to face him, the words barely finding their way through the storm of her emotions. Fionn had begged for help. Every part of her needed to answer that cry. "We're losing them."

The Shimmer flared brighter, its magic responding to the tension in the room. Color blazed high on Morran's cheekbones. "Juradoc wants Barleycorn for his own ends."

"I know." But knowing wasn't everything.

Leena's chest felt as if a wild animal were tearing it asunder. Morran was right. Somehow, Barleycorn was a weapon against Juradoc. He could not be left undefended. And Anna loved him.

But at the same time, Fionn needed her as never before. She couldn't abandon him, not even for the sake of Faery. She simply couldn't do it.

Morran's expression changed, showing he understood.

She caught his hand. "Let me go. Fionn knows me."

"Why don't you both go?" Kifi put in. "You won't be leaving the patient unguarded. Not with a hundred cats ready to answer my call."

Leena turned to face the felines. "What if Juradoc sends another assassin?"

Mo lashed his tail. "Then they will have to get through us *and* the pack of wolves Anna summoned. I hear their boots on the stairs."

"How do you know it's her pack?" Morran asked.

"The smell of muddy dog." The orange feline puffed himself into a disgruntled ball.

Kifi sat on Barleycorn's chest, as regal as a sphinx. Leena's heart squeezed at the thought of leaving her friend behind, but the cat was far safer here than in Juradoc's camp. "We'll come back for you," Leena said.

Kifi licked a paw. "Or we shall rescue you. Either way, this provides for more options. Now hurry."

Boots tromped down the corridor. Anna's wolves had arrived. At the same time, the Shimmer was beginning to dwindle.

Morran took Leena's hand. "Leave the cats to explain."

Before Leena could answer, he pulled her through the whirling light. This time, the airless dark was twice as bitter, as if Juradoc's venom had infected it, too. Leena screamed inside her mind, then a blinding flash made her fling up an arm to protect her eyes.

Pain flared through her joints as she plummeted onto hard-packed earth. The momentum sent her tumbling over and over until the cracked, sandy dirt caught her in its curving slope. Leena squinted up into a sun-washed sky, its blue paled by a haze of dust and heat. By the sun's angle, it was well into the afternoon. Gingerly, she sat up, grateful nothing was broken.

She was even more grateful that the Shades were nowhere nearby. She and Morran had returned to Faery, but it was a different landscape than they'd left. No trees broke the sea of cracked earth. Everything was painted in hues of orange and gold, as if the earth had been encased in amber. Only rocks jutted from the ground like the ribs of sunken ships. In the middle distance, she spotted four pyramids.

A shadow fell over her, blotting out the blazing sky. It was Morran, holding out his hand. When Leena gripped it, he pulled her to her feet.

"Are you all right?" she asked.

He gave a curt nod that revealed nothing. "And you?"

"I'm fine. Where are we?"

"That's the Great Temple."

Leena swallowed, her mouth dry as the desert around her. "I thought it was in Tymeera."

"Tymeera is two days' march south of here."

So much for her geography lessons. Leena frowned at the pyramids. From this distance, she could see they were set at the four corners of a perfectly square stone courtyard. They were smaller than she imagined such structures would be, each one barely twice as tall as Lord Dorth's marble palace. Their sand-colored stone was smooth and plain, with no ornament to break their perfect surface.

It didn't look at all like the tapestry the Mother had hanging in her chambers back in Eldaban. "I thought the Great Temple was one big pyramid."

"It is," Morran said, gazing down with reverence. "What you see is only part of the temple. The rest houses the Flame. That much elemental power cannot remain in Faery, but must be summoned."

Leena pondered his words. "Is it true that it's the same shape as the Wheel?"

That was the highest mountain in Faery, so named because of its round, flat top where the kings and queens had once met to govern the land. That was before the Shades, before the defeat of

High King Jorwarth, before everything had gone wrong for the fae.

Morran was watching her now, his smile gentle. "There are legends that the Great Temple and the Wheel were cast from the same clay, but they are just stories to beguile children."

Leena looked away, feeling foolish. "Is there any sign of Fionn or Anna?"

"No, but we did not cross the Shimmer at the same moment," he replied. "It's not unusual to be separated by even a small delay. Still, they should be close."

He climbed the hill, a hot breeze ruffling his dark hair. Leena followed, missing the protection of her veils. She had almost caught up when she heard the hitch of Morran's breath. She drew up beside him, then followed his gaze. Perhaps it was her imagination, but it was then she caught the smell of blood on the hot desert wind.

A dusty plain stretched to the west of the pyramids. Figures sprawled across the ground, as if the tide of battle had left them along a hellish shore. Some wore bright armor, others the dark cloaks of the Shade army. There was no sign of living soldiers. Whatever had happened was in the past.

"That's Juradoc's sigil," Morran said, pointing toward a fallen form. "I know it even at this distance."

"How did he arrive here so quickly?" Leena asked. "Even if he used a Shimmer to move his army, we've only been gone one night."

Morran met her gaze, his dark eyes troubled. "Time does not move at the same pace between worlds. A month or more must have passed."

Shock tingled down her arms. Anything at all could have happened while they were gone. "And?"

"Juradoc has moved on Tymeera. The dead fae upon the field are my own warriors." Morran's face hardened. "They came to defend the Temple of the Flame. By the look of things, neither side won. Both must have retreated to their own encampments."

Leena didn't question his assessment. No doubt Morran read a battlefield the way others might a scroll. "How long ago?"

"Not long. It appears only a few scavenger birds have arrived." He shaded his eyes, scanning the horizon. "With luck, we can join my forces. If I must deal with the Shades, I prefer an army at my back."

It went without saying that they would need shelter, food, and water as well. Leena followed Morran as he struck out toward the battlefield. "What about Fionn and Anna?"

"We will find them. They would have arrived nearby, and no one can go far in this heat."

Unless the Shades find them first. Leena's stomach twisted as her brother's despairing eyes filled her imagination. She stumbled almost blindly through the seared landscape, windblown grains of sand scouring her cheeks.

The dead were scattered as far as the eye could see. Morran didn't stop until they reached the first body. The fae had been tall and lean with skin bronzed by the sun. Now he lay with a Shade's leaf-bladed spear through a gap between his breastplate and the gorget protecting his throat. Morran pulled the weapon free, dropping it to the sand. Sun glinted from the blood-darkened tip.

Then he knelt and removed the fae's helmet, setting it aside. The high cheekbones, winged brows, and pointed ears marked the warrior as a pureblood fae noble. Morran bowed his head.

"Do you know him?" Leena asked softly.

"I trained him," Morran replied. "He was a member of my household."

"I'm sorry." She brushed away the hair that blew into her eyes and mouth in the insistent wind.

Morran rose, fresh anger kindling behind his eyes. "He deserved to have me at his back. He deserved his prince."

Leena's tribe was half-wild, more rabble than kingdom, but

she understood Morran's grief. The oath between a lord and his men ran deep. Juradoc was at fault, but the guilt remained.

Morran took the heavy sword from the dead fae's hand. "Loan me your blade," he said softly. "I will drench it with vengeance."

"Will you now?" came a cracked voice from behind Leena.

A skeletal hand fell on Leena's shoulder. She spun out from under it, but not before razor-sharp claws dug into her flesh. Springing back, she drew her knife and landed in a fighting crouch —only to feel cavernous fear well inside her. Three Shades—no doubt a patrol from Juradoc's camp—had appeared from thin air.

One was mounted on a horse as black as cinders. The foot soldier beside him held the same type of spear that had killed Morran's man. Worst, Claw Hands in front held the crooked staff of a sorcerer. Of them all, he was the most dangerous.

Morran grasped the hilt of his borrowed sword in both hands. "Three black crows, I see. Did you come to pick the bones of the dead?"

"We were looking for a different prize," Claw Hands said.

Fionn, Leena guessed. Perhaps they hadn't yet retrieved her brother or Anna.

The Shade's face was shrouded, but she felt his attention shift fully to Morran. "Never mind. You will do nicely, Morran of Tymeera."

Morran gave a laugh that was half-growl. "I've tired of Juradoc's hospitality."

Claw Hands casually dipped his staff, sending a flash of power rippling through the earth. It was almost invisible, like wind on water or a shimmer of heat. A dozen yards away, a boulder exploded in a deafening boom, throwing a shower of dust into the heat-soaked air.

It was a warning, but it fell on deaf ears.

Morran launched into action, sweeping the blade at Claw Hands. The sorcerer shrieked and vanished, leaving the bloody sword to cleave thin air. The horseman reared at the flashing steel, then plunged his mount to Morran's right. Distracted, Morran was a fraction too slow to notice the spearman move in from the other side. It was a smooth maneuver, as well-timed as any dance move.

Not one bothered with a mere dancing girl. Leena grabbed the spear Morran had pulled from the dead fae. The polished staff was hot from the sun, almost burning her palms, but she clutched it hard. Struggling with the unfamiliar balance, she stabbed at Morran's attacker, catching him under the arm as he lifted his own weapon to strike. The point missed the curve of his armor and jarred against rib and muscle. Leena twisted the point, screaming to cover the unholy sound of metal piercing flesh.

Morran dragged the rider from his horse, pulling him down just as the other assailant pitched forward. The horseman landed on Leena's foe, dragging the spear from her grip. The horse, suddenly riderless, bolted for freedom.

Morran moved in, his sword already in motion. The horseman barely had time to react before his head tumbled to the sand. Black, foul blood oozed from the stump of his neck. The spearman beneath shrieked in pain and horror before the sound was cut short by another slashing blow. Morran fell back, breathing hard as he surveyed his handiwork.

"Grab a weapon and run for the pyramids," he said under his breath. "We'll be safe from Shade magic there."

Leena understood his meaning at once. They'd killed the henchmen, but the sorcerer—the greater threat—was lying in wait. She glanced over her shoulder, estimating the distance to the Temple. The ground was flat, but the path to safety was long. It would be a hard run in the debilitating desert heat.

Morran grabbed water canteens from the dead fae while she tried to drag her spear free from the Shade's body. It was buried too deep. After a brief struggle, she gave up and took a long knife from the dead fae's belt, silently thanking him for the loan. It would serve her far better than her short blade. Barely pausing to secure the weapon, she fell into step beside Morran. As if reading one another's thoughts, they both broke into a long, loping run.

The sun was brutally hot, dragging like a physical weight on her limbs. Though she managed to keep pace with Morran, he ran with a steady, pounding gait, sweat slicking his muscled form. It was clear he meant to gain ground while he could.

But as they ran, dunes began to magically form on either side of their route toward the Great Temple. The sand seemed to boil from the earth, shrouding the flat ground of the battlefield. Running grew harder as thick tentacles of sand spilled across their path, making Leena's feet slip and slide. Before long, the muscles of her calves burned with effort.

The Shade sorcerer was playing with them, letting them struggle for the sake of amusement. Leena slipped, falling to one knee. Hot, dry air burned her nose and throat. The world narrowed to a tunnel of blinding heat and treacherous ground. Morran helped her up, and they were off again before the bite of the sand had left her palms. Everything faded but the animal need to flee and the promise of safety ahead. They kept going, barely stopping to take a drink from their borrowed canteens.

Without warning, Morran flung out an arm, nearly slamming her to the ground. Leena skidded, all but losing her balance.

"What the—" she cried, but her words ended there.

Invisible fire licked across their path, turning the sand into pools of molten glass. The moment she'd lost focus, the sorcerer had struck. Morran grabbed her hand, pulling her off the path and up the crest of a dune. Another bolt of power ignited the sand, the wave of heat like a blow against Leena's back. Morran folded her in his arms and dove, sliding on his back down the slope at breakneck speed. Behind them, Claw Hands let out a scream of frustration.

They ran as soon as their feet touched solid ground. An ominous shudder sounded behind them. Leena looked back to see a trickle of sand, then three, join and swell into a rushing river.

"Run!"

Morran's shout was almost lost beneath the growing rumble of the avalanche. Leena's legs were like water after climbing over the shifting dune, but panic granted her renewed strength. She pelted forward, stumbling as the ground rippled beneath her feet. Morran grabbed her, shielding her with his body as the wave swept them forward. At some point, they fell, rolling and sliding until they finally hit solid ground again.

Leena scrambled to her feet, bruised and scraped but otherwise unhurt thanks to Morran's embrace. The feel of his body wrapped around hers clung for a moment, both enticing and unwelcome. She shouldn't want it—he wasn't hers to keep—yet its loss left her bereft. The only saving grace was that there was no time to dwell on it.

Morran had lost his sword in the fall, and he cried out in relief when he found it half-buried a few yards away. He drew it out, a new look of defiance on his face. "Come on. We're nearly there."

He was right. The sand had carried them almost to the foot of the closest pyramid, as if the desert itself were gathering them close. The smooth stone edifice blotted out the low sun, leaving them in blessedly cooler shadows. They began to run again, closing the final distance—to what, Leena wasn't sure. There was no door that she could see.

In a flash of green fire, Claw Hands was there. He swung his sorcerer's crook sideways, blocking their path. Magic struck Leena in an invisible wall, the blow hard enough that she bit her tongue.

The Shade had finally caught them.

Morran raised his blade, but he couldn't strike.

"I must congratulate you, Prince of Tymeera," Claw Hands began. "I wondered at the value Juradoc placed on you, but now I see the attraction. Even as a tattered remnant, you are a resourceful foe."

That confirmed Leena's guess about the Shade. He'd been amusing himself, letting them come close to success just so he could snatch it away.

"Who are you?" she demanded, anger making her bold.

His shoulders stiffened, as if affronted. "My name is Olek. It will mean nothing to you because I rank far above those who deal with the fae. I am here in an investigative capacity."

"You're gathering up Juradoc's loose ends because the general has gone rogue," Morran said, his tone matter-of-fact. "Your forces are spread too thin for a war in the south, yet he insisted on attacking the most heavily defended principality. You need to know why."

Olek hesitated, his face invisible beneath his hood. "The Shades have lingered long in Faery without significant reward. It caught our interest when Juradoc made interesting claims about this place. He has a time-limited chance to win our approval."

No doubt Juradoc had made claims about the Great Temple and the Flame. Leena sensed the presence of the elemental fire, as if its energy tugged her toward the pyramid. This was what the armies of the fae had come to protect.

"What we do know is that the Phoenix Prince has the potential to become an extremely useful weapon," Olek continued. "Your father, Prince Karth, was the ideal example."

Morran flinched, and no wonder. The old prince had taken his own life.

The Shade took a step back, putting more room between them. "And although some might deem you damaged beyond repair, Juradoc believes you still have value, especially if he gets his hands on Barleycorn's treasure trove."

"What has Barleycorn or his toys to do with me?"

"A good question. I am curious enough to find out for myself. Surrender, Prince Morran."

Morran gripped his sword. "I think not."

"Then you shall be my prisoner by force."

Olek twisted the staff in his hand. Suddenly, it became a sword. It was unlike any blade Leena had seen before. Though its edges shone in the dying light, it shed a cloud of black mist that made her think of sickness and rot.

Instinctively, she stepped to the side, giving Morran room. It was only after she'd done it that Leena realized she could move again. The wall of force that had stopped them had melted away. The Shade was making room for a fight.

It was then she noticed the ground beneath Olek's robe was growing darker. The Shade was bleeding. No wonder they'd made it this far—Morran had wounded Olek during their first skirmish, and the sorcerer was weakened. Slowly, Leena drew her knife, but held it low against her side. Her primary advantage would be surprise.

Olek took a swordsman's stance, graceful despite his injury. Leena's entire body tightened, straining against an overwhelming urge to run. She forced herself to look away from the sword and scan their surroundings, ensuring there were no other enemies in sight. Thankfully, Olek was alone.

The Shade struck. The attack was a mix of magic and blade work, so fast it was no more than a blur. Morran countered, swift footwork saving him. Leena gave him space, terrified of what evil the Shade's blade might carry. One nick might poison Morran the way Juradoc had destroyed her brother.

Morran barely recovered his balance before Olek advanced again. Morran cut low, ducking beneath the smoking blade and aiming for Olek's knees. He must have struck because the Shade gave an eerie, piercing cry and fell back. The reprieve didn't last more than a heartbeat. The next second, Olek redoubled his blows, as if time were running out.

Morran parried again and again, but each blow pushed him back. Leena circled, afraid to interfere, yet wondering how to help. Then Olek charged Morran, leaving his flank exposed. She lunged with her knife.

An invisible force slammed her back twice as hard as before. She staggered, losing her footing before sprawling to the ground. Olek spun, preparing to pierce her where she lay.

He didn't take her dancer's agility into account. Leena sprang out of the way, nearly levitating in her panic.

"Back away, Shade," Morran roared.

Without warning, fire magic rushed through the air, hot as the breath of the sun itself. Then fire licked the length of Morran's blade, white against the deepening dusk.

"You dare to challenge the Phoenix Prince at his seat of power?" Morran's tone was thick with defiance as he put both hands on the hilt of the flaming sword.

Leena's lips parted in surprise. Morran's magic—the power

that had defeated the Shades for centuries—was coming back. She barely stifled a wild, hysterical laugh.

The Shade said nothing, but every angle of his form spoke of utter shock. He hadn't expected this.

Morran swung. Olek's head hit the sand with a meaty thump.

But the sorcerer was not done yet. As his body collapsed, the Shade's smoking sword blew away like mist. Then, unleashed magic spilled into the earth, releasing all the dark power the Shade had stored during a lifetime of sorcery. The ground trembled, then began to crack with an ear-splitting groan. A narrow fissure opened at their feet, but it widened within seconds, sand pouring down into unfathomable depths.

"Come!" Morran grabbed Leena's hand, pulling her across the growing gap.

They sprinted the final distance to the closest pyramid, the roar of the earthquake at their heels. At Morran's shout, a single block at the base of the pyramid slid back and disappeared within its walls, allowing a stream of golden light to fan into the falling night. Where it touched, not a single grain of earth stirred. The power of the Shades could rage all around, but not on Temple ground.

Morran didn't release her hand until they had crossed the threshold of the pyramid. Leena was very aware of the weight of the stone as she passed under the massive lintel of the entrance. Then, with a grinding sound, the huge block that formed the door to the structure slid back into place. There was an enormous *clunk* as it locked, sealing danger out.

Sealing them inside. Leena had served the Flame all her life, but she was suddenly uneasy. There was barely space to stand beside Morran without pressing against the wall of the tiny chamber. The light that had spilled out into the desert must have been made of magic because there was nothing here but tiny glowing crystals set into the walls. It was enough to see the narrow passage ahead, and nothing more.

"There are no windows," she said, keeping her voice steady with an act of will.

"Not here," he agreed. "This space is meant as a kind of checkpoint. If unwelcome guests manage to get this far, they will not reach the inner chambers."

"Are there guards?"

"This place requires no guards. It can see to its own needs."

Leena looked nervously around her. "I hope it knows we're friends."

Morran laughed. "I've been coming here since I was a boy. Follow me."

With that, he started down the passageway ahead. It was narrow enough they had to go single file. Nerves made Leena follow close enough she nearly stepped on his heels. The stifling, dimly lit stonework triggered every fear she had of being trapped. Though she had no visual reference point, the path seemed to angle upward, turning sharply twice before Morran came to a stop. When she bumped lightly against his back, he caught her hand and drew her forward.

At that moment, he moved aside to reveal that they'd come to the end of the passage. Leena drew in a welcome breath of clean, fresh air, and she stared into the heart of the pyramid. She'd always imagined the Temple of the Flame would be like this, except it was a thousand times more beautiful.

The stone on the outer face of the structure was plain and massive. Inside, it had been worked with exquisite artistry. The main chamber was enormous, the fluted pillars supporting the roof as tall as a ship's mast. The ribs of the ceiling above were as intricately carved as the legendary Pomandine lacework, each vault painted with a scene of moon and stars. The floors were a mosaic of colored marble depicting birds and beasts in a pattern of twisting vines.

"It's incredible," she said, whispering because it felt like the thing to do.

Morran smiled. For the first time, the expression seemed relaxed. Perhaps it was because he was home, on safer ground where his powers worked again. Perhaps because it was clear he genuinely loved this place, and it was good to share it. Whatever the reason, Leena was glad.

Placing a hand at the small of her back, he urged her forward. As in the temple at home, there was a central rotunda surrounded by tiered stone steps. But here, those steps framed a vast pool of water. In the middle of the pool, there was a circle of stone that housed the Flame.

"Is that—is that the core of the fire?" she asked, wishing all over again that she were powerful enough to hear the Flame's voice. What would it say, here at the seat of its power? What astounding knowledge of the healing arts might she discover?

"As I said, the Great Temple does not always dwell in Faery, but like every temple in the land, including yours in Eldaban, this pyramid provides a conduit to the Flame. That is the entrance to the inner sanctum."

She glanced up at Morran, reading the reverence in his face. "And this is where the rites of your people are performed?"

"Some. We are wary of the inner sanctum, for the Flame is hot even for our kind. It would be a fatal pit of fire if you tried to dance in it."

"I would not be so presumptuous."

Leena stared in wonder, feeling the temple's power like a vibration through her feet. The fire leaped and spat upward, the bright curls of elemental power reflecting in the still water like a living painting.

Leena pressed a hand to her breastbone, needing to ease the sudden tightness there. This sight was more powerful, serene, and lovely than she'd imagined possible. And despite everything—the Ravaged Lands, the Shades, traveling from one world to the next —she had survived to see it. This was the true Flame, the spark that gave her people life. It was the Essence, the meaning, the healing warmth of the world.

Fatigue mixed with wonder and relief, bringing on a silent storm of emotion. The sight was too exquisite, too profound to take in all at once. Wiping tears from her cheeks, Leena left Morran's side and drifted toward the pool, the soles of her borrowed shoes a whisper on the stone floor. She stopped a few yards from the edge, barely able to breathe. She stretched out a hand, as if the radiance of the Flame's reflection were something she could touch. Perhaps it was.

Morran came to stand at her side, his presence reassuring and warm. "This is what we fight to protect. The Flame, and the lives it touches with its light."

It took Leena a moment to find her voice. "Where are the priestesses and healers? Where are the temple cats?"

"There are four pyramids. One is for teaching, one for healing, and one for the archive kept by the Queen of Cats. This building is for private meditation. That said, in times of war, the Temple is evacuated. Right now, its residents will be in Tymeera. You and I are alone."

"Can anyone come here?" she asked, still overwhelmed by the quiet solitude of the place.

"Of course. The Flame is for all, but few would make the pilgrimage in wartime." He brushed her hair aside from her neck. "The Shade tore your shirt when he grabbed you back at the battlefield. He pierced your skin with his claws."

His voice was grim, as if the injury was a personal affront. Leena craned her neck to look, but the angle was impossible.

"It stings," she said, "but then everything aches right now."

"Bathe in the pool. Any hurts or poison will be cleansed by these waters."

Leena gave him an astonished stare. "I'm too filthy."

He smiled then, looking unexpectedly boyish. "What do you think a bath is for?" Then he bent to take off his boots.

"This is a sacred pool. It's disrespectful."

"Do you think the Flame can't handle a bit of sand?"

She had nothing to say to that. By then, he'd pulled off her shoes as well. Still, she wavered. Ritual bathing was common, but not women and men together. Not unless they were sworn to one another.

But then he shed his coat and weapons, and he kept stripping down until nothing remained but his linen underclothes. He waded into the pool and ducked under the water, swimming a short distance before rising in a stream of fire-lit water. It licked over the curve of his bare arms and chest in molten rivulets.

Leena's breath stopped. He was as perfect as a sculpture. An eager thrill ran through her, but she pushed it aside. He'd already declared his heart unattainable, and she had no interest in courting disappointment.

Briskly, she shed the borrowed clothes she'd put on over her brief cotton shift. She sank gratefully into the pool, letting the cool, soothing water soak away sand and grime. The buoyancy eased her aching muscles, reviving her as effectively as any of the Mother's potions. This was a place of powerful healing.

Morran swam close, as swift and sleek as a seal. He bent close to her wound, making a disapproving sound. "It's not as deep as I feared, but it still requires cleansing."

He cupped a handful of water and trickled it over the scratches, sluicing the injury. She kept still, doing her best to ignore his magnificent frame barely an inch away.

Until she felt his lips on her shoulder, trailing light kisses over the wound. Her pulse began to pound, first in alarm, then in frank desire. She turned into his arms, shaping her body to his. The move was so natural, so confident, he might have been a dance partner.

When his eyes met hers, firelight reflected in his darkened pupils, as if signaling his mood. She lifted her face and their lips met, hot, soft, and hungry. It was a foolish move, giving him that opening. He plundered her mouth with his tongue, drawing a moan from deep inside her core.

Leena should back away now. She was all too aware of her body's urgent response, the need to press her aching nipples against the hard wall of his chest. Every muscle yearned to twine herself around him, to ignite and burn in ecstatic delirium. It would be the end of reason.

"You don't want this," she whispered.

"I don't?" His expression was hazed, almost drugged, but it slowly cleared and grew puzzled as the moment slipped away.

"You said you can't trust. That you're too broken." She placed her palms against his chest, feeling the quick, sure beat of his heart. "I'm not a toy. If you do not care for me, if you cannot build an affection that lasts beyond these walls, please let me be."

Her words shocked him. She saw it in the slight movement of his eyes, quickly concealed by all the rigorous training of a prince. "I swear by the Flame itself, I am not toying with you."

It was a solemn oath, especially here. "Then what are you doing?"

He cupped her cheek, drawing close enough that his breath warmed her face. "My admiration and desire for you are pure and true."

They weren't exactly words of love, but they mattered. He had been injured in ways she could barely fathom, had barely stitched himself into a coherent whole, but he was giving her what he had. Truth. Friendship. She could walk away because he wouldn't take anything she did not give. She knew him that much.

This wasn't idle amusement on his part. The fire between them was real.

She cupped his face in her hands, feeling the rough shadow of his beard. She'd always been afraid to risk herself, but fear had no place before the Flame. She couldn't ask for something she wasn't willing to give.

Leena pulled Morran's mouth to hers.

$$\text{20}$$

ow that she had made her choice, Leena hungered for
Morran's touch. He was gifted and eager to oblige.
With him, a kiss was a word spoken over and over in a
thousand languages, each with its own nuance of meaning.

Desire surged through Leena, robbing the strength from her
limbs even as it drove her on. He scooped her from the water,
letting it sluice down their bodies, and carried her closer to the
fire. The heat was like a second caress, a blessing that healed and
erased all pain. Her body had been battered during their flight
through the desert, but that was almost forgotten now.

"Shall we retire upstairs?" he murmured, placing feather-light
kisses along her throat. He was melting her slowly with each
touch of his lips, undoing the knots of tension running down her
spine.

Leena had a sneaking fear that tension kept her upright, and
she was about to collapse into a boneless heap. "What is
upstairs?"

"A meditation chamber."

"You intend to meditate?" she asked archly. "I would have
hoped for something more gymnastic."

He frowned at the mockery. "It is far more comfortable."

She was about to protest that they were dripping wet, but the Flame had already dried them. He led her to a stone stairway that twisted to levels high above the grand hall. They ran up it as eagerly as a pair of errant children, hand in hand.

Morran took her to a room that must have been near the top of the pyramid, for the wall and ceiling were sharply slanted. Her first impression was of an explosion of brilliant, luxurious color. Every surface was hung with billowing silk of countless hues. Small onyx statues stood in niches hollowed from the stone walls, each a personification of elemental fae magic. Morran lit an oil lamp that hung on golden chains, releasing a faint scent of spice and amber. The warm glow caught the jewels and silver threads embroidered in the silks, enclosing them in shimmering radiance. Leena sank to the soft cushions strewn across the floor, her senses overwhelmed.

Beneath the statue of Earth, with her headdress of twined ivy and robes of woven flowers, there was a panel of creamy stone set into the wall. Morran pressed it, releasing a spring. The panel opened to a cupboard stocked with provisions. He withdrew a wine bottle and stone jars sealed with wax. He opened them to reveal cheeses, dates, and dried meats preserved with spices. All at once, Leena's stomach awakened, reminding her how long it had been since their last meal. Morran poured the wine into drinking cups made of stone so fine they were translucent. He knelt and presented a cup to Leena, waiting as she sipped it. It was as sweet as ripe plums.

"Do you like it?" he asked. "We keep it with our emergency provisions as it is considered restorative."

She passed the cup back to him. "I want a meal, but not quite yet."

His smile answered hers.

There was more than beauty in this place. Magic imbued the stone around them, the very air she breathed. It was a subtle vibration that seeped through flesh and bone, reminding her that she was in a sacred space. Fire magic was complex, both primal and sophisticated, raw and yet pure. It was passion itself, and it was the crucible that had birthed the firebird.

That explained so much about Morran. This was his home, his land, and his magic. Leena could see the Flame in the intensity of his eyes. He was the Prince of Fire in more than just name.

And he was here with her, watching and wanting her.

Leena opened her arms to him. He came to her slowly, gracefully, as greedily as if she were a delicacy to be enjoyed. The moment stretched as he settled beside her, sliding his hands around her waist. She rolled to face him until her body molded to his, every curve and valley finding a match. Their breath mingled, hot and intimate.

"Leena of the Kelthian," Morran began, his voice a low and intimate rumble she felt as much as heard, "every moment I spend with you restores a piece of me. You are a healer in more ways than you know."

Her lips parted to speak, but she had no words. The ache inside her had gone beyond speech or reason. She kissed him instead. When he responded, it effectively ended any conversation. With his help, she wriggled out of her shift, skin burning with the need to feel his flesh against her own. She slid her palms down his flanks, over the strong muscles that curved down to the small of his back. Tremors of desire coursed through her, every part of her anticipating a feast.

His hands closed over her breasts, possessive now. His mouth and tongue claimed her in an ecstasy of heat. The wildness in her rose to meet his, demand against demand. For that brief moment in time, Leena understood the burning, dizzying flight of the phoenix, soaring upon the wind that challenged its wings. Flight wasn't a conquest of air—it was a dance.

They showed each other how to soar.

Dawn found Morran in the room at the peak of the pyramid. Windows overlooked every direction, the openings carved in such a way that they weren't visible from the ground. He could survey the surrounding land for miles without being seen—a strategic advantage the desert warlords had often employed. Morran would, too, if he could bring himself to focus. As it was, all he saw were ragged shreds of the pink and gold dawn against a pearl-gray sky.

A sky that once had been his to conquer. *Arlanoth*. Morran's vision went dark, the sense of loss so complete that the world around him lost meaning. He bowed his head, tempted to let go and simply fall into the abyss once more.

The yearning for his other half was a constant ache, a nagging, teasing sensation like a word he could not quite recall. But now it flared into a burning pain, as if Olek's sword had cleaved him in two. He yearned for the free air, the wind lofting him into the unbound sky. He thirsted for it like a traveler stranded in the sand.

It wasn't what he wanted to feel. Not now, when he had just been in the soft realm of delight. He would have given anything to stay there in bliss, but the ache of his wound was a merciless demon.

He had meant what he'd said to Leena back at the hospital—he had been betrayed and broken, and might never have a whole heart to give to another. Beyond that, the Phoenix Prince was a powerful enemy of the Shades, and so anyone he loved was a target. Paya had been a victim. What right did he have to put Leena in danger, too?

Absolutely none, yet survival demanded light. Life demanded a future. He had reached for Leena like a plant seeking the sun, or roots finding water. She was food, drink, and air to him. She was healing. She was life.

When had that become the truth? When had he begun to take pleasure in her smiles, or feel her every bump and bruise as sharply as his own? When she'd first danced for him? When she'd taken his hand and dragged him into the human realm? When she'd picked up a spear and stabbed a Shade? She'd astonished him into feeling again.

Was that what he wanted?

Leena was no courtier's daughter. She was little more than a barbarian, and a prince couldn't afford to follow his heart. But did that matter? He was no longer the haughty warlord who had believed himself invincible. Juradoc had taught him despair.

But he'd come too far for surrender. His people, his land, were in danger, and he had to fight. He had to defend what he loved.

Yes, despite all his doubts and struggles, he'd remembered how to love.

Slender arms wrapped around him from behind. His hands went to hers, feeling the softness of her skin. Even kissed by the sun, she was moon pale, a child of the mountain snow. Given distance, rank, and history, it was miraculous they had even met. And yet—he couldn't imagine standing here with anyone else. She was his luck, a shooting star that had changed everything.

Morran pulled her to his side, enjoying the sense of familiarity in her touch. She was clean and dressed, clearly refreshed by the Temple's power. And lovely—so lovely. They fit well together, her long legs making up for her smaller form. He put an arm around her, tantalized by the silky warmth of her long, fiery hair.

"Are you watching for the Shades?" she asked. "Do you see them?"

"No," he replied. "See for yourself. There's a good view of the desert."

Leena left the circle of his arm to peer out. He knew the scenery well, having stood in this exact place so many times before.

"When I thought of the Great Temple, I imagined gold and jewels," she said, sounding wistful. "Great pillars and tamed elephants. That seems childish now."

"No," he replied, "not childish. You are thinking of the Great Temple's peacetime mood. It has many faces, so be patient. It does not show all its secrets at once."

She turned to face him with a wistful smile. "What secrets?"

"Well, for one thing, there are ramshackle tunnels beneath the inner courtyard. I was delighted to discover them as a young boy."

"What are they for?"

"I believe they were made so one can pass from one pyramid to another without interrupting a ceremony or having to push through a crowd. They've fallen into disrepair. I think the temple cats use them the most."

Her lips parted to ask another question, but they were so full and soft, he kissed them instead of letting her speak. Leena tasted of wine and dates and the spice of pure female. She pressed into his embrace, her response instant and unguarded.

A moment later, the sky darkened, plunging them into shadow. For a desire-soaked instant, Morran imagined Leena's touch had robbed him of sight, but then he turned to the window. A giant wing blotted out the sky. It was storm-gray, the membrane between the bones seeming fragile despite its size.

"What is that?" Leena's voice was a whisper.

"Dragon," he replied, leaning out the window for a better look. "If the dragons are here, that means the fae armies have come down from the north to join the Tymeeran army. We saw the remains of the last battle. The next fight will be a full-scale war."

The idea was gratifying and horrible. He watched the dragon swoop across the sky, its long tail snaking behind it. That was Ronan of the Brightwing Clan, if he wasn't mistaken, as fierce a warrior as ever sailed the clouds. The dragon angled into a tight spiral, then swooped down to land on the far side of the pyramids, beyond the northeast corner of the Temple grounds. That would be where the fae army was camped.

"You need to join your soldiers," Leena said. "You need that army at your back."

The words hit Morran like cold, clear water. He'd been thinking the same thing, but hearing it from her lips made his position all too real. He had been one of the foremost commanders of the fae, but that had been before Juradoc had torn apart his soul. He could no longer ride the phoenix into the skies and rain down fire upon the enemy. "Circumstances have changed."

Leena stood very still, her amber eyes searching his face. "Do you remember your old battles?"

"Of course," he said, his tone harsh. He hadn't meant to sound brusque, yet she had obviously read his fear. He didn't need to see it reflected in her lovely eyes.

"Then you've lost none of your experience." She leaned into him again, as if the dragon had been a momentary interruption. "My brother says it's brains that count in a battle."

"Sometimes."

Then her face fell. "Do you think we'll find Fionn?"

Guilt flared through him. He'd promised to help her brother, yet they'd spent the night in pleasure, safe within the pyramid. While darkness and danger had made that the sensible course of action, now his army beckoned. He had a chance to beat Juradoc once and for all. Would he risk a delay to go looking for one foot soldier who was corrupted beyond hope?

Surprisingly, he would. He'd barely scraped his soul back together. He couldn't afford to squander it by breaking his word. "We'll search for Fionn and Anna right away."

Leena looked up, dread in her eyes. "If one of the other fae found my brother, he's probably dead."

He hugged her close for a long moment. "The dragons will help us look. They can cover ground far faster from the air."

She nodded, but without much optimism. They gathered their weapons and made ready to leave, neither saying much. The brief time they'd spent in safety had been precious, like a spell Morran was reluctant to break.

Their final stop before leaving was at the pool surrounding the Flame. They stood side by side, fingers brushing, and watched the reflection of the fire on the water. Morran drank in the peace of the Temple, storing it up against the battle to come.

"What happens next will be chaotic," he said. "In case there is no better opportunity to say it, thank you for saving me."

Leena turned to look at him, her red hair wild around the oval of her face. "Just keep saving yourself. That's the best thanks." It was a dare and a plea.

"I will be your champion, no matter what else transpires," Morran replied. "Don't ever think you're alone."

They kissed one last time, the embrace long and hard, then left the temple's shelter. Outside, the heat was a physical slap. They set off at a determined pace, hoping to reach the fae army before the temperature mounted any higher.

As they went, Morran assembled his questions for the generals of his army. Who was in charge of reconnaissance? What was the enemy position? Who was in charge of Tymeera's forces? He had some catching up to do.

They crossed the stone courtyard that stretched between the four corners of the Temple grounds. The base of the next pyramid was just yards away when Leena shouted his name.

"What is it?" he asked, reaching for his sword.

"There."

He followed her pointing hand to see a body slumped on the ground. The pyramid's deep shadow made the dark-clothed figure hard to see, but it wore no robes. It wasn't a Shade.

Heart leaping with alarm, he broke into a run. Leena sprinted past him, skidding to a halt beside the still form. He caught up and dropped to one knee, rolling the body over so he could see the face.

It was Anna.

$\mathbf{\mathcal{H}}$ 21 $\mathbf{\mathcal{H}}$

Horror surged through Leena, negating the heat of the sun. She knelt beside Morran, automatically making a quick assessment of Anna's condition. She ran her hands over the woman's limbs, finding a broken arm. There was also a lump on the back of her skull. There was no question a brutal blow had knocked her out.

Cold horror clutched at Leena's gut, leaving her nauseous. The brother she knew—the real Fionn—would have never done this. But that child, that youth, was a memory. The thing that had taken its place had done it—but at least he hadn't killed her. Why?

She raised her eyes to Morran's face. The lines of his mouth were grim, his brow furrowed with concern as he scanned the surrounding desert. "There is no one else nearby," he said.

"No sign of Fionn?" she asked anxiously.

"No, none. We need to get Anna to the camp," he said.

"We could go back to the temple." Anna was a shifter, but she couldn't change form when she was out cold. Anna needed a healer and a stable place to recover.

"We are closer to the camp now," Morran pointed out. "We're

more exposed if we backtrack, and it's hard to run or fight with wounded in the party."

Leena had to agree. Improvising, she used Anna's jacket to immobilize her injured arm. Then Morran picked Anna up, cradling her in his arms. With that, they resumed their path toward the camp, moving as quickly as they could.

They'd only gone a hundred yards before a dragon launched from the direction of the camp, arrowing upward into the sky. Leena ducked reflexively as the shadow fell over her. It was the same gray creature she'd seen from the pyramid's window, possibly heading out again on patrol. She'd never seen a dragon's fire, but she'd heard legends of its deadly destruction.

When she glanced at Morran, he was transfixed by the spectacle, stark longing on his face. *How*, she wondered, *did a dragon's flight compare with the phoenix?* Was Morran's creature as lethal and beautiful as everyone said? Those were questions she dared not ask as Morran forced his gaze to the earth and marched onward, his face carefully blank.

The ground rose as they left the pyramids behind. From the higher vantage point, Leena saw the landscape was a patchwork of gold and ochre bleached by the harsh sun. The barren earth rolled in a series of shallow valleys that ended in distant, jagged hills.

As they crested the rise, Morran made a noise of recognition mixed with something that was almost pleasure. Tents spread out in the nearest valley, hidden from the enemy's scouts by the shape of the land. He was, after a fashion, home.

Leena's chest eased with relief. The camp was entirely different from Juradoc's. The fae's tents bloomed in silks of green, blue, and scarlet, each according to its owner's lineage and alliance. Snatches of pipe and fiddle music wafted on the breeze, urging her to dance. As they drew closer, she smelled roasting meat, the savory scent teasing her appetite.

Morran pushed forward until they were intercepted by the

camp guards. These were fae from the forest tribes—Leena recognized their small, compact frames and dark brown hair. They wore intricately etched armor studded with precious stones.

Steel whispered as the guards drew their swords. The leader stepped into Morran's path, his frown curious but still polite. Tension hummed in the air as the guard considered Anna's still form with concern. "How do you come to be here, strangers? It's a long way to the nearest dwellings."

"And it's an even longer story. I must speak with your commander," Morran said, no hesitation in his tone.

"I insist you answer my question first," the guard replied. "The commander's time is not to be squandered."

"He will know me."

"But I do not."

The impasse was broken by another figure who approached from behind the guards. Since his armor had far more gold ornament, Leena assumed he was important.

"Is there something amiss?" the newcomer asked.

"Captain Kelagras," Morran said, a note of pleasure in his voice. "You still wear the colors of Tymeera's cavalry, I see."

The officer stopped, staring at Morran. He was lithe and dark-haired, his eyes a deep amber that edged to gold. After a moment, he executed a deep bow.

"I see I have surprised you," Morran said.

"Indeed, Your Highness," Kelagras stammered. "I am more than delighted to see you."

"I have traveled hard to rejoin my men." Morran shifted Anna's weight ever so slightly.

"You have been absent a long time, my prince," Kelagras said, recovering his composure. "We heard you were a guest of the Shade they call Juradoc."

Morran's face grew stony. "Not a guest, but a prisoner."

Kelagras drew himself up as if on parade. "Are you here to take command?"

"No general can command unless his soldiers wish it."

"What would you be your first order?"

Morran nodded toward Anna. "Look after this woman. She is brave and loyal."

The captain nodded to his men, who sheathed their weapons. "A good commander sees to his soldiers first."

Two of the men took Anna from Morran's arms, then hurried toward the medical facilities. Leena met Morran's eyes. He gave a single nod in response to her silent question. Leena was a healer, and he wouldn't ask her to abandon her patient. After all, Anna was the only one who could tell her what had happened to Fionn.

Leena soon caught up to the soldiers who had borne Anna away. They accepted her presence without comment, turning her over to the medical officer like an additional piece of luggage. The hospital tent was crowded with wounded, but they found room for Anna.

"Do you have any training?" the woman in charge asked briskly. Her name was Tyla. She was an earth fae, strongly built and with a no-nonsense air that commanded instant respect.

"I am a healer, trained at the Temple in Eldaban."

"Eldaban?" Tyla asked with mild surprise. "You've come a long way."

"I have," Leena replied, silently wondering how many ways the journey had changed her.

The two women fell to work, confirming Leena's diagnosis. It was clear the medical officer understood what Leena's training meant, and she seemed glad to have another pair of able hands within her domain. Meanwhile, four other healers drifted from bed to bed, comforting the sick and injured. The pure, sweet scent of fae healing magic filled the air. Despite everything, Leena's spirits lifted.

"I don't think there's any permanent damage," Leena said to the medical officer as they set Anna's broken arm.

The pain woke Anna up, bringing her back to consciousness with a cry. Her gaze roved over Leena's face. "Where am I?"

"You're with the Tymeeran army," Tyla announced. "Your friends brought you here. Now, rest."

She rose, leaving Leena and Anna alone. With her good hand, Anna gripped Leena's wrist hard, as if she desperately needed an anchor.

"Your brother," Anna began, then trailed off uncertainly. "He didn't kill me. I know that's obvious, but I wasn't sure how it would turn out."

Leena nodded. "What happened?"

"The transformation is killing him. He's fighting it so hard." Anna closed her eyes. "That's why he didn't cut my throat. A small part of him is still clinging to Faery."

"Oh, Fionn," Leena whispered.

"He kept repeating that you'd come for him. I think that's what saved my life."

Leena squeezed her eyes shut, suddenly giddy with joy and dread. "Where is he? Do you know?"

"No." Anna shook her head, then groaned at the pain. "He ran off. I was slowing him down."

Tyla approached with a glass. "Drink this," she said to Anna, raising her from the pillow so she could swallow more easily.

As soon as Anna tasted the liquid, she tried to spit it out. "I don't want a sedative. I'm a wolf. Let me shift, and I'll heal."

"You don't need to be gadding about on four paws. You need rest," the woman chided. "And don't you be telling me you know better. This healing potion was given to me by the Mother of the Great Temple herself."

Anna balked, but the drugs were already taking effect. The hand gripping Leena's softened as Anna sank back to the pillow. She blinked, then blinked again, the second time on a massive yawn. A moment later, she was deeply asleep and breathing with a comfortable, even rhythm.

Leena straightened to find Tyla had left again. She folded her arms, glad her patient was resting but worried about Fionn. She would get no more information until Anna woke again, but that might be too late for her brother. He was sick—desperately so—and the Shades weren't far away.

She left the tent, looking around to get her bearings. The camp was quiet. The sun had risen to its noontime peak, and the heat was like a blade. Leena gazed toward the horizon, her imagination roaming beyond the rows of multi-hued tents. Somewhere in the desert, her brother walked alone.

THE FAE ARMY WAS MADE UP OF SEVERAL MILITARY FORCES loosely gathered under the direction of a joint council led by General Sabian, war leader of the Queen of Evantra. No one had taken Morran's place as the overall commander of the southern fae. For good or ill, there was only one Phoenix Prince, and none had dared to occupy the throne of Tymeera in his absence.

Captain Kelagras immediately took Morran to greet the senior officers, who were about to begin another meeting to determine the army's next moves. The pavilion where they met was a large striped affair almost entirely filled by an oval meeting table. Aides-de-camp stood at attention along the walls, ready to fulfill their officers' every need.

Of course, the meeting was disrupted by the reunion. Most encounters were the same mix of joy and confusion Morran had seen on Kelagras's face. He was the last person anyone expected to see, and miracles were nothing if not disruptive to an agenda.

Eventually, Morran took a seat at the oval table, finding a spot between Kelagras and the leader of the wood fae. The command tent was large and magically cooled. Goblets of iced wine were constantly refilled by waiting servants. Morran had never indulged in such luxuries in the field, but he held his tongue.

The meeting began. From what Morran could tell, the senior officers hadn't changed a bit. Fae memories were long—especially theirs. His record of many, many wins to one loss didn't matter. He'd been Juradoc's prisoner for too long. The onus was on Morran to clear his good name.

"Yes, I have returned," he announced. "I am ready to fight. And I am ready to lead."

The faces gathered around the meeting table ranged from relieved to deeply skeptical. A strained silence followed. A twinge of annoyance stiffened his smile, but he couldn't blame them.

"How do we know you are not Juradoc's spy?" General Sabian asked. He was a large fire fae with deep scars running from his right temple to jaw. "You might not even know it yourself."

"Indeed," cried an emissary from Kyleen, the youngest of the group. "Besides, why should we step aside? We've been holding our own just fine."

Someone cleared their throat in wordless denial.

"Don't be a fool, boy," Sabian grumbled. "There's a difference between winning and not dying right away. Don't puff yourself up like a pixie fart."

The leader of the wood fae spoke up. "If we do not trust the prince, then why spend time on this discussion? There is much to do in preparation for the next attack."

"Because Prince Morran is a better tactician than anyone at this table," Sabian replied. "Whatever side he's on, that's worth a conversation, don't you think?"

Captain Kelagras rose to his feet, clearly infuriated by the discussion. "The Phoenix Prince was the greatest warrior of us all. Where is your loyalty? He is a friend and a liege lord to most of us."

"Stop," Morran said, standing and raising his hands in a gesture of peace. "I understand your caution, my lords. In fact, I applaud it. We cannot afford to trust lightly."

"Then explain what happened at the final battle." Sabian

poured himself a goblet of wine from the pitcher on the table. "When it was time to attack, you were nowhere to be found. We saw the phoenix fly and burn in the sky, only to descend like a comet in the east. We never saw it again."

Morran looked down at the table, hoping to hide his misery. "I was betrayed, captured, and held prisoner under the thrall of Shade magic. Juradoc thought to turn me into a weapon. As a result, I no longer command the phoenix."

A mutter ran around the room. Morran could see their confidence ebb, as if the sun itself had dimmed. Shame writhed inside him.

Sabian pushed his goblet aside, his gaze steady. "Thank you for your honesty. I recall your father faced his own great loss."

Morran's mouth twisted. "I am not my father. Despair may come, but it has not come for me yet. I have a war to finish. If I need to earn your trust again, a mountain of dead Shades shall be my proof of intent."

Sabian gave a dark chuckle. "That suits me well. I'll give you a company of trusted soldiers if you'll consent to serve under me."

Morran balked as every eye turned his way, studying his reaction. He had been their supreme commander, a warrior of legend, and the mightiest sword south of Kyleen. He was no one's underling. Heat crept up the back of his neck, presaging a burst of temper.

And yet, trust had to be earned, and he couldn't command that yet. Sabian was offering what help he could, and it was up to Morran to take it. Once, his pride would have refused. Now that he'd been given a second chance at life, he understood the value of such generosity.

"I accept," Morran replied.

There was another rustle around the table, this one of relief.

"What did the Shades do to you, Prince Morran?" Sabian asked. "I half-expected you to refuse."

"Perhaps I've learned humility. I'm sure it won't last."

Laughter followed that, breaking the tension. Then, they got down to business.

Morran listened with growing dismay as Sabian and Kelagras gave a quick overview of what had happened since the Shades had arrived east of the Serpent River. As they spoke, Morran stooped over a map of the surrounding terrain. Pewter figurines marked the positions of allies and enemies. Losses on both sides had been heavy, but the Shades were bringing more and more reinforcements through Shimmers. The Shades had advanced from Eldaban to Tymeera, and would soon push across the rich agricultural plains, bringing starvation to all of Faery. They had to be stopped now, or the war would be lost.

"I have learned one thing. I understand now what drives the Shades," Morran explained.

"How so?" Kelagras asked. "We've always assumed they love destruction for its own sake."

"Let's just say that is not their only motivation. They consume fae power," Morran continued. "You might even say they crave it. Juradoc is simply bold enough to go directly for the source, regardless of the risk. He is here to strike the Great Temple and consume the Flame itself."

A babble of outrage ran around the table.

"Unthinkable," a tall, black-haired river fae said. "How could that even be done?"

"It's been a theory for some time," Sabian replied. "There's been no way to confirm it."

"I've seen it." Morran swallowed a mouthful of wine. "And yet, it was only recently that I learned what Juradoc's game is. His masters seem to regard much of what he does as dangerous."

He had the council's attention. This was insight only he could offer.

"But the other Shades are with Juradoc now," the woods fae added. "Whether they came to stop him or help him, every enemy in the south is camped on the other side of the Great Temple."

"Which means General Juradoc is far from stupid," the river fae mused. "He astonished his masters into granting him all the troops he requires."

Morran studied the assembled group one face at a time. He met each pair of eyes, ensuring every commander understood that he saw and spoke to them as individuals as well as the council as a whole. "There is one other piece to Juradoc's plot that we do not fully fathom. He sent an operative after John Barleycorn. He wants something in Barleycorn's possession to complete his plan."

"Barleycorn," Sabian murmured. "That is a name I have not heard for many a year."

"Anna, the injured woman who came here with me, is John Barleycorn's friend."

"Then summon her so we may question her," the general demanded.

"Anna was gravely hurt. My companion, Leena, is a healer from the temple at Eldaban. She will know if Anna has regained consciousness and given us any information of note." Morran turned to one of the fae who stood at attention around the room. "Bring Leena here."

The aide-de-camp left at a run, eager to be part of this new turn of events. At the same time, the tent flap opened, and a tall, dark-haired man strode in.

"Ronan," Morran exclaimed.

"Morran." The man's face looked strained, as if he'd shifted back from dragon form faster than was good for him. "That *was* you I saw from the air. It is a pleasure to have you back among us."

Despite the friendly words, the dragon shifter's tone was guarded. Like the rest, he was clearly uncertain of Morran's loyalties. That stung, coming from such an old and generous ally.

"What news?" Sabian asked.

"The Shades are on the move," Ronan said. "They march toward the Great Temple."

Morran had barely taken that in when the aide returned, his face gleaming with sweat from running in the blistering heat.

"I'm sorry, my prince," the young fae panted. "Your companion, Leena, is nowhere to be found. She left the medical tent."

Morran's chest tightened. "Are you certain?"

"She might have left the camp," Kelagras interjected. "The patrol rarely questions those who leave, only those who enter."

The world dropped from beneath Morran, momentarily stranding him in cold, black nothing. He sucked in a rattling breath to curse himself. He had promised to help Fionn—a vow he'd still failed to keep. "Her brother went missing not far from here. She might have gone to search for him."

And, if Ronan were correct, she'd walk right into the arms of the Shades.

22

Leena struggled through the heat, feeling the weight of it like a thick, stifling blanket. Everyone knew Shades hated the bright sun, which made this a safer time to leave the fae encampment. Sadly, they were not the only hazard. She was used to sweltering temperatures, but not like this. It left her sluggish and lightheaded, as if she'd drunk bad wine. Her search had to be brief and smart.

She and Morran had left one pyramid, and they'd found Anna in the shadow of another. Fionn's path suggested he had been moving toward a third, which was set diagonally across the square courtyard to the one she'd slept in last night. Leena turned her steps to this southeast corner of the square, which was thankfully closest to the camp.

Not even snakes or insects moved at the peak of the day. She put one foot in front of the other, the rhythm both grueling and hypnotic as she made a slow circuit of the structure. There was nothing but dry, sandy earth and the twisted thorn bushes that dotted the land like skeletons. Morran said they bloomed in rainbows of color when it rained, but, right now, that was hard to believe.

She found no sign of Fionn. Before she gave in to the dusty heat, she made the long trek to the last of the pyramids in the northeast. From there, she would have no choice but to return to the camp as she was ill-equipped to wander the open desert. She was still wearing the clothes Anna had loaned her, and she missed her own lighter clothing and veils. Already, she could feel her skin growing tender from the sun. Making it back to the camp from even this distance would test her endurance.

When Leena reached the building's shadow, she half-collapsed in the shade. With clumsy fingers, she unscrewed the top of her leather flask and sipped a mouthful of the warm water. It tasted as good as fine liquor. She closed her eyes and leaned her head back against the stone, gathering her strength.

"You should have obeyed my orders," said the voice of the Mother.

Leena's eyes snapped open in surprise. "Where are you?"

"Where I always am, my daughter. I am where you need me to be."

That was an odd answer. "Are you in Eldaban?"

"You should have obeyed my order and taken care of the Phoenix Prince."

Which meant using the poison from her chatelaine. "But he's not evil. I understand how you might have thought so when he was at Juradoc's side. There is no cause for that worry now. He is free of the enemy's influence."

"He can never truly be free. Not when his soul has been broken in half. There is still time to do your duty."

Fear and anger roiled through Leena's chest. The Mother had trained her from the time she was a child. She'd almost been a mother in truth. Leena would never, ever have imagined such words coming from her mentor. Her hands dug into the lifeless soil beside her, as if she needed the anchor. "Is it truly my duty to murder an innocent man?"

Silence followed her disobedient words. Despite the heat,

Leena shivered, shocked by her boldness. The heat was making her drunk, imprudent.

Her mind raced. The conversation she'd had with the Mother at Juradoc's camp had barely made sense. She'd put some of that down to distance—details could be lost when speaking to someone so far away. Yes, the Mother had admitted her power had been stretched to its limit. They were much farther apart now, so how was communication even possible?

"He has betrayed you," the Mother said, her voice thick with sorrow. "He has not kept his promise to save Fionn."

Those words stung as no others could. Leena drew her knees to her chest, then wrapped her arms around them. No, Morran hadn't done everything she'd hoped he would do. But then again, he had fought for her life, taken her to safety, and made love to her in the sensuous beauty of the Temple.

"He is a prince, and you are nothing," the Mother continued. "Will he remember you once he takes back his throne?"

Sharp pain lanced beneath Leena's breastbone—fear, loneliness, the echo of old losses. Loving Morran would leave her vulnerable to it all. The Mother knew precisely how to twist the knife.

But she'd never spoken of this to the Mother. In fact, when they'd last met in Eldaban, Leena had not met Morran—not in any meaningful way. So how did the Mother know her feelings? Even if she'd divined them from afar, wouldn't she also understand how Morran had changed? Nothing here made sense.

Leena took a mental step back. What was going on? Communication over an improbable distance. Giving orders out of character. Information that couldn't be known. Was there trickery at work?

"What Morran thinks of me in the future is of secondary importance," Leena said, ensuring her tone was calm and even. "He is, as you say, a prince. All of Tymeera—indeed, all of Faery—depends on him to lead his armies against our foe."

Slowly, Leena got to her feet, careful not to make a sound. Now that she was on her guard, she noticed a fine wisp of power nearby. It was so faint it was hard to detect, much less identify its nature. However, once found, Leena could follow it. It was coming from her right.

Leena inched along the side of the pyramid, keeping to the shadows. When she reached the corner of the structure, she peered around the edge of the stone, whispering a barely perceptible spell to reveal what was hidden. Terror jolted through her when she saw a dark-clad figure on a coal-black horse.

She shrank away, pressing her back to the hard wall of the pyramid. What had she just seen? The image of the rider skittered and danced in her imagination, refusing recognition. Was that a spell or her own dread?

She took a second glance, too anxious to breathe. It was a struggle to see past the enchantment meant to hide what was there, but Leena managed. Such magic rarely worked once the viewer knew there was something to see.

The rider was Juradoc himself. Leena swallowed, her dry throat painful.

"You are very quiet," said the voice of the Mother, but the figure's hood moved ever so slightly. It was his lips that formed the words, making them seem to come just inches from her ears.

Chills of disgust pebbled Leena's skin, even as she scrambled to shield her thoughts. The only way to end this conversation and get away safely was to agree.

"You are correct about one thing," she replied. "Morran has not kept his word. He promised to find my brother, but now I'm forced to search for him alone."

"He is heartless. Heartless and faithless."

Fine words coming from a Shade, Leena thought wryly. "Morran lured me here and abandoned me."

"You say all of Faery looks to this haughty prince for protection, but he is a broken abomination. He will betray them all because he is incapable of doing anything else. Do you see, my dove, how essential it is to carry out your mission?"

Disagreement would be as good as a death sentence. "Yes."

"Do it today."

"I need to find my brother."

Impatience darkened the threat of magic. "He is lost to you."

"I do not abandon those I love. That is why I despise Morran so much. That is why I will obey your orders."

Leena sensed a burst of anger through the spell, but it vanished as quickly as it had flared. "I sense your brother's life-force is all but extinguished."

"Where?"

"If I tell you, will you obey?"

"Yes, I will."

"Today?"

"Tonight," Leena said, thinking of Morran's story of Paya and her chalice of poison. "It will be simpler when he is relaxed and on the edge of sleep."

"Do it at once. Immediately."

"Very well, but first tell me where to find my brother."

"Look to the north."

Was this a trap? Then again, if Juradoc wanted her dead, she'd be a bloodstain on the sand. Leena released her breath. "Thank you, Mother."

"The Flame go with you, daughter."

A moment later, the horse's harness jingled—a single chime of metal on metal before magic silenced it. Very carefully, Leena looked around the corner of the pyramid once more. The horse and rider were heading west. She pulled back, keeping herself hidden. The Shades had to be close if he had braved the hot sun to ride here.

Had Juradoc been watching for her? Had he met her by acci-dent? Had he been scouting the Great Temple, searching for some means to access the Flame? Only two things were plain.

First, he knew Fionn's location, yet was leaving him to die. Fionn had no more value in his eyes.

Second, he'd left Leena alive to kill Morran.

He'd first tried to convince her back at the camp. She'd been the one to initiate contact with the Mother, but Juradoc had clearly intercepted the spell. Now that she thought about it, the so-called Mother's orders fit Juradoc's cruel streak. Leena would be tortured by the mission, but so would Morran when he was betrayed by another woman he trusted. And while Juradoc didn't know she already carried poison, he knew she understood how to mix medicines. He'd gambled on both her skill and obedience to the Mother.

But then why order Morran's death at that moment when they were still far from the Great Temple? Because Morran was regaining his strength? Or was it like Anna said, some gambit to bring the phoenix back when Morran died? Perhaps Juradoc could have magically delayed the death until the perfect moment.

Leena watched a ripple of heat and magic swallow the last of Juradoc's form in the distance. She shaded her eyes, staring at the spot where he'd vanished like a mirage.

He'd urged her to kill Morran again. Was he ready to set his plan in motion, even though Fionn had failed to kidnap Barleycorn?

One thing was certain. The Shade would stop at nothing to make his last, lethal assault on the Flame before the Phoenix Prince could stop him. This was his end game.

Well, at least she'd learned Fionn's location. She'd look north, just for a minute, and then she'd return to the camp to tell Morran what she'd learned.

Leena searched the north side of the pyramid, but she found nothing, just as before. She was about to surrender and return to the camp when she took one last sweeping look of the desert beyond, spotting something on the cracked dirt. It was a dark smudge that looked like a shadow—perhaps a ripple in the land.

Her instincts said not. She struck out to investigate.

At first, Fionn was so still she thought he was dead. Leena bent to look closer, but she was forced away by the urge to gag. All she could do was stand and stare in shriveling horror. The spell Juradoc had cast to accelerate Fionn's infection had worked all too well, consuming everything but a few strands of familiar hair.

The hot, dry air smothered her sob to a cough. Leena's eyes blurred and stung. This was the last of her world crumbling away. She had lost her home, her people, and her parents. Only her brother had been left, and, like everything else, he was gone. Not even Morran's magic could fix this—ironic when they were this close to the Flame's heart. This was where fire fae magic was the most powerful.

Steeling herself, Leena knelt and touched the edge of Fionn's robe—the hated black garment that marked him as Juradoc's property. She longed to rip it away or use it to cover his pitiful face, but the bone-dry air turned her sob into a cough before she could decide.

It was then she sensed a faint stir of breath. Fionn was not dead yet, but he was dying. And yet, as a priestess of the Flame, she could give a dying man one last gift. She could give him the Flame's blessing and final rites.

Leena rose, closing her eyes so she could envision the Flame in her mind. Instead, all she could see was Fionn. As a babe, warm and squirming in her arms. As a boy, splashing through Eldaban's fountains despite the scolding adults. Tears wet her cheeks, but they dried to salt almost at once.

Her brother had finally slipped beyond her grasp. When she'd left for Juradoc's camps, she'd still hoped to retrieve him, but she'd lost. The only thing left was surrender.

In the Great Temple, she'd felt the source of the Flame, the ecstasy of the leaping fire. Pushing down her sorrow, she conjured the image. Memories of Morran's arms and lips wove with it, but that fit. The Flame was joy and passion, the wild, trusting leap into the unknown—even if the unknown was death.

All her life, Leena had searched for certainty, stability, a home despite her homeless state. Fear had made her a hard worker, and sheer force of will had kept her and Fionn safe and fed. However, fear would never bring joy. Fear was the opposite of Flame, and that had limited her magic.

Here, now, with the memory of Morran's kiss and the immediacy of Fionn's passing before her, Leena understood that fear on a gut level. She'd never taken chances before setting out from Eldaban. That had been the first time she'd defied her belief that she was helpless.

Now, it was time to be brave again and accept what the Flame had decreed. This was the humility and openness the Mother— the real Mother—had spoken of. This was the peace of the Flame that spared the heart even as the world burned.

But how could she accept Fionn's death? Leena's tears fell freely now, too abundant for even the thirsty desert wind to steal. She summoned the circle of fire, holding the mystery of the Flame in her mind, but sorrow in her heart.

Perhaps it was careless to set a fire with the enemy nearby, but she was too miserable to care. She whispered her memories and words of love, slowly losing her sense of time. It was as if she held the past by a fraying thread and the Flame was urging her to let go. Her duty now was as a priestess, here to ease her brother's passing. Abandoning her claim on Fionn—on who she'd wanted him to become—was essential. They both needed that release.

At last, Leena surrendered, her heart giving a final wrench of grief.

There is no judgment, the Flame whispered. *Grief is a sign of your love.*

Leena's breath stuttered. The Flame had never spoken to her before—not in the dance, not even in the Great Temple. She was not that powerful a priestess.

Yet, the Flame spoke again. *There are no limits to your power unless you draw that boundary yourself.*

This time, Leena flinched. There was a terrifying wildness in that voice. It held destruction and creation, pain and comfort, the immediate and the eternal. They were all ideas she honored as a priestess, but this was up close and in person.

Her sudden start broke the connection. She tried to grab it again, but that was the opposite of what she had to do. She wasn't fighting Juradoc now. There was no need to clench her mental fist against invasion.

Leena took a breath and held it, easing her pulse back into a steady beat. The Flame was an elemental, a force that existed outside herself. She had no right of expectation. She could ask, but not compel. As with Morran, she could invite it, woo it, and finally surrender to it with trust and abandon.

The thought barely formed when the Flame returned in all its ferocity. Leena staggered, but then forced herself to remain still. She acknowledged the Flame's power without trying to hold it.

Good, it whispered in a voice that held infinity. *That is how it is done.*

Leena's heart thundered, but she let the terror drain away. She let her mind drift as the Flame whispered, some of the words nonsense, others wise. She regarded them all the same, gathering the elemental power into herself and feeding it into the circle of fire she'd made around herself and Fionn. This close to the Great Temple, that power was enormous.

At last, when she had fed the circle all it could hold, the Flame burst forth, filling the air and setting herself and Fionn ablaze. She was on fire, apart from it and yet a part of it. For the briefest instant, she was aware of pain, but she surrendered to that, too, letting it flow through her.

The world as she knew it vanished.

23

Morran fought panic with limited success. Leena was beyond the camp's protection, either alone or with her insane brother.

He stormed from the command tent, bellowing for a horse and armor. Guilt pricked like a dagger's point. He'd promised to help find Fionn, but he'd been too slow and now Leena was in danger.

Sabian was at his side in an instant. "Are you going somewhere?"

Morran stopped cold, remembering he was no longer in command. In fact, he answered to someone else. "Forgive me. I would like to ensure Leena's safety."

The scarred general pointed toward a crest of land to his right. "Ronan of Brightwing's report concerns me. I plan to ride to the vantage point on that ridge to see the lay of the land for myself. Why don't you come with me? From there, we can see the enemy's camp. Plus, we'll be able to spot your friend if she's within view."

Pages came running with a set of battle gear for Morran to wear while a groom arrived with a dark bay stallion for Sabian and a dappled gray for Morran. Both steeds had the long legs and arched neck of the finest desert horses. Kelagras ordered his own mount, and the request was echoed by others. Soon, half a dozen of the commanders were mounted and following Sabian and Morran across the scrub and sand.

Just as they were passing the patrol gate, a wolf loped from somewhere inside the camp. It limped slightly, but not enough that it couldn't keep pace. Its fur was mostly gray, with just a touch of brown, and it bore a star of white on its brow.

"Anna?" Morran asked.

The wolf yipped. For an instant, Morran's spirits rose with relief. At least one companion was out of danger.

They spurred their horses to the highest vantage point. As they reined in, the other officers crowded behind them. Morran surveyed the landscape, searching for Leena but seeing only the enemy. The patch of ground where they'd fought Olek was restored, with no sign of great dunes or cracks in the earth. The Great Temple had healed the surrounding desert, but could it withstand whatever the Shades had in store?

Sabian took out a battered brass spyglass, then swept it across the field. Then he handed it to Morran.

Morran raised the spyglass and counted Shades until he gave up. There were too many, and he had limited time. Ronan's report had been correct. The black cloaks of the Shades resembled a swarm of insects surging across the sand. They were setting up some basic defenses, but the bulk of their forces guarded a phalanx of sorcerers, identifiable by their crooked staffs. He saw at once they were marching toward the pyramids and the source of the Flame. Juradoc was executing his wild plan.

"Shall we send the dragons?" Kelagras asked.

"No," Sabian replied. "Dragon fire is most effective when the enemy has committed themselves too far to stage an effective retreat. Let them grow overconfident first."

"Then how should we prepare?" another asked.

Sabian turned in his saddle, regarding Morran. "Suggestions?"

Morran took a last look, assessing the enemy's position. He also took a last, desperate look for Leena, but found nothing. "Coordinate an attack that will close in on the Shades from three sides."

Sabian cocked an eyebrow. "Elaborate."

Morran did, his old expertise reviving as he spoke. It felt right and natural, like falling back into his native tongue after a long journey to foreign parts.

The plan was simple but elegant. By the expressions on the faces around him, the others understood his choices, although they hadn't seen his precise solution before now.

"Excellent. Of course, I would have suggested something similar," Sabian said. At his approving nod, the officers rode away, eager to ready their troops.

"All right," the general added in a low voice only Morran could hear. "Maybe nothing quite that good."

Morran's satisfaction was grim. He had studied Juradoc long enough to understand his arrogance. The Shades wouldn't expect this short, sharp shock of resistance, followed by a torrent of dragon fire the instant the Shades turned to run. In the old days, he would have been in the air, riding Arlanoth and raining down an equally lethal blaze. The phoenix was the only creature as deadly as the dragons, able to match them, fire for fire. Together, they had been unstoppable.

Had been.

Morran turned cold with grief, barely managing to steel himself. Today, he would have his revenge—or not. Either way, Juradoc and Morran would meet and only one would ride away.

He took one more look with the spyglass. Just as he was finishing the sweep, he caught sight of fire to the north. Morran adjusted the instrument's focus to be sure of what he saw. Leena was stepping away from the blaze, flame streaming from her like water.

Something significant had happened. Leena was powerful, but this was on a new level. He warmed with pride, but it was tempered with caution. The show of magic had made her the enemy's target, and there was a party of Shades coming her way.

He had to get Leena to safety. He turned to Sabian, returning the spyglass. "With your permission, I will ride north."

Sabian turned to Kelagras. "Gather your men and ride with the prince."

"At once," the captain said eagerly, his color high with excitement. He rode away at a gallop.

Sabian clapped Morran on the shoulder. "Here's where you amass that pile of dead Shades." With that, Sabian wheeled his horse and galloped back to camp.

Morran glanced down at Anna, who sat patiently at his horse's feet, snout raised to watch his every expression.

"Now we ride like the desert wind."

◈

Leena emerged from the fire. Her return to the conscious present was like waking from a dream. She felt energized, bewildered, and exhausted all at the same time. She had danced in the Flame before, but this heat was a thousand times greater, as if her skin should be blackened and flaking away. Unbelievably, she was intact. She crackled with life, yet felt oddly weightless. She took a few steps away, not quite steady, then sensed the flames wink out behind her. She spun, expecting to see nothing but molten sand.

Instead, her brother still lay there—but he had changed. Leena fell back a step, her entire body suddenly limp with surprise.

He was not the monster she had seen before—not the wreck he had become. Fionn was as she'd known him in Eldaban. His sandy hair curled around his face, a little too long for neatness.

His tanned face was kissed with the flush of sleep. His clothes were still rags, but the skin that showed from beneath them was clean and whole.

Leena ran back to him, too stupefied to make a sound. She fell to her knees, grasping his hand. It was warm, but not overly so. At the press of her fingers, his eyes flew open. They were clear, sky blue, and gazed into hers with wondering surprise. He sat up, coughed twice, and then scrambled to his feet, pulling her up with him.

Tears filled Leena's eyes. She was feeling too many things in a single space of time. Relief. Apprehension. Shock. Despite the sun, she was suddenly cold, as if her blood had stopped flowing. "H-how do you feel?" she asked, voice cracking.

"Am I healed?" Fionn whispered.

"Are you?"

He looked down at his hands, turning them over to view his palms. Tremors shook his body. "I am."

His stunned expression crumpled as he broke into sobs. Tears streamed down his face as he doubled over, trying to push Leena away even as she folded him in her arms. Then he gave in and sagged into her, weeping like a small child.

"Thank you," he gasped. "Thank you."

"It was the Flame. It answered me."

His gaze met hers. They had both learned much since they'd last embraced as brother and sister, and the remorse and grief on his face were plain.

"I'm sorry," Fionn said. "It's not enough, but I don't know any other words for it."

"Hush," Leena said, her throat tight with everything she wanted to say. "There will be time enough to talk later. Right now, we need to get out of here."

Though they hugged tightly, she could see over his shoulder. There was movement in the direction she'd seen Juradoc disappear. Black dots were moving toward the pyramids, some faster than others. Riders—and some were moving their way.

At the same time, fae troops poured from the camp, splitting into groups. From her position, Leena could see what the Shades could not—the fae army was circling the enemy like a vise. It was a perfectly choreographed dance, economical and swift. It was also no place to be a bystander. They had to return to the camp before the battle started.

She grabbed Fionn's hand. "This way."

He made no protest, but he stumbled when he attempted to walk.

"What's wrong?" she asked, sliding an arm around her brother to keep him steady.

Fionn gave a rueful laugh. "It's like my legs forgot how to work. They're healed, but they need to learn again."

Nevertheless, he shuffled forward, leaning on her in a game attempt to keep going. Their progress was slower than Leena liked, although, with every step, Fionn seemed to be regaining his strength.

They had reached the closest pyramid when they saw Morran riding at the head of his party, the wolf loping beside him. Leena's heart soared. Anna was well, Fionn was healed, and Morran was back in charge of his men. The first sliver of real hope warmed her heart. She waved, catching Morran's eye. When she felt his gaze find her, it was like she glowed from the inside.

When Morran barked an order, his party of horsemen wheeled, the movement as precise as if they shared a single mind. But Leena's elation faded as the riders drew their sabers, the sun flashing off their wickedly sharp blades. They had seen Fionn's tattered cloak.

"What's this?" the captain—Morran had called him Kelagras —bellowed. "A Shade turncoat?"

Fionn held up his hands in a gesture of surrender. "I accept whatever punishment the prince deems suitable for my crimes." His voice rang clear and calm.

Morran's expression was grim, only his eyes showing joyous relief at finding her. Then his brow furrowed as he shot her a questioning look, clearly asking what had happened.

"Who is she?" asked a junior officer Leena didn't recognize. "She is with this traitor."

Morran's lips parted to reply, but Fionn pushed forward, stepping between Leena and the aggressor. "She is a priestess of the temple. She saved my life."

Morran swept a hand for silence. "Captain, take your men and guard our position. This won't take long."

Kelagras glanced from Fionn to Leena, clearly reluctant to miss any details, but he obeyed at once. A moment later, only a handful of horsemen remained behind as Morran's personal guard. Two got down from their horses to stand on either side of Fionn. He was effectively a prisoner now.

Morran dismounted, one hand on his sword hilt as he gave Fionn a studied glare. "Thank your sister that I do not behead you at once."

Leena stepped out from behind her brother. "Please don't."

Without warning, Morran swept her into an embrace, burying his face in her hair.

Fionn bristled, suddenly protective. "Leena!"

"Did you heal him?" Morran murmured in her ear.

"I was merely a conduit for the Flame," Leena replied.

He smiled, his voice rich with pleasure. "You didn't need my help after all. You did it yourself. Well done."

"You helped me more than you know." She said it with perfect certainty. If Morran hadn't been there—pushing her, needing her, and honoring her courage—she would have never made it this far. He had shown her the beauty of trust and surrender. Without that, the Flame's power might have stayed beyond her reach.

"You came for me," she added.

"Did you believe I wouldn't?" he murmured, kissing both her hands. "If so, we have much to speak of. But, for now, I must get you to safety."

A shout went up from Morran's men. Leena spun to look, sucking in a gasp. Captain Kelagras had been charged with their defense, but his cavalry had already been scattered. By trickery or magic, the Shades Leena had seen in the far distance had closed that gap unseen. The fight was upon them.

A handful of the Shades had heavy recurved bows designed to shoot an arrow through armor. The first flight of arrows plucked two of the fae from their mounts with ease, feathered shafts piercing their throat and chest. Morran's horse reared in panic. Leena grabbed its bridle to keep it from bolting or trampling the unwary with its iron-shod hooves. As the Shades charged, Anna leaped to Leena's defense, chasing the enemy off with fangs and claws.

A blade swept down, striking the soldier beside Fionn. The fae fell instantly as the blade cleaved him from shoulder to hip. Fionn grabbed the wounded fae's sword and turned on his attacker, driving him back. No one objected to Fionn's help. Even with Morran and the wolf, there were two Shades for every fae.

Morran mounted his horse, then wheeled it toward their attackers. Immediately, the Shade officer charged. Morran slashed his saber, severing the Shade's sword arm. That instantly made Morran the chief target until Fionn moved in, covering his flank.

One Shade fell at Fionn's thrust, and then another as Anna tore it to pieces. Leena grabbed a blade to defend herself, but she was no soldier. She ducked as cold iron whistled over her head, then leaped away to avoid trampling hooves. If only she had learned how to throw fireballs or call down lightning—but she hadn't, and it was all she could do to stay alive.

Morran's latest opponent thudded to the ground in a splash of stagnant, rotting blood. "Follow me," Morran bellowed above the crash of steel. "Get to safety."

A firm hand grasped Leena's arm. Fionn had mounted a riderless horse, and he leaned down to pull Leena up behind him. She dropped her sword, needing both hands to clamber onto the back of the tall steed. With Anna beside them, they pushed through the crush, Morran in the lead. Leena clung to Fionn as he struck at looming enemies at one side, then the other. The moment they reached open ground, they gave the horses their heads.

More Shades swarmed the battlefield like a tide rising before them. Morran swerved to avoid them, circling close to the pyramid where he and Leena had taken refuge the night before. From there, Leena glimpsed twenty or thirty sorcerers standing in rows. They faced the Great Temple from a distance of a hundred feet, their crooked staffs raised above their heads. The gray-green haze above them indicated some kind of spell.

She saw no more. An arrow whistled past Fionn's horse, cutting a deep graze across its rump. The animal reared, shrieking in pain. Leena fell, crashing to the hard-packed earth and instinctively rolling out of harm's way as the animal plunged. Fionn fought to keep his seat, unable to turn back for a handful of seconds. By then, he and Morran were far ahead.

Leena struggled to pick herself up as Shades flowed around her like an inky river.

✣ 24 ✣

If the Shades saw Leena, she was as good—or worse—than dead.

Leena crawled away, ignoring the stabbing pains that said her ribs and hip had suffered in the fall. She kept low until she reached the pyramid's wall, where she curled into as small a target as she could. Morran, Fionn, and Anna were gone, swallowed up in the fight. They were in peril, but at least they had the skills to protect themselves and each other.

With no weapon and no horse, Leena was a helpless target.

Another body fell just feet away. This one was a woods fae, eyes wide with the horror of his death. Fear closed Leena's throat, reducing her breaths to jagged sobs. There was nothing she could do to help Morran and her brother. There was little she could do to save herself. Her simple plan to look for Fionn amid the pyramids had gone horribly wrong.

She covered her ears against the screams and crash of battle, pressing herself against the stone. At least the pyramid protected her back, even while it guarded the Flame within it. The fire's power seeped through the stones, calming her enough to think.

The temple had sheltered her and Morran the night before, hadn't it? It had saved them from Olek's avalanche.

The first hint of an idea formed, and she grabbed at it. If she could find the pyramid's entrance again, she could take refuge until there was a chance to get away. Leena looked from left to right, calculating her position along the structure's base.

The entrance was on the opposite side from where she sat. In the midst of battle, that was a long, dangerous path. She could end up marooned there for who knew how long, surrounded by Shades and unable to rejoin the fae. The only certainty was that the enemy couldn't get in—making it both a haven and a possible tomb.

A bad idea was better than no idea. If she kept sitting there while the bodies piled up, she'd join the ranks of the dead within minutes. Slowly, Leena rose to a crouch and crept along the pyramid's base, praying she was too insignificant to notice. She kept one hand on the stone beside her, as much for luck as for balance.

The distance to the first corner seemed like a mile. Stray arrows cracked into the stone, rebounding as their tips failed to pierce the hard surface. After the first one, Leena risked more speed. She was almost to the corner when a new sound joined the cacophony of steel on steel—heavy, rasping breaths immediately behind her. Blind panic seized Leena, turning her numb. She spun, a shriek rising in her throat.

It was Anna, inches away and panting hard. Leena bit down on her scream, reducing it to a muffled squeak. Anna sniffed her face and hands, licking a scrape where Leena had fallen from the horse.

"Are you hurt?" Leena asked, burying a hand in the wolf's thick fur. It had to be brutally hot in this climate.

The wolf shook its head. Giving Leena a push with her snout, Anna urged her onward. Leena obeyed, keeping the wall of the pyramid to her left. Around the corner, the fighting was farther away from the structure. That gave them a clear path, though it was more exposed. They sprinted forward, reaching the halfway mark before they met resistance.

A Shade soldier stumbled from the crush of battle to Leena's right, one hand clutching his head, the other gripping a sword. He staggered, swiping his blade at the empty air. Leena jumped back, the tip narrowly missing her chin.

Anna gave a sharp, growling *woof*, pressing close to Leena's side. The Shade caught his balance, and the shadowy hood turned their way.

"Hello, there," the Shade said, the words almost lost beneath the din. Then he reached for Leena.

Anna launched into the air, catching the Shade's arm by his leather gauntlet. He screamed, a high, agonized shriek of fury, and swept his blade down toward the wolf's back.

Pure reflex took over. Leena hurled herself forward, catching the fist holding the weapon. The momentum knocked all three to the ground. The Shade tried to push them off, but without success. Leena grabbed the sword from his hand, but he was too strong for her to keep it for long. When she finally wrenched the blade away, she hurled it out of his reach.

Bones crunched as the wolf bit down on the Shade's fore-arm. The Shade smashed his free arm into Anna's side, but Leena doubted the blow carried much force by then. Anna let go, and they burst into a run, leaving their attacker to writhe in the dirt.

Leena felt sick as they rounded the last corner. She was a healer, not someone who caused pain—but here, fighting meant survival. She swallowed down her misgivings and began searching the place where the door was supposed to be.

"I'm not sure how to open it," Leena confessed, earning a frus-trated whine from Anna.

From here, they could see the encroaching line of Shades, like a murky flood seeping across the red-brown earth. Green magic swirled above them, promising destruction.

Leena had no time for trial and error—they had to get safely inside.

What had Morran done? He'd shouted something, and a block of stone had slid aside. Was there a magic word? A spell? He'd said anyone could enter. It didn't take royal blood.

Leena racked her brain. Secret doors were a fae tradition, and the fire fae had their fair share—but there was no time to try every magic word she knew. She pressed her palms against the stone, feeling the presence of the Flame inside. "Please."

Stone rumbled as it rolled aside mere feet from where Leena stood. Anna gave an excited bark as she plunged inside. Leena followed, and the stone rolled shut behind them.

The cramped, dark passage to the pyramid's heart was just as before. When they emerged, Leena ran to the edge of the pool and sank to the steps, her strength finally run out. Silence enveloped her, free of the noise of pain and war. It was cool here, lit only by the Flame and its reflection on the glimmering water.

She was aware of Anna inquisitively roaming the space, but otherwise, Leena's awareness unraveled. She'd been braced for danger for so many hours, its absence left her unmoored. When she wiped a hand across her face, it came away wet with tears. A floodgate opened, and Leena began to shake with the release of all the fear she'd held at arm's length. Now that it was free, terror and grief had their way with her, and she began to weep in earnest.

Without warning, a black, furry body crashed into Leena's chest. She yelped in surprise. "Kifi!"

The cat rubbed her cheek against Leena's, purring madly. Leena clutched her friend, grateful for her soft warmth.

"How did you get in here?" Leena asked, rubbing Kifi's ears. "Did Mo come, too?"

It was then she noticed Kifi held something in her mouth. The cat dropped it into Leena's hand. It was an ornate golden medallion.

Kifi licked her whiskers, as if the metal had left a questionable taste behind. "Fang of Deadly Retribution stayed behind to guard Barleycorn."

"Did you come through the Shimmer after Morran and I crossed over to Faery?"

"Not at all. Barleycorn made a new one that brought me straight here. He knows everything there is about portals." Kifi's tone implied Barleycorn and his talents were somehow her idea.

"He is awake?" Anna asked from the shadows.

Leena looked up to see Anna was once more in human form. She wore loose-fitting pants and tunic similar to those of the local desert fae—no doubt raided from one of the upstairs rooms.

"Your friend is awake but weak," Kifi said. "He said the activities of the smelly Shade general disturbed his rest—particularly when he opened the portal that brought Fionn and the rest of us to the Mortal Realms."

"That explains the storm and earthquake," Leena replied. "That was Barleycorn preparing to wake." She looked down at the medallion. It was the size of a large coin and had a loop at the top, as if it were meant to be worn on a chain.

Anna gave a short, harsh laugh. "Though he keeps his power to himself, John has unusual earth magic. The storms and quakes were but symptoms of his rising consciousness."

"And there is nothing like an enchanted assassin to provoke bad dreams."

Kifi hopped down from Leena's lap. The cat sat between the two women, wrapping her tail neatly around her paws. "He said to tell you that he has been awaiting this battle. This is the moment Juradoc plans to seize the power of the phoenix and turn it against the fae."

"Morran is no longer under his control."

"But the phoenix could be. The Shades have tried harnessing the firebird before, but that success was short-lived. According to Barleycorn, Juradoc intends to go further and make Arlanoth his own familiar, not Morran's. Barleycorn knows how to make it happen."

Leena gave a soft cry. "He means to actually *steal* Morran's familiar?"

"Then he could fully use it to draw power from the Flame."

Anna caught her breath. "That's why Juradoc sent your brother to my world. He wants Barleycorn's secret to binding the phoenix."

"Yes," Kifi said, her lamp-bright eyes staring at the dancing reflections in the pool. "But Juradoc does not have a cat to explain the folly of his ways."

A long silence followed, in which Anna fidgeted with impatience. "So what is this secret John's been hiding?"

"Can we repair the bond between Morran and Arlanoth?" Leena asked at the same moment.

Kifi began carefully cleaning her paw. "The phoenix was irreparably damaged when it was parted from the prince. It was killed."

"What?" Leena cried. "It's dead?"

"Barleycorn says it has been reborn as an egg," Kifi said with obvious patience. "That is its nature—to live and die and rise again, over and over."

"There must still be a bond of some kind between Arlanoth and Morran. That's how Morran's death would summon it. Juradoc would take the opportunity to seize the fledgling and make it his own."

Kifi gave a grave nod. "Any newborn creature is defenseless. The bird wouldn't stand a chance."

"We need to find the egg before the Shades do." Leena pressed a hand to her stomach. For the first time, she saw a thread of hope for Morran, and it was giving her butterflies. "How hard can finding an egg be?"

"Not hard at all. It's in the Sanctum of this temple."

Leena stared at Kifi. "Is that why you're here?"

"Yes." The cat's tail flicked once, a sign of impatience at the stupidity of non-cats. "That is why Barleycorn sent me directly into this pyramid."

"No one can enter the Sanctum," Anna said, sitting beside Leena. "Even I know that."

"It requires a key." Kifi's tone was reasonable. "You're holding it."

Leena held up the medallion. "Was this on Barleycorn's chain? The one he wore around his neck?"

Anna plucked it from Leena's hand. "Yes. He called it his souvenir from the battle of Ildaran Falls. It was among the palace treasures the fae saved from the Shades."

"Did he always wear it?"

The wolf turned the gold piece over in her hand, then handed it back to Leena. "He never took it off."

Leena gripped the warm gold. "Perhaps he foresaw this need."

"But the key isn't enough." Heaving a sigh, Anna ran a hand through her dark hair. "When the Shades first arrived, the priestesses lay an enchantment upon the Great Temple. They decreed that no Shade could enter without surrendering their life, nor any who might be corrupted by them. Trespassing means death."

Leena frowned at that. "I don't see the problem. We aren't Shades."

"No Shades can enter," Anna replied, "but neither can humans or fae. We're all susceptible to corruption."

Leena's heart seemed to stumble. "Then how..."

"Cats cannot be corrupted." Kifi rose with an extravagant stretch. "That's why the Shades hate us."

"Oh no." Leena reached for Kifi, needing to hold her. "Cats are hardly innocent, and the Sanctum isn't like the Flame I summon in the dance. We can easily survive that, but not this Flame. Morran warned me. Even if the spell lets you pass, the Flame itself will devour you."

Kifi lashed out a paw, knocking the medallion—the key to the

Sanctum—from Leena's hand. "The Mother of Cats dwells in the Sanctum. I set my paws upon this path with a longing to feel her breath upon me."

Suddenly wary, Leena reached for Kifi again as the feline grabbed the key in her jaws. Even as Leena's hands closed on the cat's sleek black coat, Kifi shot from her grasp with surprising strength.

"*Kifi*," Leena screamed as the cat bounded toward the pit of Flame, tail waving like an inky streamer. Anna pounced, but not even her wolf-quick reflexes could catch the temple cat. Kifi leaped into the Flame, her lithe body a perfect arc of black against the burning orange. Leena froze, stunned to silence.

Kifi was gone.

❧ 25 ❧

Morran lost his horse somewhere in the fight. It was not dead, but it had fled. He didn't blame it.

"Leena?" he called, voice cracking from overuse. "Anna?"

He paused to cut a Shade from the back of his mount, driving the tip through the monster's throat for good measure. Cartilage crunched in a way that made his stomach roll. He pulled the blade out, using his boot to hold the body still.

He had fought long and hard, shoulder to shoulder with the other fae. He wore no general's cloak, nor a prince's golden trappings. The anonymous armor he had borrowed turned him from a target to a hidden weapon turned loose among the Shades. Sadly, one swordsman—even an exceptionally lethal specimen—could not turn the tide of war.

"Leena?"

The fae were losing. There were too many Shades arriving through countless Shimmers. By Morran's count, three fresh soldiers replaced every one the fae killed—which meant the Shades were committing everything they had to this fight. Somehow, Juradoc had convinced them to take the risk.

A brilliant battle plan meant nothing against an infinite enemy. Sabian had ordered the dragons to attack at will, but they couldn't incinerate the Shades without frying the fae as well. The two sides were impossibly entwined on the battlefield.

"Anna?"

Morran had crossed the bloody ground a thousand times, Fionn at his side, desperate to find the women. He'd returned time and again to the last place he'd seen Leena, but she was gone. A sword thrust through the gut would have carried less pain.

"Leena?"

Morran had left a trail of death behind him, but nothing could balance the exchange of her life for that of a thousand putrid monsters.

Now the fighting was confined to an area before the pyramids, the fae pushing hard against the rising tide of Shades. Dragons had attacked the sorcerers, but their fire could not pierce the green cloud of magic swirling over the Shade forces. With Fionn at his side, Morran climbed a rise in the land to look down on the carnage.

Leena's brother had fought bravely, almost recklessly. Though he had saved Morran's life more than once, it would take time to atone for his association with the Shades. That was something Morran understood all too well, and he had promised to help him. While Leena had healed Fionn's body, Morran might be able to mend his spirit. Letting the lad restore his honor in battle was a start.

As they climbed, Morran gripped his bare sword in one hand. Though he had taken no wounds, thick, dark liquid trailed from the blade. The Shades' blood burned the trampled earth where it fell.

Morran and Fionn turned to face the fray. It was concentrated around the ranks of sorcerers, as if nothing else mattered but the spell they cast. None of the enemies had any interest in two lone figures escaping the fight.

Leena's red hair would blaze like a beacon among the filth of battle, but, just as before, there was no sign of her. Nor could he see Anna, in wolf or fae form. He suspected Anna had turned back to find Leena—something neither Morran nor Fionn had been able to do in the thick of the fight—but he couldn't be sure. It was as if they had both vanished through a Shimmer.

His gaze returned to the Shades, snagged by fresh movement. The sorcerers bellowed and pointed their staffs toward the pyramids, aiming for a point in the middle of the square. The green mist that had gathered above the Shades floated toward the four structures. The mist spun and billowed like a fishing net cast over the sea, except it floated up and up, carried by an unnatural wind. And then, it settled.

Fionn gasped in amazement. For an instant, the mist hung above the Great Temple's courtyard, a storm above the stone blocks that lay half-buried in sand and dust. Then it seeped downward like an artist's pen sketching in green ink, delineating the point and four walls of a new pyramid—one far grander and heavily ornamented with carving and statues, one that touched the clouds in its majesty. Grand steps led up the face of the structure, ending in a platform before the apex. The point itself was open to the sky, a mouth where the Flame could erupt. The four existing pyramids sat like miniatures at the corners of its base, no bigger than an apple beside the tree that bore it. It flickered like a living illustration made of hovering, transparent threads of murky green light. All across the battlefield, the fae cried out with one voice.

Fionn fell to his knees, face white with awe. "The Great Temple. I never thought to see it."

"You should not have seen it like this." Outrage stormed through Morran. The Temple's hidden beauty had been dragged forth by the filthy green magic. There was violence in the act, defilement. The Shades had forced its will, pulling it from another time and space with brute strength.

As if in protest, the green threads flared orange, turning to solid flame. The fire licked up the lines that defined the pyramid, erasing the structure once more. The Shades roared in protest. Morran's heart almost lifted, but then a big smash of power from the sorcerers stripped the orange blaze away.

A black, zigzagging line formed in thin air, breaking an invisible shield suspended in front of the Great Temple. It split, the edges parting until the line was a visible gap. Then it spiderwebbed across the breadth of the pyramid, a million cracks covering the unseen surface.

"What's happening?" Fionn asked.

Morran's heart faltered, but he found the courage to reply. "The wards that guard the Great Temple are failing."

"Isn't that why Juradoc wanted you? So that the phoenix would get him through the temple's front door?"

"That was the first reason, but he's grown impatient and found another method."

"And here's proof it takes hundred Shade sorcerers to equal one firebird."

Fionn managed a jaunty grin, but it didn't last long. The invisible wall shattered, each particle flaking and floating away like ash in the air. It was a strange sight, the huge structure of the Great Temple emerging into view one scrap at a time. Flames flared up here and there, an effort at self-defense, but the wards could not hold against the enemy's combined power.

Fighting had stopped on both sides, the Shades and fae alike too stunned by the spectacle to carry on. Morran was no exception. He was used to battle, even magical battle, but he'd never seen anything like this. The warrior in him wanted to fight, but another instinct held him back. There was something here he needed to understand.

Once the Great Temple was fully revealed, Morran could see the wavering heat of the Flame above it. Tongues of fire leaped into the sky, evidence of the Flame within. This was its source and the beating heart of the fire fae.

General Juradoc marched forward to stand before the ranks of the sorcerers. No Shade had ever been able to approach the temple. Like Olek, they had all been rebuffed. Even now, Juradoc kept a respectful distance.

But he reached out his hands, palms forward, and a strange pressure filled the air. Morran felt it like a subtle wind against his face, and he knew what it meant. He'd felt it many times in his long years as a prisoner of the Shades. This was the technique the Shade had been hoping to perfect by using the fire dancers.

A roar rose from the Shades, giving voice to their amazement. Juradoc was sucking at the Flame, drawing it into his own power, absorbing it like a thirsty man lapping at a rare desert spring. No —that image was far too innocent. He was a demon of legend, draining the life of Faery itself. Morran's heart pounded, his blood thundering in his head. This was his worst nightmare made flesh.

And Juradoc had done it without Morran or Arlanoth, when only the phoenix should have been able to withstand the pure power of the Flame. Even fae could not withstand the heat of the Flame fresh from its core. How was Juradoc doing it?

It seemed an eternity before Juradoc dropped his hands long enough to push back his hood. Then, with a shrug, he shed his cloak altogether. In all the time Morran had endured the Shade's company, he'd never seen what that cloak concealed. It was obvious why.

Despite the distance, fae eyesight had little trouble noting every detail. The little flesh remaining on Juradoc's bones was blackened with rot, like carrion left in the sun. Morran's gorge rose as the Shade approached the Temple's steps. Juradoc was a caricature, a moving skeleton that should not have possessed the motions of a living body. Yet, he did, mounting the stairs higher and higher until he stood on the platform level with the pyramid's tip. Fire backlit his ghastly figure as he climbed, the wavering heat blurring his form in and out of focus. Morran blinked, aware of something strange as Juradoc reached the top. The Shade turned, raising his arms in victory.

Surely, he should be burning by now, consumed by the fire? But that was the farthest thing from the truth.

Perfect silence rang as loud as any bell. Morran stood stock still, open-mouthed with the rest. What he saw was not the horror of moments before, but a shining, beautiful creature. Silvery hair cascaded down Juradoc's back, reaching his knees. Sleekly muscled flesh filled out a tall, powerful frame. His face was striking, though alien, with high, arched cheekbones and brow. Large, silvery eyes gazed upon the crowd with pure triumph. Just as Leena had cured Fionn, Juradoc had healed himself by devouring the Flame's power.

For the first time, Morran understood what it was the Shades desired, what had led them from world to world, destroying everything in their wake. They were seeking elemental magic powerful enough to save their lives. For an instant, Morran pitied the enemy. What had happened to them?

A great shrieking cry ended the awestruck silence. As one, the Shade sorcerers threw down their staffs and surged toward the pyramid. A heartbeat later, the Shade soldiers dropped their blades and followed. The fae and the battle were insignificant in the face of imminent salvation.

If the Shades had once believed Juradoc a crazy rebel, that time was over. He had proven his risky, wild dream was possible. Now, they stampeded forward, pushing each other aside. Those who fell dragged themselves up to stumble forward again. They all had one desire—to drink the Flame's power. Anyone in their path would be cut down.

Morran had learned enough. It was time to regroup.

As if reading Morran's thoughts, Sabian raised his sword.

"Retreat," he bellowed, using magic to push the command across the field.

They had lost.

$\mathscr{H}$ 26 $\mathscr{H}$

Leena screamed as the fire devoured her little friend whole, leaving nothing but a whiff of smoke curling in the air.

She lunged forward, but Anna caught her from behind. "Stop. Stop."

"She'll burn. Morran said the fire in the Sanctum isn't safe."

"Hush," Anna said, squeezing her gently. "Kifi has the key. The Flame knows her. It will be fine."

The key was an abstract idea. Kifi roasting was a concrete image in Leena's mind. She hiccupped, teetering on the verge of hysterics.

Anna let go, taking her hand instead. "Let's go upstairs, away from here."

Leena wavered, possessed by the notion that Kifi would pop back out of the flames with a mischievous bound. That was something the little brat would do.

No, she wouldn't. That was madness, and nothing about the temple felt safe now, not even the glittering pool. Leena allowed Anna to lead her up the stairs.

"There must be windows up here?" Anna asked.

Leena replied with a nod. She reached out to the Flame, hoping for reassurance. But the voices weren't talking to her now, as if the Flame's attention had gone somewhere else.

Anna cast her a glance. "Maybe we can see a path through the battle. If it's safe enough, there might be a way back to the fae encampment."

That would mean leaving Kifi behind. Her friend was gone. Surrendered.

Talk to me, Leena urged the Flame, but no voices came.

"In here." It was Leena's turn to take the lead, pulling Anna into the room where she'd seen the dragon and kissed Morran. It felt like a million years ago, but the sun still slanted into the room, a little brighter because it was afternoon.

They approached the window, glimpsing blue sky. Within seconds, the image vanished in a flare of sickly green light, leaving blank stone behind. The shock of it stopped them cold.

"No, no, no," Leena cried, slamming a palm toward where the opening should have been.

Anna caught her hand before it touched the glowing green magic. "Don't. You don't know where that's been."

Leena wrenched free. "Now what do we do?"

THE FAE OFFICERS BARELY KEPT THE RETREAT TO THEIR CAMP from becoming a rout. Their warriors were brave, but they had failed when they could least afford it. If the Flame were extinguished, all of Faery would be snuffed out. Such staggering consequences made discipline hard. Still, it was Morran's immediate duty to keep order, so he led the march and harried the stragglers with the tenacity of a sheepdog.

After that, the problems got harder.

"Has anyone seen Leena?" he demanded once they'd reached

the camp. He'd hoped against hope that she and Anna had made it back safely.

They stood in the command tent, which looked exactly the same as before, with its maps and empty wine jugs. After such a loss, it should have been different somehow.

"No, my prince, your lady is nowhere to be found," Kelagras responded. The captain had a bad cut across his left cheek, but he had not wavered in his tasks. "What are your orders?"

Morran cursed under his breath. The two women had vanished. There had to be somewhere he hadn't already looked.

Sabian entered the tent. "What supplies do we have?"

"Enough for a week," answered the officer in charge of supplies.

A week was too much and not enough. Morran folded his arms, joining the other commanders gathered around Sabian.

The general glanced from face to face, reading the same weariness he felt in every expression. "I will ask the dragons to fly to Evantra to summon every sorcerer they can find. Plus, Tymeera must send reserves. We need more troops to free the Great Temple."

"That's a long march across open desert," Kelagras replied.

"Do you have another suggestion?" Sabian asked.

The commanders shook their heads.

"There's some chance the Shades are too occupied with the Temple to bother with us," Sabian said wryly. "If we're lucky, the dragons might find a sorcerer who can use a Shimmer. Then they could port the troops straight from Tymeera—or anywhere else—to our front lines."

A ripple of agreement went through the group.

"Meanwhile, double patrols and prepare the camp for an attack. Sooner or later, the Shades will look our way."

Sabian dismissed them. Morran conferred with Kelagras around the deployment of the remaining cavalry. Then he deputized Fionn to get a tally of the wounded and report back to the command council. It would be good for them to see the lad making himself useful.

That left Morran blessedly alone to make plans.

Although he'd known the Shades had hungered for elemental power, he'd hadn't foreseen Juradoc's move. Morran wasn't convinced the Shades had understood, either. Not given their response to the general's transformation.

Juradoc had wanted the phoenix. Now that Morran had regained his memory, he fully understood why. It went far beyond today's invasion.

Not only would the phoenix open the door to the Flame's heart in the Sanctum of the Great Temple, but it would ensure its master survived the experience. Juradoc had gone ahead without the firebird, breaking through the Flame's wards using the combined might of the fae sorcerers. And he was consuming its power. A risk, to say the least.

Although Juradoc's move was clearly about healing, it might also be about ambition. Juradoc had failed to get the phoenix, and he'd failed to secure Barleycorn and whatever objects or knowledge the earth fae could offer. Now he was moving ahead without either of those plans—and whatever protections they offered—in place. Why? According to Olek, Juradoc had the interest of his masters. He'd thrown caution to the wind, and he was proving his theory while he had their attention.

Somewhere in that desperation was a weakness Morran could use. Morran himself had lost too much—his life, his love, most of his power, and half his soul. He would be the worst kind of opponent—the one who had already survived an enemy's worst blow.

Morran looked beyond the tent flap to see Captain Kelagras lead his mounted patrol into the desert. The captain's face had been hastily bandaged, but the wound was likely to leave a scar. No doubt it would add to his roguish appeal if they all survived long enough to tell war stories.

Not *if*, but *when*. Morran wasn't giving up without a fight.

LEENA HURT IN PLACES SHE'D BARELY KNOWN SHE POSSESSED.

As Morran had promised, there were indeed tunnels beneath the Temple. Leena had located the steep stairway hidden behind a sliding panel in the rotunda. It must have been the perfect secret passageway for a mischievous young Morran to explore.

It was impossible to know if the Shade magic had touched the underground passages, but Leena thought not. Though filthy and full of scorpions, they seemed ordinary enough. Some were big enough to walk upright while others were little more than drain-pipes. In some places, the openings were so small she'd had to wriggle through like a snake.

Anna had fared a little better, having two forms to choose from, but they'd both been battered and filthy by the time they'd made the diagonal crossing that brought them closer to the camp of the fae. When Anna had kicked the tunnel door open, they'd expected another stairway leading to ground level.

Instead, heat washed over them like the breath of demons. Leena stumbled into the sun, blinking away tears at the sudden brightness. Before them was a vast sweep of cracked earth and sagebrush. The tunnel had taken them far into the desert.

"Maybe there was magic in the tunnels after all," Anna muttered. "Maybe the Flame wanted us out of the way. We sure didn't travel this far on our own."

Something moved behind Leena. She spun around to find the door to the tunnel had vanished.

There was no going back.

Although Morran was still under Sabian's command, it seemed he'd earned back trust through his performance on the battlefield. Now, everyone wanted his opinion. Ronan of

Brightwing turned up asking about the safety of sending his dragons over the Great Temple. Even the cook stopped by, wondering whether supplies could be brought in if they found a sorcerer who could work a Shimmer. Evidently, they'd mistaken Morran for an all-seeing oracle.

Thus, it was some time before he finally left the command tent to begin his search for Leena and Anna. The sun was past its peak, but the heat was still stifling. He filled his waterskin, then drank it dry before reaching the edge of the camp. From there, he could see the Great Temple with ease. It occupied the courtyard that had once stretched between the smaller pyramids. If Leena and Anna were to be found, they would be in the desert beyond.

Something bumped Morran's shin. Too tired to startle, he reached down out of instinct. There, he found warm, soft fur. "What the—"

He looked down to see Kifi draped over his ankles, golden eyes gazing up in an expression of dwindling patience. The cat's fur was crisped. Had she been near a fire? Since she was already sooty black, it was hard to tell.

"I could ask what you're doing here," he said, "but something tells me that I don't have time for the complete answer."

Kifi sat up. By the shakiness of her movements, he guessed the cat was exhausted. Around her neck was a drawstring bag made of gold silk.

"What's this?" When he reached out to touch the bag, she stretched up, making her neck long.

"The gift is for you," the cat said in her high, childlike voice.

He slid the string free of her ears, then cupped the silk in his palm. The oval sphere inside was surprisingly heavy. Morran straightened, instantly aware of what it was. It was the egg of a phoenix. *His* egg.

His head felt suddenly, dangerously light. "How did you get this?"

"I fulfilled my mission," Kifi said. "I met the Queen of Cats, you know." Her voice throbbed with excitement. Obviously, the experience had been everything she'd hoped for.

"And?" Morran prompted after a silent pause.

"She'd been keeping the egg in the heart of the Flame. She told me it was for you."

The egg meant Arlanoth hadn't survived their separation. Fury twisted in Morran's chest, hot as the phoenix's wing. He stared down at the little cat, imagining her trotting through roaring flames. "You went to the Sanctum?"

Her ears twitched in what might have been amusement. "I had to. I was the only one who could."

"How did you survive?" Morran noticed the cat's whiskers seemed oddly shriveled.

"I had the key." A crumb of whisker fell off.

Morran cradled the bag with reverence. The egg was no bigger than that of a small chicken, but he knew without looking that the shell would be pure gold. The phoenix curled inside was fragile yet powerful. It was part of Morran, yet not. It was Arlanoth, ready to be reborn.

Emotion surged inside him, closing his throat with the impulse to weep at the sheer improbability of this moment. The fae were on the cusp of oblivion, and he held the potential of everything new.

Careful of the egg, he bent and picked up the cat, cradling her in his free arm. "Brave, noble Kifi."

She licked her paw, shedding a tiny sprinkle of charred fur. "I thought going on an adventure was my dream, but I am wiser now. I gave what I could because Leena needed my help. So did you. That was adventure enough."

Morran was struck speechless. Kifi yawned, showing a lot of pink tongue. "I wouldn't mind a bit of fish, though. Heroics takes energy."

Despite himself, Morran chuckled. "You deserve the finest treats Faery can provide."

"Of course I do."

"If I settle you in with food and drink, do you think you could guard the egg a moment longer?"

"Why?"

"I have something to do that cannot wait. Not even for this."

Kifi's tail twitched in disapproval. "The Queen of Cats has one more message. The Flame will survive the Shades only if the phoenix is reborn. Don't miss your chance, Prince Morran. The queen doesn't hand out magical eggs willy-nilly."

"No, I suppose she doesn't."

"And yet, you hesitate."

"Leena is missing. I have to find her before I do anything else."

Morran's own words surprised him. Half his being was gone, but Leena's loss was more grievous. She had restored him in ways he could not name. Now that she needed him, he wouldn't walk away.

Kifi's ears flattened. "Are you certain Leena is gone? She was with the wolf woman."

"Where?"

"Inside the temple. She was there when I jumped into the Flame."

Appalled, Morran spun to glare at the pyramid. "The temple now swarmed by the Shades?"

Kifi snuggled deeper into the crook of his arm. "Details."

❧ 27 ☙

Morran carried the cat back to the tent, pausing only to demand an astonished sub-lieutenant fetch fish and milk.

"And a cushion," Kifi called after the junior officer. "A comfy one, please."

"I suppose you'll demand royal treatment for the rest of your days," Morran grumbled.

"At least a lifetime's worth," Kifi replied. "I used up at least one of my traditional nine on your behalf."

They trudged on, retracing all the progress Morran had made toward the desert. The flap of the tent had barely fallen closed behind them when a dirt-streaked apparition flung her arms around him.

"Morran, thank the Flame you're safe," Leena said, her voice faint with emotion.

Morran stared, half-convinced he was hallucinating. Relief hit him like strong wine. "Leena."

Then she snatched Kifi from his grasp and covered the cat in kisses. "Oh, kitten," she cooed. "You came back, you darling little thing."

The little monster shot Morran a smug look as Leena planted another kiss between her ears.

"Oh, Kif-kif, your poor whiskers are singed."

"Leena," Morran said again, louder this time. "How did you get here?"

Leena raised her head from Kifi's fur. Her face was dark with grime, giving her a comical resemblance to the cat. "Forgive me, the last time I saw Kifi, I was certain she'd perished."

He gazed down into Leena's eyes, feeling sudden weightlessness, as if she could give him the power to fly. "I know what Kifi did."

"I'm right here," the cat said dryly as Leena set her down on the table.

They ignored her. Morran ran his hands down Leena's arms, careful of the scrapes and scratches. Her red hair had come loose from its braids and hung in dusty tendrils down her back. "What happened to you?"

"We escaped through the tunnels, only to find ourselves in the desert. Captain Kelagras found us and brought us back."

Morran made a mental note to commend him. "And Anna?"

"She has gone to bathe. The captain insisted I stay here because you were searching for me."

"Good man," Morran murmured, carefully setting the silk bag with the egg on the table next to Kifi. The cat wrapped a paw around it, keeping it safe.

Leena reached up, cupping his face in her hands. "Perhaps I would be more appealing in fresh clothes."

Between the battle and a trip through the tunnels, her garments had been torn to shreds. He doubted he looked much better. "There is nothing lovelier to me than your presence. That is more than enough."

Her hands slid down, clasping behind his neck. The gesture pulled them closer. "I am very happy to see you in one piece."

"I was preparing to go in search for you, but you found your own solution yet again. I despair of ever playing the hero."

He kissed her then, tasting the sweetness of her lips. There was sand and salt, too, earthy and real. She felt like life itself against him, yielding, warm, and lithe, every inch of her indisputably female. Leena's fingers wound in his hair, coaxing and possessive. Her tongue flicked against his, promising her need for him was as urgent as his for her. When they parted, it was reluctant.

This was why he faced death on the field of war. So they could have life.

They were interrupted by the young officer arriving with Kifi's meal. He was followed by other servants bearing refreshments for the prince and his guest. One brought a pillow trimmed in gold tassels. Another brought water and towels to wash in. Once they had set down their offerings, Morran dismissed them.

"There is much we need to discuss," he began, pouring Leena a cup of wine. "Eat and drink your fill as we talk. We may not have much time."

As he told Leena about the Great Temple and Juradoc's triumph, her face grew white beneath the grime. "I tried to speak to the Flame, but could not get a response. No doubt it was busy defending itself against the Shades."

By this time, Kifi had licked her plate clean. She took up the tale then, telling Leena all she'd told Morran about the egg. Leena listened without speaking a word until the end.

"I see," she finally said. "So let me test my understanding. Juradoc's aim all along has been to find a cure for the Shades, which will secure his fortune among their ranks. He knows he has to do this by accessing the strongest possible source of fae power. The Flame meets his needs, but it's deadly in its pure form. He tests his theory, using fire dancers to summon a safer level of energy, but he needs the phoenix for any serious and safe power draw. He needs your death, plus whatever knowledge Barleycorn has to bind the firebird as his own familiar."

"But nothing works out," Morran said, picking up the thread. "I escape, and Fionn fails to kidnap Barleycorn. And yet, he's still moving ahead. He's smashed his way into the temple—incredible enough—and he's soaking up raw power. This shouldn't be possible."

Kifi spoke up. "Perhaps the Shades combined are strong enough to withstand the heat of raw Flame for a time. Juradoc's counting on his mob as a shield while he works."

"Works at what?" Morran asked.

Kifi's whiskers lifted in smug satisfaction. "I believe he's searching for the egg, but I got there first."

Morran's gaze shot to the egg nestled in the curve of Kifi's side. The idea of Juradoc stealing his other half twisted and slithered down his nerves.

"So how does this joining happen?" Leena asked. "If we're to save the Flame, it must take place with as little delay as possible."

Morran sat, numb with apprehension. He didn't remember *how* he had joined with Arlanoth. It had happened at birth, an automatic union forged in ritual and ceremony. "Adults don't join with a familiar. It's impossible to unite if the two candidates are at different life stages."

"How so?"

"One would perceive the world as a child does, the other not. More significantly, the patterns of power solidify over time. Magic and power grow to maturity along with the rest of us. The younger half of the bond would be crushed, the older half broken in the attempt to adapt. Both would perish."

He picked up the silk bag from the table, then slid the egg out. It gleamed in the faint light of the tent, perfect, golden, and impossible to access. There was no lid to open, no lock to turn. Within, he could sense his other half sleeping beyond his reach. The impulse to break it free was almost irresistible, yet any attempt to tamper would destroy it. "There must be a means to unlock its secrets."

"Can we hatch it, then wait till it grows up?" Kifi suggested. "A chick might be an entertaining playmate."

Morran shook his head. "The Shades will have destroyed us by then."

"Then what do we know about the phoenix?" Leena asked. "They are creatures of the Flame. They die and are reborn."

Leena came to stand beside Morran, reaching out one tentative finger to lightly brush the egg's gleaming shell. "There was one more prophecy that was made regarding the Prince of Tymeera."

Leena's gaze moved from the egg to Morran's face. "May I pick it up?"

Morran nodded, conscious of the slide of her fingers over the egg's delicate shell. Her brows drew together, an expression of deep concentration pushing all other emotions from her features.

"What is it?" Morran braced himself, reluctant to hear the answer.

Her attention returned to him. Morran stared down into her eyes, trying to read all the layers of meaning there. He couldn't.

As if sensing his confusion, she took a step back, gathering herself. "Before I left to follow Fionn among the Shades, I visited the Temple at Eldaban. The prophecy came from the Mother."

"And?"

Leena touched the chatelaine at her belt. "She said the poison I carry is for you."

❧

NOW IT ALL MADE SENSE TO LEENA. YES, JURADOC HAD twisted the idea into an order to murder Morran, but that didn't matter now. The Mother's original words had been plain: *I dreamed of poison and the prince, of his fall into the Flame. You were part of the dream, sowing his ashes in a newly plowed field.* She had been speaking of rebirth, of death supporting new life.

Leena drew a long breath, her fear of the prophecy finally releasing. An ache seemed to vanish, letting her breathe. The egg seemed to grow heavier, more solid. However threatened the Flame might be, it still whispered to the tiny creature inside, lulling it with the song of fire.

"Poison?" Morran eyes widened with surprise. "May I point out that if I am dead, my ability to fight the Shades will be greatly reduced."

You know what to do. The Flame's rasping voice was clear in her head.

Leena gazed down at the egg in her hand. To her surprise, she did know. It was the simplest of equations. Carefully, she set the egg down on the table beside Kifi, who had fallen asleep on her pillow.

"You will only perish for the briefest moment."

"Is that meant to comfort me?" Morran's tone was light, but it couldn't hide his alarm.

"Do you trust me?"

This had to be a moment of complete trust, or nothing would work.

By way of reply, Morran cupped her face in his hands and bent to kiss her once more. It was gentle and brief. "I am afraid that death will be too similar to the abyss. I can't be a prisoner again. I can't exist with no will of my own."

She reached up, placing her hands over his. Morran's skin was as cool as if shock had robbed him of warmth. This had happened to him before—Paya, the poison, Juradoc breaking him in two. "I understand."

"Do you?"

Her fingers traced his lips, then trailed over his shoulders, caressing, soothing. Leena knew what it was to need some scrap of control over her existence. She also knew how that fear had blocked her powers. Then again, she wasn't taking this risk. Who could blame his caution? After such betrayal, how could he trust her?

You know what to do.

Except—if this failed, she would lose him. She would be the one whose hand held the poisoned cup. Doubt curled its tail around her heart. *I can't risk this.*

There is light after the abyss.

Morran's hand went to the chatelaine at her belt. With a swift jerk, he broke the chain that held the silver vial. He held it up, studying it. It looked small and harmless in his sword-calloused hand. "Do I drink it all?"

Leena's lips trembled. She pressed a hand to her mouth, forcing down her panic, until Morran raised an eyebrow. She dropped her hand, a wave of helplessness leaving her trembling.

"You don't have to do this," she whispered.

"I could blame the Shades for this predicament, but they aren't keeping me from the phoenix today. My own bad memories of betrayal and ruin are at fault. I can't allow them to stand in my way."

"Morran," she began.

He pulled the stopper on the vial, letting it drop to the ground.

She swallowed, her throat painfully dry. "Drink it all."

"I trust you," he said before he swallowed it down, grimacing at the bitter taste.

Within seconds, he began to sway. Leena caught his arm. She helped him sit on the ground, then cushioned his head as he gradually lost consciousness. Before long, he was on his back, stretched out and breathing lightly. His face was peaceful, the lines of tension softened.

"What have I done?" Leena murmured under her breath. Terror clawed through her.

And then it fled as the voice of the Flame grew, the sound

swelling to fill her mind. There was urgency in it now, a recognition of its own dire needs.

The Flame needed its defender, the Phoenix Prince.

Leena picked up the egg and placed it on his chest, folding his hands around it. Instinctively, they clutched the golden sphere above his heart. She sat for a long moment, hypnotized by the fire's whispers as the rise and fall of his strong chest stilled. Panic surged in a sudden wave.

Now, she said to the Flame. *Now you must come.*

The command tent was smaller than she liked, but Leena drew the circle of Flame around Morran's still form. It came with instant obedience, tongues of white and orange flickering as high as her waist. The voice multiplied to a chorus in her mind, rejoicing and commanding. Beneath was a dark thread of pain, fury at Juradoc's crime.

Leena began to dance, using it all. Anger was a spice, a spark to leaven the rest.

It began slowly, as it always did, the shuffle and stamp of her feet against the hard-packed earth. All else fell away but the essence of her purpose. She was fire fae, and, in the dance, she was more elemental than flesh. She wound the Flame through her fingers, letting it cascade through her hair and lick along her skin.

As she leaped and swayed, the Flame sang to her of the binding that was their mission. This creation, this joining of souls was a mad spark on a knife's edge between order and chaos. So Leena danced for passion and for flight.

She could feel Morran in the midst of it, the sun to her spinning orbit. As she willed him back to life, she encountered the unfamiliar mind that was Arlanoth. He was a true being of fire, the eternally burning raptor. He hungered for prey, needing the air and height and flight to hunt.

She danced, winding the spiral of flames around her limbs, and found Morran—familiar, strong, and dear to her. In the dance, she could see his life and his mighty will. She could see how his purpose was essential to the Flame's strength.

Yes, yes, yes, the fire's voice crackled. *We need him now.*

Morran had to survive. Leena's dance grew in power, driven by her intense emotions. Ecstasy of movement pulled her into a whirlpool that held them all—dancer, bird, and prince. The common element was the fire—they shared it, she was part of Morran, part of the phoenix, and still solely herself. This was the binding—their fae blood and breath and life essence.

With an enormous crack and crash, fire fountained to the ceiling of the tent, licking across it and down the walls. All at once, they were inside a ball of flame. Leena shrieked, releasing the enormous energy she had summoned with the dance. The egg cracked, releasing an incandescent glow. Through the golden veils of Flame, the light grew in intensity, forcing Leena to shield her eyes.

Then, with a roar, the Flame vanished, leaving the tent untouched, as if there had never been a single spark of fire. Kifi sat up on her pillow, awake and blinking in astonishment.

Morran was gone. In his place was a molten, golden light the same shade as the egg's golden shell. It roiled and twisted, forming and reforming in a thick, luminous fog. Leena felt its presence against her mind—both the bird and Morran, yet not either. This was something new created through the binding, and she was not part of it.

With a fluttering, whistling sound, it shot out of the tent and into the sky. Leena stumbled to the tent's entrance, nearly tripping over Kifi. Then she gazed up, sinking to her knees.

The golden light had become the firebird.

Leena's heart soared with the fiery creature, tears of wonder blurring her vision. The Flame had healed the broken places within Morran—she had felt it. Finally, he was whole, his pain banished forever.

She put her hand up to shield her eyes, following the bird's flight through the cloudless sky. The creature's general shape resembled a crested eagle, and its wingspan was as broad as a small dragon. Where the sun hit its feathers, it shone like beaten gold. That was fearsome enough for any bird of prey, but the phoenix was more than sinew and feathers. Where it flew, its wings and tail left a trail of fire like a banner made of Flame.

"Magnificent," she said aloud, but none of the fae soldiers heard her. They had all poured from their tents to stare, open-mouthed, at the sky. A reverent silence fell over the camp, leaving only the jingle of the horses' tack. The return of the phoenix was an answered prayer.

Kifi brushed against Leena's leg. She picked up the cat, welcoming something to hold. Kifi smelled of soot, but Leena didn't care.

"I see the phoenix," Leena said softly, "but where did Morran go?"

"He died and turned into a bird. Haven't you been paying attention?"

"I know, but..." She could not quite grasp that the creature she saw shooting like a star through the heavens was both Arlanoth *and* Morran in one body. The two were made one in every sense. She was no stranger to magic, and this was wondrous.

Yet, the ache in her chest spoke of loss. Morran was gone, far beyond her reach, and not just his physical being. The bargain between them was complete. Both the prince and her brother were cured.

The outcome was what they had asked for, but it was an ending. Despite what they'd shared, the penniless temple dancer had no more claim on her prince. Vertigo swept through her, leaving her cold. The rush of adrenaline from the ritual had passed, leaving weariness in its wake.

Anna, washed and dressed in a clean tunic, came to stand at Leena's side. She stared up at the golden spark swooping through the sky. "Was this your doing?"

"In part. Kifi brought the egg."

The wolf fae gave the cat a considering look. "Well done, Bite-size."

"Is there any word on the Shades?" Leena asked.

Anna's jaw tensed. "The temple is overrun by the enemy."

Leena swallowed hard, barely trusting her voice. "Was the phoenix restored too late?"

"I can't see the future. That's Barleycorn's department, not mine." Anna gestured toward the sky. "But from everything I know, our survival is up to him now."

Leena grew queasy. Morran had described Juradoc's transformation after he'd gobbled down the Flame's magic—from something monstrous to a creature of godlike splendor. How could anything stop the Shades now? How vulnerable was the phoenix to attack?

Doubt fluttered inside Leena. "Anna, you understand shapeshifting. Will he change back to a fae after the battle?"

Anna shook her head. "I've not seen a case like his before. All I know is it won't matter if he can't stop the Shades."

There was movement in the encampment now, as astonishment over the phoenix turned to inspiration. Troops rode out, taking up their battle positions. Despite the staggering odds, they clearly expected the Phoenix Prince to lead a new charge.

With unspoken agreement, Anna and Leena, the latter with Kifi in her arms, moved to higher ground for a better view of the field.

The firebird had flown in a wide circle from one horizon to the next, finally returning to hover over the Great Temple's fiery peak.

The Flame within was hard to see now, barely rising above the platform where Juradoc still stood, arms upraised like the conductor of an infernal choir. Between the Shades and Morran's restoration, the sacred fire had used up much of its power. If Morran planned to make a move, it had to be soon.

As if it heard Leena's thoughts, the phoenix folded its wings and dove into the heart of the Flame.

❧

ENEMY. THE SIGHT AND SCENT OF THE SHADES BROUGHT BACK the terror of being torn apart and hunted. Arlanoth's only refuge had been death and the egg. Now the urge to rend and kill was fierce.

Yes, enemy, Morran replied.

Not good to eat. Arlanoth never put one of the nasty rotters in his beak if he could help it.

Morran agreed, but he didn't try to form words. He was more

than the bird's passenger, but he was far from in control. Sensation swamped him—the air beneath them, the fresh-born, untrammeled strength of the bird, the relief of being whole again. It was more than an absence of pain. It was jubilation. Despite everything, the moment held celebration.

Rotters don't belong. The phoenix shrieked its fury. *They hurt our home.*

Home meant the Flame. Many of the Shades had followed Juradoc's example, and they were gulping down the fire's power. As an elemental being, Arlanoth was the Flame's extension, its child and avatar. The Shades attacked the core of his being—and, by extension, Morran's. *We will hunt them.*

Go to great fire?

Great fire.

Arlanoth dove straight down into the Flame.

A sudden feeling of falling head-first, the wind rushing up to meet them. Inside his head, Morran whooped in pure intoxication. He was nothing but fire, air, and bird.

It would be easy to forget his other self—the fae prince who walked on the ground. This was the fight, the balancing act of what he was. So much practice with that struggle had kept him from annihilation while under Juradoc's spell. He'd had a mind to come back to.

Then, there was only heat as they fell into the Flame. It might have been Arlanoth's home, but Morran still felt the fire's bite. Wind ruffled the bird's feathers, combing through them like scorching fingers. He was left breathless, stripped of all but essential functions.

Find the threat. Kill the threat.

Arlanoth's sight was raptor sharp. The rippling tendril of Juradoc's magic was like a black serpent coiling into the Flame. It went deep into the white-hot core, searching, seeking, gorging on the elemental power like a worm in a rosebud. Morran could feel it leeching the living energy of the Flame, and, by extension, all of

Faery. It was a sickening, dizzy sensation, like the sudden loss of blood.

Arlanoth wasted no more time on thought. The bird lashed out with its curving talons, striking at the snake-like rope of power. Claws dug into the reeking abomination, dragging it free. It wasn't easy. Juradoc resisted with astonishing force. It coiled and bunched, writhing until the phoenix tore it in two with its beak. Fire leaked out of the mangled serpent, deflating until it sagged and flattened like a burst balloon.

The struggle took strength, and every Shade was sending its own dark snake into the Flame's core. As Kifi suggested, there seemed to be strength in numbers, as if the sheer number of attackers balanced out the Flame's lethal strength. None were burning, and they were all growing stronger.

Arlanoth shuddered, hating the parasites and dreading the effort it would take to root them out. There were hundreds, perhaps thousands, of fine tendrils worming in, waiting to fatten.

But Juradoc had other ideas. His wounded snake began absorbing the others, sucking them all into his. A silent shriek of protest vibrated through Morran's skull—the other Shades being robbed of their supper—but Juradoc had no pity. Suddenly strong again, his serpent reared up and lashed out, striking at the phoenix with fangs extended.

Magic sparked, and Morran caught a glimpse of Juradoc's hate and disappointment. He wanted—*needed*—the firebird, and Morran had it. Once he had enough power, Juradoc would seize it for himself.

Swerving out of reach, Arlanoth screamed in fury, but Morran took the helm this time. It wouldn't be so easy to defeat Juradoc again. The element of surprise was gone. Strategy was necessary.

He ordered the phoenix to dive into the Flame's blue-white heart. It scalded beyond the boundaries of pain, beyond his ability to howl or even breathe. But the Flame would not harm Arlanoth.

Morran reached for the fire's power, calling it to himself before the Shades could steal it.

The woven serpent of Shade magic detected the intrusion. It reared up, hood flaring like a cobra, but the threat was pointless. The Flame rushed toward Morran, ebbing away from the serpent like a vanishing tide. Juradoc's hungry fury raged—just as Morran hoped. Anger was a poor tactic in a fight.

Juradoc faltered just long enough for Morran to unleash his strike. All the fiery power Morran had taken for himself blasted free at a rate the serpent couldn't hope to absorb. Tendrils of Shade magic fried and withered as the phoenix shot back toward the sun. Flame fountained after it, reaching the sky.

Morran exulted as the phoenix wheeled in the azure heavens, fire shimmering from its wingtips. The pure, bright power was like strong brandy, leaving everything sharp-edged and surreal.

Burn. Burn them all, quick, quick.

An image formed in Morran's thoughts—a firestorm rolling over the Shades, searing life from the desert in one definitive blow. His instincts leaped to make it so. The Flame would obey. It would be clean and final.

Rend. Kill. Be done.

But there were others. His soldiers. The cat and the wolf. Leena.

What are they against the health of the land?

That was right, but not kind. Once, Morran had thought that way, but no longer. When he'd been at his worst, Leena had pieced him together like a broken cup.

Fire might burn, but it also warmed with gentleness. He could do better than crude violence.

They wheeled, gazing down at the battlefield with an eagle's eyesight. Miraculously, Juradoc had survived the blast. His features were visible as he glared up at them, hatred etched in every line of his luminous face.

The Shade picked up a sorcerer's staff and thrust it into the air, unleashing a jagged bolt of green lightning. The phoenix banked, easily dodging the strike. In return, Arlanoth breathed Flame, splashing fire at Juradoc's feet. The Shade sprang away, cursing.

They were evenly matched, the advantage a little on Morran's side. But there were many Shades, and only one Phoenix Prince. This wouldn't be resolved by an ordinary exchange of blows. This required a concentrated, definitive strike.

Morran went back to the reason the Shades were there—they wanted power. Juradoc had plunged his magic deep into the Flame's core to devour its magic. In fact, he'd sucked the magic-seeking tendrils of his fellow Shades into his own, securing the lion's share of the power for himself.

Greed was Juradoc's mistake. Morran seized on it.

All he had to do was deliver more of what Juradoc wanted.

Morran opened himself, dropping his mental shields to let the Flame fully inside. Arlanoth seemed to grow lighter, becoming more fire than bird, a pure conduit for elemental might. Morran became a strategic intelligence in a greater being. His will amplified the Flame's power, giving it purpose.

Arlanoth opened his beak, and Flame poured forth. It wasn't the fireball that would scorch the desert clean, but a fine beam of concentrated heat aimed squarely at Juradoc. The Shade threw his arms wide, bracing himself to drink in as much of the power as he could, but that bravado didn't last. There was a shift of posture, the shoulders hunching in, then a step back before he was cowering, arms flung up to stop the flow. Juradoc's armor began to smoke.

The other Shades wailed. Their power was still entwined with the general's, imprisoned as they'd burrowed into the Flame's core. The Shades began to crisp and burn, falling to ash one by one.

Morran wasn't immune to the overload of raw magic. It blazed inside his being, saturating him from the inside out. His sense of self thinned and slipped away, holding on just long enough to see Juradoc smoke, blaze, then burst into cinders that scattered in a puff of wind. Sparks swirled and snuffed out, disappearing to nothing.

Juradoc's army of Shades wasn't simply defeated. It was completely annihilated.

Morran followed, his mind unraveling into cobwebs that melted in the deluge of Flame. Everything that had happened—Juradoc, the miracle of the egg, the battle, and Leena—dissolved into mist. He was fire and wind and freedom—nothing more.

Like a shooting star, the phoenix vanished into the limitless sky.

❦ 29 ❦

Leena sank to the dry, dusty rise of land, watching as the blazing phoenix disappeared into the bright sky. Kifi curled under her arm, sheltering from the heat that washed over the desert in pulsing waves. Anna was there, too, pressing close. Leena huddled, grateful for their presence.

When she finally looked away from the vanishing bird, an afterimage remained burned on her soul. But even as her sight recovered, she knew that moment of wonder would remain.

Fionn stumbled to where they sat. He dropped to the earth beside Leena, putting an arm over her shoulders. His other arm bore an angry red slash from shoulder to elbow. It wasn't deep, and the oozing blood was reassuringly normal—not the black sludge of Shade corruption. Leena had her brother back.

The Great Temple continued to glow, though the heat faded. Leena lifted her head at the sound of cracking stone. A fissure running from the peak to the base split open to emit a pure white radiance. The brilliance grew, washing the sky a faint gray and the sandy earth white. Leena ducked her head again, bending over the cat to shelter it once more. The wonder she felt edged toward fear.

The phoenix is reborn, the Flame whispered in Leena's mind, the voice so unexpected that she jumped. *My fire can once again reach beyond the confines of my temples.*

All the fae sheltered their eyes from the brutal glare, cowering until it slowly dimmed. It felt like hours, *years*, of blinding, hammering light. Leena blinked hard, straining to find color in her surroundings once more, but when she did, every trace of the Shades was gone. Even their black cloaks and blood-soaked weapons had evaporated. The light had burned them from existence.

Now for the wounded children of my sister, Earth. I claim them back in her name.

The beasts the Shades had enslaved—horses, dogs, and oxen— had been spared by the light. Gone were their yokes and collars and the bits from their mouths. In a sudden, wild burst, those creatures ran free. Some went to the fae, knowing they would be cared for. The horses galloped into the desert to join the wild herds. There they would live untouched and unbridled with the desert winds in their manes.

Kifi twitched, called with the rest of the animals, but she burrowed deeper into Leena's arms. Above all, she was a temple cat.

I have finished, the Flame said. *All is safe.*

Leena and her friends rose, looking about them. Everywhere, the fae were doing the same, blinking in wonderment and wiping the tears from their cheeks. Not all the tears were from the light. Most were from joy. The Flame had cleansed the land, and the desert was once again pure.

But from horizon to horizon, there was nothing but empty blue sky, with no sign of the phoenix.

"Where is he?" Leena asked the Flame.

Morran is my servant, and he has rediscovered my wildness. There is a reason the phoenix is a bird of prey, and that Morran chose to join with that form instead of remaining a man. Your prince is truly himself for the first time in centuries. He is free to fly and hunt at his pleasure.

"But he is also a leader," Leena protested, earning a sidelong glance from Fionn, who only heard half the conversation. "Tymeera and its people require him."

She required him, but Leena barely let the thought take shape. It seemed impossibly selfish.

The Flame's response was just as blunt. *Only he can decide if a hearth fire is as enticing as the blaze of a righteous war. Only he can choose to return.*

With that, the Flame's whisper fell silent.

Oblivious to Leena's loss, cheers of victory broke out among the fae, the sound cresting and ebbing like a tide. It was slow at first, the survivors needing time to grasp what had happened. Then their cries rose in wave after wave of joy. The dragons spun and dove above them in a spectacle of aerial acrobatics. There would be feasting that night for sure.

Leena remained still, staring at the revelers. Numbness seeped down her limbs, as if she might turn to stone beneath the desert sun, becoming a marble ghost at the skirts of the temple. While her mind was relieved Faery was safe, any joy she might have felt had flown over the horizon with Morran.

Then, in an eye blink, the Great Temple was gone, leaving nothing but the open courtyard and four smaller pyramids at its corners. It was as if the battle and Morran's transformation had never been.

Leena felt his presence like a wave receding from the shore. Longing rose within her, sharp and intense.

Kifi squirmed, so Leena set her down. "What now?" the cat asked.

"Yes, what now?" Fionn pulled her close in a one-armed hug, kissing the top of her head.

It was a good question. She'd done what she'd set out to achieve. All she'd had to do was sacrifice her heart.

"I want to go home."

"TELL ME ABOUT THE TEMPLE ONE MORE TIME," LITTLE RIYA pleaded. "Come on, Leena, please?"

Leena laughed. For a moment, she was glad to be back in Eldaban. It had been easy to forget her normal life while she was having an adventure. Now that she'd returned, she realized how much she valued its simplicity.

She sat on the steps of her apartment building with Elodie and Riya, enjoying the cooling breeze and watching the crowds go by. Afternoon sunlight washed the streets, painting the buildings and people in a shimmering glow. Her heart might be broken, but at least she was not alone. There was a place she belonged and people she loved, including Elodie and her small family.

There was an air of festivity in the streets because Lord Dorth was gone. After Juradoc's defeat, he had been marched to the edge of town and sent away. The people had let him take provisions and a handful of his followers, but no one cared where he went or what he did next. There was no question that the council who'd taken his place would do a better job running the city. For one thing, they had no allegiance to the Shades. For another, it would be hard to do worse.

Elodie grabbed Riya's hand, bending low to speak to her daughter. "Come, little one, you've heard that story enough. Give Leena some peace."

"It's no trouble at all," Leena said with a smile.

"It was no trouble the first dozen times," said Grandmother Vira, who stood in the building's entrance, arms folded. "And you have an appointment with Master Tovas, do you not?"

Riya looked from her mother to her grandmother, lower lip pouting. After a heavy sigh, Grandmother Vira picked up the child and took her inside, muttering about a bath.

Vira was right. It was time Leena left for her appointment. Of course, Tovas was used to her habit of arriving for any engagement at the last possible moment.

"Do you want to perform in Tovas's revels?" Elodie asked as Leena got to her feet.

"The new council is having a banquet to honor the victors of the war. Quite a few of the armies are passing this way as they return to their own lands. It's a way to show gratitude and to signal that Eldaban is ready to fight with the fae in the future. Lord Dorth's exile has changed everything."

Elodie's brows lifted. "Shouldn't you be a guest and not an entertainer? You had as much to do with the outcome as anyone."

"I don't need applause for what I did. Serving the Flame is the role of a priestess."

Her tone was harsher than intended, and Elodie drew back. "My apologies. It just bothers me to see you back here, in your old life, with no reward."

Leena squeezed her friend's hand, silently apologizing for her sharpness. "Coming home was my choice."

"I know." Elodie hugged her close. "I just want you to be happy."

"I will be," Leena replied. "But I think it will take time."

With that, Leena left to meet Tovas. The fragile serenity she'd managed to create on that sunny afternoon crumbled. She would dance for her old friend that night because she owed him so many favors. As Master of Revels, he'd given her work when she needed it, and Leena didn't forget her friends. But what she could barely admit to herself, much less Elodie, was that her heart wasn't rooted in Eldaban anymore.

She had found the core of her magic, come into her power, and used those gains to heal the Phoenix Prince. That was exactly what Morran had needed—and all of Faery. Together, Leena and her prince had saved the Flame. By every measure, it was an astounding victory.

It had changed her, but not in the material ways Elodie wished for her. Though Morran, a powerful prince, was entirely beyond her as a lifetime mate, he had been perfect in ways she could not describe. Their spirits had matched. So had their bodies. She would always crave him, and that knowledge left her unsettled.

In response, she'd thrown herself into learning what her powers could do. If she could reclaim her brother from the Shades, could the cleansing Flame restore the Kelthian lands? Maybe—just maybe—she could walk again in the green valleys of her home and smell wildflowers in the cold mountain air.

Kifi all but tripped her, then yowled loudly when Leena stepped on her tail. Once they had both regained their balance, Kifi stared up at her with big gold eyes. "What are you thinking about?"

"My home in the mountains," Leena answered.

"Really?"

"Very well. I was *mostly* thinking about my home."

"You're fussing about the bird again." Kifi's tone was flat. "Cats are better."

"Well, don't worry. Prince Morran is not coming back." Annoyed, Leena quickened her pace, threading her way through the crowded street.

Kifi kept up with no trouble. "You don't know that. He might have needed a rest after all that egg business at the end."

"Egg business?"

"You know, the poisoning, getting sucked into a bird, and having to die. It's a lot."

"I had to poison him," Leena said firmly.

"Still, people tend to take that the wrong way."

Leena was saved from the conversation by a noise like the beating of war drums. She stopped in her tracks, Kifi bumping into her from behind. The cat leaned against Leena's leg as they both gazed up toward the source of the sound.

"Thunder?" Kifi asked.

"No," Leena replied. "Wings. Dragons. A whole flight."

Leena recognized Ronan of Brightwing, but he was not alone. There was a slender female with spotted wings flying beside him, as well as at least twenty others. Brown, blue, green, and black dragons landed on rooftops and in courtyards. Some of the citizens screamed and ran, but more stood by in openmouthed awe. Up close, the rippling scales were beautiful.

The dragons were carrying cargo in slings. As Leena approached the closest arrival, she saw it carried dozens of flat boxes—and Anna.

"What are you doing here?" Leena cried in delight as Anna leaped to the ground.

Anna hugged Leena, then crouched to pet Kifi. "I wouldn't miss this party for the world. Besides, there is someone I want you to meet."

A figure dismounted from another dragon and walked toward them. It was John Barleycorn. He gave a respectful nod to Kifi as he drew near, and then stopped before Leena with a low bow. "Very well met, Leena of the Flame."

"I'm delighted to see you looking so well, my lord," Leena said. "But what brings you here?"

"I woke to find that, for months, I had lain helpless in a hospital bed. I have a score to settle with those who put me there."

Leena sensed Barleycorn had far more power than an ordinary fae. That begged the question of what had done him such harm.

"Shades?" she asked.

"Among others." He gave a cold grin. "But they are foremost among my enemies."

"Haven't we destroyed Juradoc and his friends?" Leena asked, but she already knew the answer. They had indeed squashed the Shades who had invaded the south, but that was only one part of Faery. The war wasn't over yet.

Barleycorn smiled again, but this time his expression was kind.

Leena noticed that he held Anna's hand, indicating the two were more than just friends.

"The fae won a significant victory," he said. "That gives us hope when all seems dark. It also means that it is time for me to contribute to the fight."

Leena wondered what that meant.

"What's that smell?" the cat demanded, thus derailing the conversation.

Leena turned, following the direction of Kifi's golden stare. While they'd been talking, guardsmen had emerged from the nearby banquet hall to free the dragons from their cargo. There was an enticing scent wafting from the mountain of boxes. It took her back to the hospital, with Morran under the tree and the strange lights that glowed everywhere in the modern world.

"Pizza," the cat cried, bouncing forward to leap atop the tower of cardboard. She immediately began digging at the box with her claws.

Leena gaped at Anna in astonishment. "You had the dragons deliver pizza?"

"Hey, can you think of a more convenient food for a feast?" Anna replied with a smile.

"Besides," another voice piped up, "the heat from the dragons keeps the food warm."

Leena whirled. "*Morran.*"

§ 30 §

Leena's heart hammered in her ears, even as her breath refused to fill her lungs. "You're back."

He stood a dozen feet away. Somehow, she knew it was to give her space. Leena took a hesitant step forward and then stopped, unsure. Perhaps he felt as unmoored as she did at that moment. Maybe he wanted to keep his distance from an entanglement he didn't need.

But then Morran smiled, the grin uncomplicated and joyful and so different from any expression she'd ever seen on his face. As if that smile permitted her feet to move, she lunged into his arms. *"You're back."*

Her words were all but inaudible, mumbled into the front of his tunic because she was gripping him so hard.

"Evidently." He squeezed her hard, burying his face in her hair.

"How? You disappeared. There was only the phoenix."

"And it's still there," he said, signaling upward.

A flash of blazing light filled the sky, and a cry went up from the crowd. Leena craned her neck to catch sight of the firebird. It flew over the rooftops of Eldaban, sparks flying from its feathers like a rain of falling stars. It made one final lap around the city before it streaked away, as swift and bright as a shooting star. The sheer beauty of it left her awestruck.

"A fae and their familiar are bound but separate. We only join our physical forms in times of great need." Morran smoothed a wisp of hair from her face. "I believe the episode with the temple qualified."

"I killed you."

"With permission. Please don't repeat the exercise."

"I wasn't sure I'd see you again." Leena kept the days and weeks of doubt from her words. To her surprise, her heart was simply glad.

"Why not?"

"You are a prince. Your obligations don't extend to a temple dancer from Eldaban."

She stepped back from the embrace at last. His expression was solemn, but there was laughter under the surface.

"You must think me a fool," he said.

She folded her arms. "How so, my lord?"

"As much as I despised my jailor, he taught me an important lesson. I learned what it is to be powerless."

Leena averted her gaze. "Then you understand my situation."

"Not in the way you think. You showed me your great powers from the night we met, Leena, and every night after. You lifted me from despair with your kindness. Do you think it so strange that I should come back to you?"

Tongue-tied, she could only gaze into his dark eyes.

Morran leaned down, his voice confidential. "I assume you know your way around the banquet hall?"

Leena nodded in surprise.

"Then show me," he said.

"Do you wish an introduction to the new council?" She knew most of the members, at least by sight.

He shook his head. "No, not at the moment. Take me in the back way. I would rather avoid any formality."

A little mystified, she led him through the servant's entrance she always used.

"These are the kitchens." She took his hand, pulling him through the bustle of the corridor. Few paused to give them a second glance. Those who did nodded to her and regarded Morran with curiosity, but no recognition. Morran wasn't dressed like the formidable prince who had glowered from Juradoc's head table. He was tall and imposing and very clearly a warrior, but, if he was with Leena, he was a friend.

"And where did you go when you were to perform?" he asked.

She led him through the building, remembering the night they had met. So much had changed, yet so much had not.

She pointed out a few features of interest as they walked. He followed, nodding and asking the odd question, but it was clear he had something on his mind. When they got to the room where she'd wait her turn to perform, Morran kicked the door shut and turned to her. "At last, some privacy."

He backed Leena against the wall, then moved in for a kiss. His lips were soft, his hands firm against the small of her back. She arched into him, tracing the line of his shoulders with her palms. His breath fanned over her cheek as his eyelashes brushed against hers. She threaded her fingers through his hair, once more learning the feel of him. They'd had such a short time together, and there was still so much to know.

He pulled away, cupping her face in his hands. "I am so sorry I left for so long, but I had to surrender to Arlanoth for a time. I had to heal, then I had to remember who and what I was."

"But you are whole now. You have your power. Your throne awaits."

"Not quite." His smile was soft now, almost shy. "Once I have you, then I'll be whole."

"I'm a Kelthian barbarian, not a princess."

"I beg to differ," he said, opening the door and leading her into the empty banquet hall. From there, he pushed open the double doors to the balcony and held out his hand to her. "Come."

Tentatively, she joined him. From where they stood, they could see the dragons, the pizza boxes, Kifi perched on a dragon's head, and all the people of Eldaban crowding the streets. Those same people caught sight and waved cheerfully, for Leena knew everyone and Morran was the hero of the hour.

"You see," he said, "they see you as you are, a woman nobler than many of royal blood. You have suffered and bled for the sake of this land."

"I don't seek fame," she replied, voice shaking. Hope and apprehension made a powerful brew in her veins. If only he genuinely loved her. If only he meant to stay.

One corner of his mouth rose. "Then what is it you want?"

"Before I met you, I would have said certainty. But I've learned that if my home slides away from beneath my feet, I will survive it. I will survive war and Shades. I will survive the Flame itself."

"And?" he prompted, taking both her hands before dropping to one knee.

The supplication in his dark brown eyes undid her. "I don't want to have to survive any of it alone."

"Then take me as your husband."

"Your people will never accept a temple dancer as their prince's mate."

Morran's face fell, but he kissed both her hands and rose to face the curious onlookers crowding the street below. He steered her right up to the balcony rail, one hand on her back to keep her from running away.

"Behold," Morran cried in a voice meant to carry through a battle. "I wish to take this brave woman as my wife. What do you say, people of this fair city?"

Every throat in Eldaban cheered in approval.

"So you see, your fears are groundless, Leena of Eldaban,"

Morran said, turning her to face him so their lips were but inches apart. "They see the princess you are."

Leena tried to speak, but could not. She was feeling too many things at once—humbled, terrified, hopeful, and in love.

"What do you say?" he asked, his eyes bright.

"Yes," she said, surrendering one last time.

LATER THAT DAY, BARLEYCORN OPENED A SHIMMER, AND LEENA and Morran followed him through the silvery portal. It was early evening with a hint of dusk in the sky. The first thing she sensed was cold mountain air. She drank it down greedily, long-forgotten memories of her childhood coming alive. But one glance told her these were not the mountains of her home.

The mountaintop was actually a vast flat plateau. Ancient stone buildings surrounded an open courtyard. The courtyard itself was bare rock. A circle was carved into it, the design divided into four quadrants that corresponded to the fae elemental tribes —air, water, fire, and earth. Tall torches lit the space, bathing everything in a shifting glow.

"Where are we?" Leena asked.

"This is the Wheel," Morran said, "the ancient seat of the high king of the Fae."

Leena had heard tales of the place. Every child had. "Why are we here?"

"All four tribes of the fae must light the beacon fire to summon High King Jorwarth," Barleycorn said. "It is time he returned to defend his people. The final fight for our land has begun."

"Air and water have lit their signals," Morran replied. "Fire will join them."

The beacon fire stood in the middle of the courtyard. There was a place for four separate blazes. Two were already lit, and two were dark. Morran picked up an unlit torch from beside the fire, then turned to Leena. "Would you care to do the honors?"

When Leena summoned her magic, the torch burst into Flame. Then Morran took it from her, lowering it to the beacon. With a whoosh, fire rocketed into the sky to challenge the dark.

"From the ash will rise the flame," Morran said. "It is the old war cry of Faery."

"It must refer to the phoenix," Leena added. "The fae need its power to win."

"We lack only Earth before the prophecy is fulfilled." Morran looked at Barleycorn. "Where is the King of Earth?"

"The stage is set," Barleycorn said. "Leave it to me to summon the players."

With that, Barleycorn stepped back through the Shimmer, leaving them alone on the mountaintop. The portal vanished behind him. Leena leaned into Morran, suddenly feeling the night chill.

He leaned down, catching her mouth with his. The cold vanished from Leena's mind as they kissed, nipping and exploring. A slow ache throbbed low in her belly, making her long for a soft bed, Morran, and perhaps a jug of wine.

"You do recall the promise you made on the balcony?" Morran said, a sly look in his dark eyes.

"I believe I agreed that you desired me to be your princess and that the people of Eldaban approve. I think that is how you put the question."

Leena grinned as he raised his brows.

"Do you question my intentions, madam?"

"Perhaps your grammar."

"Then let me try again." Morran sank to one knee before the beacon fire, the light playing over the sharp planes of his face. All playfulness left his expression. "Will you be my mate, my life companion, my heart, and my princess, Leena of the Flame?"

Faery spread out around the Wheel, hidden beneath a blanket

of starry darkness. For that moment, the entire realm was theirs alone. Leena knelt so she faced Morran, folding his hands in hers.

"I will be all those things, Morran of Tymeera, if you will be my husband and lover and, most of all, my friend."

"So be it. We shall wed, fire dancer. Our love shall never lack magic." He drew her to her feet.

Leena wound her arms around Morran's neck, giving him her sweetest smile. "One question, my lord."

"What is it?"

"Are we supposed to walk down this mountain?"

Laughing, Morran gave a piercing whistle. To Leena's delight, a star seemed to separate from the heavens as it hurtled their way. Within seconds, she realized it was the phoenix. It circled the top of the Wheel, trailing fire as it landed upon the rock.

It was the most beautiful creature Leena had ever seen. It bowed as she approached, giving a gentle trill. Morran helped her onto its back, mounting behind her so she was secure in his arms. Together, they launched into the sky and soared into the heavens.

They were the brightest star of all.

THE END

THE CROWN OF FAE NOVELS BEGAN WITH *SHIMMER* AND WILL continue with *Quake*. If you missed Alana and Prince Ronan's adventure, check out *Shimmer* to find out how it all began!

AFTERWORD

Thank you so much for reading *Smolder.* It's the biggest adventure so far in the series, and it leads us to the final battles with the Shades.

If you enjoyed the story, please tell a friend or leave a review. Reviews help other readers find good stories and are incredibly important to authors. Your opinion matters.

Also, if you'd like to keep up on what's happening with my books, please sign up for my newsletter on my website at www.SharonAshwood.com.

I promise that I won't share your email or information, and I won't send you spam.

If you're curious about what happens next in Faery, the series continues with *Quake.*

FLICKER

CROWN OF FAE, BOOK 0.5

When hope is just a flicker, trust a dragon to light the flame.

Fliss is the youngest princess of Bright Wing, a tribe of dragon shifters defending Faery against the enemy Shades. She yearns to fight, but now she's stuck at school far away. The situation is ridiculous. Intolerable. How can she save the world when she's forbidden to fly after curfew?

The school at Penriva House is far outside the battle lines. The students are safe, or so everyone believes. But Shades attack Fliss before she arrives at the school, and now there are signs the enemy is hiding just beyond its walls. When the headmistress ignores the evidence, Fliss has to wonder whose side she's on.

Terrified, Fliss is unsure where to turn with the secret she uncovers. There's no clear way to save her newfound friends, much less herself. Does Fliss run, or risk all and fly into battle, one small dragon against a host of perilous foe?

SHIMMER

CROWN OF FAE, BOOK 1

Three wishes, two warriors, one chance at redemption

Fae martial artist Alana Beech demands justice when her teammate dies during a rigged fight, but no one cares. Injured and alone, Alana is forced to accept a last-chance job at a curiosity shop. There she finds a magic lamp—and a spark of hope—in a box of abandoned junk.

Ronan is a dragon prince imprisoned during the destruction of the fae homeland. He's the genie bound to the lamp and forced to grant three wishes to every comer. As handsome as he is hazardous, Ronan joins Alana's search for answers.

While their alliance turns passionate, Alana's quest reveals a mystery that goes far beyond murder. The lamp is a lethal weapon, and Ronan's enemies are on the hunt. Alana will do anything to guard her lover's back, but sometimes a warrior's courage—like the genie's wishes—carries an unexpected price.

SHATTER
CROWN OF FAE, BOOK 2

One lover is lying. The other will kill them all.

Tessa Harrison takes a cruise to Alaska and—just like her love life—the voyage seems doomed. The fact that her ex followed her aboard is bad enough, but this time he's brought sea monsters.

Tessa's former lover—who reveals himself as the Sea King of the fae—isn't her only surprise visitor on the ship. Maxwell Stokes, captain of the ghost ship *Solitude*, is a guardian of the gateway between the fae and human worlds. Betrayed by the Sea King, Stokes is determined to get vengeance until Tessa disrupts his plans. She's fire to his ice, and the result is unexpected steam.

Tessa's survival means unlocking a destiny she never suspected. Fiercely independent, she holds the key to both men's future —or their destruction. Both want her power. Both claim she is the only woman they desire. Which one is telling the truth?

Tessa must choose—and the wrong choice could destroy two worlds.

QUAKE

CROWN OF FAE, BOOK 4

A king with no mercy. A queen with no fear.

Sorcha's last hope for her people is an alliance, but the earth fae have never stood united. She is Ildaran's Queen, bitter enemy of the Ice Realm, and not even war against a common foe has brought peace between the two kingdoms. But her armies are losing, and King Bronnik's cold lands are her only refuge—and possibly a fatal trap.

Her mission is to unite their armies, but Bronnik refuses. A cruel enemy, he is renowned as a matchless warrior, stern, powerful and—when he chooses—seductive. Yet he's hiding secrets that keep him secluded within his ice-walled castle, and Sorcha has to discover the truth before both kingdoms fall.

Trust is impossible. Passion is unthinkable. A queen never risks losing her heart to an enemy, and she never, ever gambles with her realm. But before she can win Bronnik's alliance, Sorcha will have to do both.

ABOUT THE AUTHOR

USA Today Bestselling author Sharon Ashwood is a novelist, desk jockey and enthusiast for the weird and spooky. She has an English literature degree but plays with numbers for her living. Interests include insulating the walls with her to-be-read books and building a graveyard diorama over much of her desk. As a vegetarian, she freely admits the whole vampire/werewolf fantasy would never work out, so she writes paranormal romances instead.

Sharon is a winner of the RITA® Award for Paranormal Romance. She lives in the Pacific Northwest and is owned by a pair of naughty black cats.

www.SharonAshwood.com
Sharon@SharonAshwood.com

facebook.com/authorsharonashwood
x.com/RowanAshArt
instagram.com/rowanashart
bookbub.com/authors/sharon-ashwood
pinterest.com/rowanashart

Crown of Fae Series

Flicker

Shimmer

Shatter

Smolder

Quake

Dark Forgotten Series

Ravenous

Scorched

Unchained

Frostbound

Gifted

Fragile Magic (short story)

Hidden

Camelot Reborn series

Enchanted Warrior

Enchanted Guardian

Royal Enchantment

Enchanter Redeemed

Horsemen series

Possessed by a Warrior

Possessed by an Immortal

Possessed by a Wolf

Possessed by the Fallen

Dragon Lords novellas

Lord Dragon's Conquest

Valkyrie's Conquest

Audiobook

Enchanted Warrior

Corsair's Cove miniseries

Kiss in the Dark

Secret Seed

Long Road Home